Enjoy the
history and
The mystery!

A PHANTOM WALKS AMONG US

A PHANTOM WALKS AMONG US

Rod Vick

Laikituk Creek Publishing

A PHANTOM WALKS AMONG US

By Rod Vick

Laikituk Creek Publishing
Mukwonago, Wisconsin

ISBN-13: **978-1706704980**

For Phyllis

A Note from the Author

I love to write, and I love a good mystery. Thus, it seemed a natural thing—and fun—to write a mystery story set in my hometown, one that brings a treasure trove of local landmarks and history to the table.

However, one danger of writing such a book is that readers will think my characters represent real people. They do not. I have tried to give my cast of heroes and villains interesting lives, flaws, back story and personalities, but any similarity to people you know or have known is coincidence. This is true even if I've accidentally given a character a similar-sounding name to that of a real village resident. Or if I've nailed your chocolate creme-filled pastry addiction, your slavish dedication to a daily routine, or your fanatic adoration of rummage sales. These characteristics are shared by millions of people, oddly enough, and if you share them as well, it is pure happenstance.

I also wanted to make it clear that this book is in no way intended to portray Mukwonago or its institutions in a negative light. I've lived in Mukwonago or within a few miles of it my whole life. I have tremendous respect for the Mukwonago Village Police Department, Mukwonago Area Schools and its teachers, and members of Mukwonago's business community. This book chronicles fictional individuals conducting a fictional murder investigation, and while I have attempted to create believable interactions, I have also allowed them to make human mistakes. These are not meant to reflect the behaviors of actual individuals who live in Mukwonago and represent its institutions.

Please note that while some characters in the book grumble about development and the loss of the small-town feel that often accompanies it, it is not my intention to make a political point, offer criticism or endorsement of any development policy. Such discussions by characters in the book are simply meant to reflect the unavoidable conversations and attitudes that are a part of small-town life when people are confronted by change.

Speaking of change, this novel was written in 2019, and reflects the physical state of the village at that time. As years pass, even the many familiar and beloved landmarks mentioned in this book may be altered or disappear.

The whole point here is to have fun. Instead of imagining intriguing, thrilling and dangerous events occurring in far-off places, to imagine them occurring along streets we have walked.

Although many thank-yous are noted at the conclusion of the novel, I did want to give up-front acknowledgement to three. First, thank you to Jon Stock, who entrusted me with three Mukwonago history books that had been the property of his mother, Hazel Stock. These were an immense help in providing historical depth to the novel. Second, thank you to Mukwonago Police Chief Kevin Schmidt who met with me to answer questions about local police procedure and who continued to be a valuable resource in follow-up questioning. It should be noted that while I tried to have my police officers act according to established procedure, there may be cases where I have deviated slightly in order to facilitate the action of the novel. In all cases, I have endeavored to portray the department in a positive light; yet it is important again to note that the officers in the novel are fictional characters whose actions and decisions do not reflect those of the real-life police department. Third, thank you to PARS International Corp. and Gannett Newspapers for permission to use the *Mukwonago Chief* name in this novel.

Finally, while most of the locations and historical occurrences described in the book represent real places and events, I've also created a few, and have embellished a bit of the local history. To discuss those now would, I think, detract from the story. However, I have included an explanation at the end of the novel that examines what is real and what is fictionalized, and why such choices were made.

I hope you enjoy the book.

Rod Vick

"People in small towns, much more than in cities, share a destiny."
- **Richard Russo**

The Phantom watched the solitary jogger from a shadowy, hidden spot behind towering pin oaks that had begun their own journeys more than a century earlier. Tonight, the nearly full moon hung above the lake like a misshapen orange. It was true that moonlight represented a complication. But complications, the Phantom observed, only doomed the inept, the lazy, and the stupid. The Phantom was none of these.

Everything had been carefully planned.

Almost everyone in Mukwonago knew the jogger, Sandy Sewell. However, the Phantom had made it an obsession to know more about the young woman than virtually anyone except Sandy herself.

Sandy had grown up in the village of about 6,000, waitressing at a popular local restaurant where her smile and comfortable chatter had charmed young and old, making everyone feel that she really *was* interested in how they were feeling or where they had gone on their recent vacation or in the photos of grandchildren they readily shared from their phones or wallets. Her winning demeanor had earned her generous tips and paid for most of her college. Degree in hand, she had returned to her hometown, certified as a realtor, and seven years later at the age of 29, was selling as many properties in a year as the grizzled realty veterans. As of late, she was known to be dating a physical education teacher from the high school, a young fellow who, according to local gossip, was decent, church-going, and well-respected by his colleagues. The idea that these two might end up together generated a lot of smiles among locals.

That was the sad part, of course. A beautiful young woman, someone who should marry, have children, laugh a lot, live a long life filled with friends, travel, and dreams fulfilled. But the Phantom knew that was not how it was destined to play out.

While the Phantom knew Sandy's personal and work history, there were other useful details of which fewer were probably aware. For instance, the Phantom had learned through weeks of clandestine watchfulness that Sandy jogged seven days a week, rain or shine. Her schedule was rigid, perhaps a bit obsessive. That's how it often was with type-A individuals, the Phantom had noted. Obsessive dedication to a routine made one predictable.

One might have called it a fatal flaw.

On Saturdays and Sundays, Sandy ran at 7:00 a.m., and always the five-mile loop that started at Field Park, followed the sidewalks along Veterans Way to what locals referred to as "the bypass," continued on Bay View, and then weaved through town back to the park. On weekdays, however, she ran in the evening, conducting showings or finishing up office work until 7:00 or 8:00 p.m., and then changing into her running gear at her house near Miniwaukan Park. She had a set route for every weekday night, although she always began with a warm-up jog to Field Park where she paused for a rigorous ten-minute stretching routine. After that, on Mondays she ran the bike path west along Veterans Way, past the high school, wove her way through that subdivision—the one with all the famous golf course street names—took Eagle Lake Avenue east to Rochester, and then back to the park.

Always the same, every Monday.

Tuesdays it was the Mukwonago Heights subdivision, where streets were dedicated to NASA astronauts with names like "Lovell Court" and "Armstrong Court".

Tonight was Thursday. And on Thursdays, without fail, Sandy ran down Andrews Street to the little park on the edge of Phantom Lake—Phantom Glen Park, where both Sandy and the Phantom rested now, though only one of them was aware of this. The Phantom had watched her run this route on a dozen Thursdays. Always, at the end of Andrews Street, Sandy would swing left into the park, run beneath the oak canopies bordering the paved lots, then cross the grass to the fishing pier that jutted south into the lake. There, she would pause her workout to admire the view, sometimes tarrying a minute or two if the skies were particularly star-filled and spectacular.

They were particularly star-filled and spectacular tonight.

The Phantom watched.

Had this been Detroit or New York or most other big cities, the Phantom guessed that Sandy would have been less enthusiastic about lingering in the darkness. And it was dark indeed. While the lights of homes along the far shore of Phantom Lake reflected off its waters, there were no security lights at the pier, no electronic cameras. But this was not Detroit or New York. It was Mukwonago. Nothing to worry about here.

And this was true, thought the Phantom. Tonight was *not* the night to worry. Tonight was an evening of diamond-studded skies and distant barking dogs. Of the soft, overhead rush of a jet engine dying to silence, carrying with it weary passengers to sunny tomorrows in distant places. Of gentle June breezes, only occasionally flexing enough muscle to rustle a few leaves.

In short, a beautiful night where worries were as far away as the three solar furnaces that had birthed the radiance that defined Orion's Belt.

Yet, the Phantom knew there would come a night when there was truly something to worry about. A night when the mortal fears of village residents would not be a thousand light years away, but would be as close their next step, their next breath, their next whispered question into the darkness.

And that night would come very soon.

#

Like everyone else in Mukwonago, Nate Janowsky had been a little surprised to learn that the community's weekly newspaper, the *Chief*, would be publishing again after being absent for several years. It was, for most, a pleasant surprise.

The paper had put out its first issue on New Year's Day 1889 under the editorship of Dan and Lucy Camp and had published every Wednesday for about a century and a quarter, usually under the ownership of local entrepreneurs. More recently, however, it had been sold to a news giant for whom—in the age of digital news platforms with 24/7 coverage—it had apparently represented a more 19th- than 21st-century approach to news dissemination. And so the operation had been shuttered, much to the chagrin of many village residents who had enjoyed the local slant on everything from high school sports to contentious board meetings to profiles of citizens prominent and otherwise who had passed on. It had been regular reading material in restaurants, coffee shops, the waiting rooms of doctors and dentists, convenience stores, family rooms, and bathrooms, bringing the community a little closer together and making everyone neighbors.

The paper's demise left a hole in the town, something hard to define yet undeniable. Almost overnight, it had seemed like there were more strangers. That there were fewer interesting things happening *here*, and perhaps it would be better to look *elsewhere* if you wanted real entertainment.

Then, about a month ago, the news broke that the big paper had sold rights to the *Mukwonago Chief* name, and that it would begin publishing twice a week, Mondays and Thursdays, starting in June.

But not all the news had been good. The new publisher was allegedly a woman in her early forties who came from Madison, the state's capital. A bad sign. An "anything goes" kind of city whose values weren't exactly a good match for those of a small town. There were assurances from the usual self-designated gatekeepers of community standards that she would be given a chance, but they would be keeping an eye on her. Any suggestion from the paper's editorial pages that the Second Amendment wasn't an absolute right or that Nativity scenes weren't appropriate for the town square—even though the village didn't technically have a "square" anymore—and perhaps it would be time for the paper to cease operations again.

The woman—Star Calloway, if Nate remembered correctly—had apparently met with dozens of local business owners, drumming up advertising for the newspaper's reboot. At the same time, a rumor began to circulate that she had been arrested and subsequently fired from her previous news job. Another red flag.

Despite all of the lingering doubts and questions, the first issue of the new *Mukwonago Chief* had arrived on newsstands last Monday to a mostly positive reception. No exposes or Communist manifestos. What it *did* have was board meetings, obituaries, police reports, local sports, and a double spread of photos of the Mukwonago High School graduation ceremony, held in Milwaukee at Miller Park since even the new high school gym was too small to handle the anticipated crowds. And lots of ads, mostly themed around a "welcome back" to the paper itself. In short, the new *Chief* contained everything that was really important to folks who called Mukwonago home.

Nate had not met Star Calloway previously, but that would change today. She had called the police station and reported receiving a "possibly threatening" letter. Mukwonago's police force consisted of fifteen individuals: Chief Gary Beckman, two lieutenants, eleven officers—of which Nate was one—and a dispatcher. Since "possibly threatening" letters were fairly low on the priority scale, Chief Beckman had routed the complaint away from his desk, past the two lieutenants, and it had fallen into the hands of the nearest available officer.

That had been Nate.

After eighteen years on the force, Nate had hoped he would have achieved the rank of lieutenant and be able to pass assignments like this on to one of the underlings. Yet, he was still a garden variety patrolman, and he knew part of it was his own fault. He was a big man, significantly bigger than the department's "proportional height-to-weight restrictions" would have allowed if he were a new recruit. He could still throw a jack-hammer punch, and he moved pretty fast for a guy over two hundred, but if moving meant more than thirty yards at a sprint, he was done for. It wasn't as if he didn't try. He worked out three times a week at the Mukwonago Y—when the sometimes mercurial schedule of his police job permitted. But damn, there were way too many good pizza and burger joints in such a small town.

He recalled the conversation he had had with Ms. Calloway about a week ago when he had returned the initial call on the advice of Chief Beckman.

"Thank you for getting back to me," Calloway had said, her voice deeper and somewhat more rusty-sounding than he had expected. "I just...well, I'm new here. I'm not sure what sort of thing is considered...normal."

"No problem, Ms. Calloway," Nate had replied. "I'm guessing you'll find what's 'normal' around here is pretty much what you'd find as 'normal' where you come from."

Calloway had remained silent for a beat. *"Where I come from.* Ah."

Something in her tone had suggested to Nate that he might have phrased his response in a way that offended her. He had decided to press ahead. "So this email that you received—"

"It was a letter," Calloway had corrected him, perhaps a shade too brusquely, he thought. "An actual, physical letter on actual paper. In an envelope. It was left tucked between the front door and the jamb of the *Chief* office. Part of it was resting on the door handle, so I couldn't miss it."

"An actual, physical letter," Nate had repeated, rolling his eyes. He had been glad he was only talking to her over the phone. She sounded like one of his grade school teachers from years ago, a snooty, middle-aged woman whose gray-streaked hair was tied back in a bun so tightly that it had seemed to stretch her whole face into a grim mask. When making a point, she had liked to rap the knuckles of daydreaming future police officers with a ruler. "When did you find this letter?"

"Yesterday, Wednesday morning," Calloway had replied. "It was all typed. Even the address on the envelope. *To the Chief. For the Editorial Page* it said on the envelope."

"Okay," Nate had said, making a note on a pad on the desk in front of him. "Do you know who wrote the letter?"

"It was unsigned. Actually, that's not true. It was signed, but with a pseudonym."

"A what now?"

Nate had heard a sigh of exasperation and figured Ms. Calloway was rolling her eyes. He had imagined that she probably sported a troubling wart beneath her left eye, just like his snooty teacher.

"A fake name. It was signed *Ho-ma-ba*."

"Ho-ma-ba? What the hell does that mean?"

"You tell me. I'm not from around here. I thought it was maybe some local thing."

"How do you spell it?"

She had spelled it for him.

Nate had stared at the apparent name, considering it for a moment. "And was it the name that you found threatening?"

"What? For God's sake, no! That name doesn't even make the top 100 unusual names I've heard!"

Nate remembered that she was from Madison, and judged that she was probably not exaggerating. She had then read him the letter.

"To the Chief,

"As someone who has called Mukwonago home for many years, I've developed a deep respect and even love for this village. As a result, it saddens me to see many of the community's most cherished landmarks, private residences, and beautiful public lands being treated with such indifference and even callousness by some citizens, by village planners, and by developers.

"I believe this is the result of two kinds of ignorance that run rampant among our neighbors. The first is ignorance of our village's rich history. A house is just a house, right? That's true if you have no knowledge of village history. However, one hundred and thirty years ago, Mukwonago had an opera house! Imagine it! Folks who lived here, in this town, in the 1880s, pulling their horse-drawn rigs up to the house, dressed in their finest clothes, listening to The Marriage of Figaro for a night's entertainment! And that opera house is still here on Rochester Street, although now it is a private residence. If we are ignorant of its role in local history, well, it's just another house, and we don't care what happens to it! Sure, tear it down if you wish. Or 'renovate' it to look like an IKEA store. But if we know it was an opera house, that it was an attempt by our forbears to bring culture to what was then a town of dirt streets, why, then to tear it down or renovate it into something perversely modern would be sacrilege.

"This form of ignorance has begun to kill our village. We've seen it in the loss of beautiful houses and cherished natural areas, bulldozed or bastardized to bring us the newest burger bar. But it pales by comparison to the second form of ignorance, which is the ignorance of the fact that our village has a soul, is a living thing! Certainly you have felt it? The beating of its heart beneath our feet!

"And like any living thing, our village will not go quietly. It will fight with all the power of nature and beyond. To those who wish to kill the village, it will respond in kind.

"But all is not lost. Perhaps we, the current generation of inhabitants, can redeem ourselves. And so I pose to you a series of riddles to determine whether we are worthy. I will submit one for publication for each Monday. Any community member may volunteer an answer by letter or email to the Chief. If the correct answer is printed in the Thursday edition of the same week, this will show an understanding of our shared heritage, and the soul of the village will be assuaged.

"But ignorance will only breed anger and death.

"Here is the riddle:

"Five little hearts, all in a row.

"The first one said, 'I love you so!'

"The second one said, 'Pledge your love by these shores.'

"The third one said, 'If you do, then it's war!'

"The father said, 'Flee with your last breaths!'

"The reaper said, ''Neath the waves, they met death.'"

A long pause had seemed to indicate that Star had finished the letter. Nate had chuckled. "Oh yeah, there are going to be a lot of winners in this contest. I have to ask this: This isn't some sort of promotional gimmick for the paper, is it?"

Calloway's response had been indignant. "Are you seriously asking if I wrote the letter?"

"I'm sorry," Nate had said, though he really wasn't. "Just covering all the bases. You have any idea what that riddle means?"

"Not a clue."

Nate had thought for a bit. "What is it about the letter that concerns you?"

"Well, for openers, it's pretty dark. The village is going to fight to survive. If you try and kill it, it will respond in kind. Sounds kind of threatening."

"Probably just speaking metaphorically," Nate had suggested. "I mean, it's not like anyone was threatened by name. 'Ignorance will only bring anger and death'. So what's it saying? If we're too ignorant to solve the riddle, the village is going to die?"

"So you aren't concerned?"

"Well, it is sort of creepy. And the letter isn't technically signed."

"I've printed unsigned letters before."

Not surprised, Nate had thought. *Madison*. And he recalled that she had allegedly been fired from her previous job.

"I think this is your call," Nate had concluded. "I don't see anything that's a violation of the law. So far it's not against the law to be a crackpot. I'd probably throw it in the recycling bin, but I'm not in the news business."

The letter had been printed in Monday's paper on the "Opinions" page, alongside a letter from a local schoolteacher saying what a great school year it had been and thanking Mukwonago parents for having such wonderful kids, and a letter from a village man who had gotten a speeding ticket along the divided highway near Wal-mart, and who thought that the 25-mile-per-hour limit there was ridiculous.

Thursday's paper had come out this morning. Nate had glanced at it while finishing a slice of leftover birthday cake that one of the patrolmen had brought in to the station. On the front page, a photo of carnies setting up rides for Summerfest in Field Park. On the "Opinions" page, no answers to the riddle.

Well, whosever idea that was, it was a pretty big dud.

Three

Full moon summer nights were the best, thought Sandy Sewell as she turned off Main Street and began her jog down Andrews. Tonight, however, the familiar orb made only sporadic appearances through wispy fissures in the banks of steadily eastward-drifting clouds, responding, it seemed, to winds belonging to a different world than the still and muggy one occupied by ground-dwelling mortals. Porch and street lighting offered a soft beacon here and there, yet the moist night felt haunted bayou-lonely and rather untamed. That was part of the beauty of living in a small town like Mukwonago, she thought—the sensation that even though you were in the center of a community, at certain times and in certain places, you could still feel like you were miles from everything. Most folks were settling down for the night, some probably in bed already, although it was only a little after nine. Yet, muted and windless as it was, Sandy felt like she had the whole town to herself, like in one of those post-apocalyptic movies where the people disappear but the silent buildings remain.

She kept a pretty good pace on the slight downhill slope toward Phantom Glen Park and the lake. Sucking in deep, cool breaths, she had never felt fitter. *I should hold back a bit*, she told herself. In just two days, she planned to run the ten-mile event at Racine's Lighthouse Run, and so she didn't want to expend too much energy during a period where she should be tapering. She hadn't expected to be able to run the Lighthouse ten-miler, but then the Hackenfuss property had sold this past week—an executive property that would give her a handsome commission—and she had cancelled the open house that had been scheduled for Saturday. The Lighthouse Run had gone back on the calendar, a little present for herself, and part of a mileage build-up that would eventually ready her for running a full marathon in the fall.

The Hackenfuss commission would also pay for a nice little bed and breakfast getaway in Iowa for her and Rick next month, a vacation that they had both been looking forward to for some time. There would be a riverboat trip on a stopover in Dubuque, a side-trip to Dyersville to see the Field of Dreams baseball diamond—mostly for Rick, who was a baseball nut—and two nights snuggling beneath a hand-stitched, down comforter at a quaint and pricy B&B. Sandy smiled. Oh, yes, she was going to enjoy it.

She slowed as she approached the little park, hardly more than a couple acres in size. The mature pin oaks gave it a "woodsy" feel, particularly at night, where they formed a streetlight-blocking canopy that arched over most of the park. As was her habit, she crossed the parking lot and headed down the narrow asphalt path toward the pier that jutted south into Phantom Lake. When weather permitted, she enjoyed pausing on the pier for a few minutes, drinking in the vastness of the universe, rare moments of down time, of stepping off the spinning treadmill that defined her life as a salesperson and a competitive runner.

No street traffic disturbed the stillness. Andrews Street ended at four posts with reflectors set deep into the ground to keep the inattentive from coasting into the lake, and so at this hour, it was one of the quietest streets in the village. The houses along the street were well-kept ranch-style homes, their owners a mix of the young and the retired. Only one faced the park, and its front windows were dark tonight. The hum of window air conditioner units, noticeable on the street, was muffled by the leaf cover.

Sandy stepped onto the pier, slowing to a walk, reaching the railing at the end. where she leaned, staring out over the water.

Deep breath. Now breathe out. Slowly.

On starry nights, the lake was dark-blue glass studded with shimmering pinpoints of bijouterie. Tonight, under a starless sky, it was a dense slab of polished obsidian, beautiful in its own rite, she thought. She could not help smiling. Not even thirty, and she had it all: a rockin' boyfriend who had just coached the high school baseball team to another successful season, a career that generated more money than she had ever dreamed of, dozens of loyal friends, and a romantic weekend in Iowa to look forward to.

She sensed the presence before hearing a sound, and then turned instinctively at the light footsteps behind her on the pier, letting out a congenial laugh.

"Oh, it's you! You startled me! Well isn't this a nice surprise? Hard to stay indoors on a summer night, isn't it?"

"That it is," said the new arrival. "I hope you don't mind sharing the view for a few moments? I can't stay long."

"Be my guest!" said Sandy, moving over to allow the other a place at the railing. They stood silently for a few moments before Sandy spoke again. "Even without stars, there's a beautiful serenity to it, isn't there?"

The other nodded.

"Do you come here often at night?" asked Sandy.

"Yes," said the other. "Quite often."

"Surprised I haven't seen you before," said Sandy, noting that unlike the bright-colored gear that she wore as a nighttime jogger, the other's clothes were dark, not the safest choice for a night walk. "Well, nice to see you! I suppose it's time to get back to my run!"

"Before you go," said the other, "take a look over the railing. Just below us."

Sandy leaned out a bit, looked down. "A canoe," she said, matter of factly.

"Doesn't that seem odd to you?" asked the other. "That someone would leave their canoe tied up here overnight? Can you make out any markings on it?"

Sandy leaned a little lower. "I can't—" She felt something soft suddenly cover her nose and mouth, and then the world went fuzzy and, a moment later, away.

*

She woke, endeavored to blink things into focus. For a moment, she felt pleasantly groggy. But only for a moment. Her senses returned rapidly, no doubt accelerated by the suddenly terrifying oddness of her situation. The cloudy sky filled her field of vision, framed by something she could not identify at first. The sound of lapping waves, the undulating motion of the vessel, and the dampness from a quarter inch of accumulated water quickly revealed that she was lying on her back in the bottom of a canoe. She recalled that her acquaintance had pointed to a canoe just moments before the world had blinked out.

The face of the other appeared above her. "Welcome back."

Sandy could say nothing. It seemed her mouth had been taped shut. She twisted to see what was restraining her hands and saw that her wrists had been zip-tied to the crossbar at the front of the canoe. Her feet had been similarly secured at the other end. The other noticed her terrified, questioning eyes.

"Chloroform," explained the other. "Works quickly, doesn't it? The effects don't last long, but it was long enough for me to get you into the canoe."

Sandy began to make high-pitched, muffled, whining sounds.

"Oh, stop that right now," said the other. "Or I'll chloroform you again. You don't want that, do you?"

The whining subsided. The terror in her eyes remained.

"You're probably wondering what this is all about," said the other, who sighed resignedly. "Did you see the Monday newspaper? The riddle? You're the answer to that riddle!"

She thought back to Monday. She had read the *Chief*. Something about the village being alive. And a children's rhyme, but with weird changes. It had all sounded like foolishness to Sandy. And to hear that strange rhyme mentioned in this even stranger present moment filled her with real fear, more intense than anything she had ever experienced.

"I don't have the time to explain everything to you right now," said the other. "I have to finish here quickly. No sense pressing my luck and being discovered. Let me just say that you're part of something big. Bigger than you can imagine. And you're about to become part of village folklore by re-enacting a bit of local mythology!"

Sandy had no idea what the other was talking about, and in fact, could hardly see with tears filling her eyes.

"I have to leave you now," said the other, and as Sandy raised her head from the bottom of the canoe, she saw the other drawing a rowboat beside. The vessel apparently had been towed behind. The other lay down the paddle and carefully maneuvered into the rowboat, leaving Sandy alone in the canoe. "Goodbye, I-wo-so," said the other, pushing off and disappearing from view instantly. The sound of oars dipping into water diminished after a few moments, and then there was only silence and stars.

I-wo-so? Everything about this episode seemed beyond bizarre. Was that supposed to be some sort of name or insult or what? *And how am I going to get out of these zip ties?* Would she be stuck out on the lake all night? Now she felt a surge of anger. She wouldn't get a wink of sleep, tied up as she was. She'd have to reschedule tomorrow's appointments. And it would put her behind on some important paperwork. If this was supposed to have been a prank, it was not at all funny. But she would try to relax. Perhaps some meditation. Surely some early-bird fisherman would spot the drifting canoe and rescue her around sunrise.

And then she would go to the police. This was an unthinkable violation, and there were going to be consequences.

She noticed, then, that her backside seemed wetter than it had when she had first awakened in the canoe. Sandy jerked her head up, water sloshing off her ponytail. There had been perhaps a quarter inch of water in the bottom of the vessel earlier. Now it seemed more like two inches. Thrashing her head around, she saw them: rocks packed into the space beneath the seat at the back of the canoe. She twisted toward the front. More rocks. The truth stole her breath away.

The other had put a hole in the canoe. It was sinking. More rapidly now, for the water almost covered her shoulders. She tried to cry out but could make only pathetic, muffled sounds that she knew would not carry or, if they did, would be too faint and ambiguous to be understood.

The water lapped at her chin.

This can't be happening!

Water began to rush over the stern.

From the safety of shadows beneath the great oaks in Phantom Glen Park, the Phantom watched the canoe slip under, then silently disappeared into the perfect June night as the clouds finally parted to reveal a gift of stars.

Four

Nate Janowsky was thinking of a chocolate, creme-filled doughnut as he strode toward the entrance of the Mukwonago Police Department. They were his weakness, one of about 14,000 weaknesses he guessed. One would undoubtedly be waiting for him when he arrived. Someone always brought a couple dozen doughnuts on Fridays, and that someone knew he was partial to chocolate creme-filled. Nate was sure the person was just trying to be a good friend. Unfortunately, good friends seemed to play a role in destroying his good diet intentions. Like his next-door condo neighbor, Pete, who frequently invited him over for "meat on the grill", always starting him out with a double bratwurst—two large, juicy sausages in one bun. And damn it, they were always too delicious to refuse.

He'd always been big. Not obese, but probably twenty pounds north of where the insurance charts said he was supposed to be. He'd been a conference wrestling champ for Mukwonago High School in the 185-pound class, despite not starting the sport until he was a junior. His introduction to wrestling had come about in a somewhat unusual way. Because he had always been big and doughy, he knew what it was like to be picked on. He had earned nicknames like "Thumper" and "Lardzilla" and "Jan-COW-sky" and many too cruel to repeat. Thus, he occasionally had come to the defense of others who were bullied, which usually involved simply stepping in and telling the bully to knock it off. Because of Nate's size, most of the time they did, though often their retreat was marked by some vulgar parting shot and a raised middle finger.

On one particular day, Nate had been in the high school commons, at that time a crowded area just inside the school's main entrance with long tables set in rows where students ate their lunches. It was not uncommon for students to sit with groups of friends who shared similar interests, and Nate had been sitting with five of his teammates from the junior varsity football squad. There were a few students, however, who sat alone at an otherwise unoccupied end of a long table, and one of these was a sophomore girl named Amber. Nate had heard a bit about her history. Her childhood had been as normal as one might experience in Mukwonago—youth soccer, violin lessons, Girl Scouts. And Amber had excelled, not only as a star on her U12 team, but also in performing on the violin with the Milwaukee Youth Symphony Orchestra. And she had possessed a ready smile and golden, wavy hair often tied back in a ponytail.

Then, the summer before 8th grade, while crossing in the walk lines to meet friends in downtown Mukwonago, a drunk driver had run the light, plowing into her at forty miles an hour. She had never seen it coming.

Amber had spent months in the hospital where doctors wired together her shattered jaw, pelvis, and femur as best they could. They knitted her back together with more than 100 stitches. But the worst was the swelling around her brain, for which they had to remove a section of her skull until it subsided. For the first month, she had lingered in a coma, and most had doubted that she would live. However, even against these incredible odds, Amber had excelled.

She'll never walk. Over the course of two and a half years, Amber progressed from wheelchair to walker to crutches, to a modestly hesitant gait aided by only a cane.

She'll never talk. The speech therapy had been just as grueling, and while it was true that Amber's colloquy would never be described as eloquent, she spoke short, soft, articulate, monotone sentences when it was necessary.

She'll have to be institutionalized for the rest of her life. Again defying the odds, Amber had received tutoring at home after eighteen months, and then had returned to school as a sophomore, first in the special education classrooms, and then, gradually, being immersed into regular education classes. She had even clawed her way into the same algebra class as Nate, despite her setbacks and being a year younger. He had said hi to her on her first day back, but she had not responded. He noted how different she had looked: her long hair, now cropped short. A stocking cap to partially hide some of the scars. An expression that suggested she was half asleep even though it was obvious she was working hard, taking notes. A slightly different curve to her face as a result of the severity of her broken jaw, nose, and left eye orbit.

That day in the cafeteria, Amber had sat alone, but perhaps five feet away from her, at the far end of the same table, were four junior boys making lewd comments about one of their teachers and laughing loudly. Suddenly, one of the boys—Sylvester Spliving, Nate recalled—had turned to Amber.

"Don't you think that's funny?"

Amber had said nothing, continuing to work on her sandwich, taking small bites with her head slightly inclined toward the table.

"Hey, Bride of Frankenstein! I'm talking to you!"

Amber had continued to say nothing. Sylvester had slid over on the seat to within a foot of her.

"I heard they stitched you together out of the corpses of a bunch of other dead girls who were so ugly that they committed suicide!"

His buddies had snickered.

"Why are you here? Aren't there special places for mutants? This is a school for normal kids! Are you trying to scare the shit out of them?"

Nate had heard enough. He was out of his seat in an instant. Sylvester had no time to react. Nate had grabbed him by the back of the neck, hitched his free hand to Sylvester's belt, and pitched him like a sack of trash. Sylvester slid across the top of a neighboring table, causing students to scatter, and bounced unceremoniously against a recycling bin. Sylvester's buddies sat frozen to their seats, their eyes wide, none moving to intervene.

Nate had turned then to Amber. "You can sit with us, if you want."

Amber had hesitated a moment, then had used her cane to rise to a standing position and followed him to his table. "Thank you," she said in a careful, quiet voice after she was seated again.

She had eaten with Nate and his friends the rest of the year.

Curiously, no teacher had come to Sylvester's rescue or had dragged Nate off to the associate principal's office, the general feeling being that Sylvester, long a pain in almost everyone's derriere, had it coming to him, that justice had been served. However, at the end of the lunch period, the wrestling coach, who had been one of the supervisors on duty and who had seen the whole thing, stopped Nate on his way to his next class. "You threw that kid like he was a pencil box."

"Sorry."

"Wrestling practice starts November 20th."

Nate supposed that experiences like that were why he had decided to become a police officer. It gave you an opportunity to help. Of course, he spent a lot more time writing speeding tickets and giving anti-drug lectures to middle schoolers than he did tossing bad guys into the trash. He guessed that was the way it was when you were a cop in Mayberry.

He was just about to the door of the police station when it opened and Chief Beckman burst out, clearly in a hurry.

"Come on!"

Nate fell into step with him. "What's up?"

"Fisherman found a body in the lake."

"Phantom Lake?" Nate asked.

Beckman nodded. "Diving team is going to meet us there."

They belted themselves into Beckman's squad.

"Makes me sick to my stomach," said Nate. "Every summer there's at least one accidental drowning. Was it a kid? Alcohol involved?"

"We don't know if alcohol was involved," said Beckman, switching on the lights and wheeling out of the lot. "But it doesn't look like it was a kid. And it doesn't look like an accident."

Nate's eyes widened. Mayberry suddenly seemed a lot more like Gotham City.

Five

The news would make virtually everyone in town sick with grief. And because it was murder, it would fundamentally change life in the village. Mukwonago was not a community where murders occurred frequently. Nate recalled perhaps one in the past decade. What made it worse was that this was Sandy Sewell.

There had never been any question, either about the body's identity or whether it was homicide. No one commits suicide by zip-tying their own ankles and wrists to opposite ends of a sinking canoe. Not physically possible. No one loads rocks into a canoe by accident. This had been carefully planned, right down to making sure the body would be found this morning.

They had finished collecting and photographing evidence, and Sandy's body was in the ambulance, waiting to be whisked away for autopsy. The two divers had packed up their gear and were making small talk punctuated by occasional laughter, seemingly enjoying the beautiful weather lakeside with no place they were anxious to be. Probably from Waukesha with no emotional attachment to the victim. Jack Guenther, the owner of the big tow truck, was solemnly rewinding the cable that had been used to help bring the canoe out. It had been loaded onto a flatbed truck and would be taken back for further analysis. A lakeside resident, Albert Sutherland, who lived several doors down from Phantom Glen Park had already identified it as his canoe, whose theft he claimed he had been unaware of. A second local squad plus a Waukesha County Sheriff's SUV were also parked nearby, lights continuing to flash in the brilliant sunlight. Barriers strung together by yellow police tape had been set up to close the west end of Andrews Street. Behind these stood a modest crowd of neighbors and others who had heard the news, which was surely sweeping rapidly through the village. Two local officers, Art Schnell and Jason Bell—often referred to as Schnell and Bell or, when Chief Beckman was in a hurry or irritated, "Schnabell!"—were identifying neighbors in the crowd and going door to door, trying to determine whether anyone had seen or heard anything.

Nate felt sick. The circumstances of Sandy's death were gruesome enough. He could barely bring himself to imagine her last moments—mouth taped shut, wrists and ankles bound, dark water covering her. There was no other way to describe it than cold-blooded cruelty.

But it was the other thing. The killer had not tried to hide the body to delay detection or conceal potential evidence. He had read about rural drug dealers or meth manufacturers in nearby communities who had weighted down bodies with cement blocks and dumped them in ponds on their farms, or who had soaked the corpses with gasoline and burned them to ash, or who had buried their enemies in leaf-covered graves deep in the woods. Whoever had killed Sandy had made sure the body would be found today.

A fisherman, John Aldenberg, had noticed what he had at first thought was garbage floating in the water, though it had a rather odd look to it, even from a distance. One of those pinwheels on a slim wooden stick, maybe a foot or so high, sticking out of a piece of thick Styrofoam, a photograph attacked below the stick. When Aldenberg had trolled closer, he saw that the photo was of the Caul house, which, with its high roof lines and intricate gingerbread trim painted powder blue and white, had been a village landmark for 140 years, though it had been torn down seven months earlier to make way for apartments. When Aldenberg had tried to lift the odd item into his boat, he realized that fishing line was attached to the crude raft, which seemed to anchor it in place. The water was about twelve feet deep and murky, though Aldenberg had thought he saw what looked like a canoe resting on the bottom. And maybe something more, something that disturbed him. He had a glass jar full of dirt and earthworms that he dumped onto the bottom of his own boat, rinsed out the jar in the lake, and then put the bottom of the jar into the water, looking through the open top as if it were a scope. His anguished cry was heard in Bucherville.

A variety of similarly powerful emotional reactions, Nate guessed, would erupt all over town. One of the first things people would ask is "Why?" Drug deals or robberies gone bad, they could understand that. But Sandy Sewell was not a criminal. Everybody admired her friendliness, her drive, and the fact that she was a hometown girl who they had watched grow into a vibrant and successful adult. Everybody loved Sandy.

Well, thought Nate, *apparently not everybody.*

His phone dinged and Carol, their dispatcher, interrupted his thoughts. "Star Calloway has requested that you stop by the *Chief* office as soon as possible."

Oh, for God's sake! He imagined her puffy face and the wart below her eye. "We're kind of busy this morning, Carol, as you know."

"She said it's very important. She said it's something you needed to see right away."

Everybody always thought their problems needed to be addressed right away. *I'll bet it's a real emergency.*

He was about to make some excuse to push off the meeting to at least later in the afternoon when Chief Beckman returned from the direction of the lake. "Carol?" he asked, seeing Nate on the phone.

Nate nodded.

"Is it about the hippie?"

Nate didn't understand. "The hippie?"

"The Madison gal from the newspaper," said Beckman. "She called the station before you got in today. You were the one who talked to her last time, right?"

Nate nodded.

"You can take that call," he said, turning Nate toward the squad as he passed. "Things are under control here. Schnabell are taking statements. We might as well make ourselves useful. I suppose I'd better write a department statement for later when the Milwaukee news cameras get here. Shit, what a nightmare! C'mon, I'll drop you at the station."

#

He pulled the black police SUV to the curb in the historic downtown area. Nate had heard that, originally, the intersection of Rochester Street and Main Street had formed a round-about with a grassy island and bandstand at its center. However, in 1974, the island had been bulldozed and a standard intersection had been created, an intersection which somehow managed to be both significantly less appealing to the eye and significantly less functional.

For years, the *Chief* had been published out of a storefront on the east side of this intersection. However, after the paper had closed down, another business had swooped in. Fortunately, Star Calloway had found a vacant building just across the street, a building that for years had housed Horn Hardware and, more recently, a succession of gift shops. The building was narrow but long, its front door sandwiched between two glass display windows. Banners proclaiming MUKWONAGO CHIEF – BACK IN BUSINESS! along with the front page of the new first issue were on display in the windows.

A tiny brass bell above the door jingled as Nate made his way inside. He was greeted by a modest waiting area with four uncomfortable-looking folding chairs set on the bare wooden floor. Overseeing this was a thin, dark-haired woman with severe features, a hawk-like nose, and glasses that sat low enough so that she peered over them at everything.

She's about what I had imagined.

The woman sat at a 1950s-era gray, metal desk, behind which stood a waist-level wooden railing supported by balusters that prevented visitors from accessing the rest of the building without checking in.

"May I help you?" asked the woman, peering accusingly.

"I'm Officer Janowsky," said Nate. "Are you Mrs. Calloway?"

"It's *Miss* Calloway, and no, I'm Judith Patrick, the office manager. But Star is expecting you."

She pushed a button on her desk phone. "Officer Janowsky is here." After a pause, the reply: "All right." She turned back to Nate. "You can go all the way back."

Nate thanked her and stepped around the right side of her desk, through an opening in the barrier, and faced an eight-foot-wide vinyl banner that reached almost from floor to ceiling, upon which the words of the First Amendment were written in a classy script against a background made to appear like the parchment of the original Constitution. The banner served to screen at least some of the work area from the front of the building. Weaving past this, he faced three modern work stations with the latest

Apple computers. Two were empty. At the third, a man who appeared to be in his mid-thirties, with dark, slightly receding hair appeared to be working on an ad for one of the local restaurants. Beyond the desks sat a long table with eight chairs and an oversized flat monitor perched on one end, possibly for staff meetings.

At the far end of the long, narrow building was, of all things, a fireplace, in front of which rested a somewhat nicer desk, simple, but with a polished, onyx-colored surface. Two comfortable chairs faced this desk, all resting on a braided country-style rug of reds, gold, and browns. Star Calloway rose from behind the desk as Nate approached.

He had to make an effort to keep his jaw from hitting the wooden floor.

However he had imagined Star Calloway, it had never been like this. Rather than graying hair pulled back in a bun, the real Star Calloway had fawn-colored hair that tumbled past her shoulders. Instead of a puffy scowl and warts, the genuine Star Calloway had the lean, attractive face of a movie star with full eyebrows and Cindy Crawford lips. *Why is she hidden away here writing the news? She should be in front of a camera anchoring!*

She wore a serious expression, and as Nate approached, she moved around the corner of her desk to shake his hand. She wore a white, long-sleeve blouse with tan pants and red Nikes. Something in her movements seemed slightly less fluid than he would have expected. He also noticed that she trailed her left hand, perhaps out of habit. At first, he wondered whether she had at some point suffered a stroke. However, after a second look, he was almost sure her left hand was a prosthetic.

She caught his gaze, which had lingered just a moment too long.

"Iraq."

Nate blinked. "I beg your pardon?"

"I did a tour in Iraq. That's where I lost the left hand." She held up the very real-looking prosthesis whose fingers actually moved. "Don't worry. Everyone looks. Electronic. Responds to signals in the existing muscles. Gets them mixed up occasionally. Thank God I'm right handed."

Nate found himself momentarily not knowing what to say. She relieved him of the responsibility by continuing.

"Lost the left leg, too. Just below the knee. Same IED took 'em both."

"I-I'm sorry."

"Lots of others got worse," she said matter-of-factly. "And my leg prosthetic is pretty sweet. I can swap out this foot for one that I can run on."

Nate nodded dumbly, then found his voice.

"Thank you for your service, Ms. Calloway."

"Star," she corrected him.

Nate cleared his throat. "Er, you said you needed to see me right away?"

She picked up a file folder from her desk and motioned him to a seat at the long table, settling herself next to him.

"I heard what happened," she said. "A woman tied into a canoe. There's a rumor that it was Sandy Sewell."

"I can't officially confirm anything until the deceased has been positively identified and relatives have been notified. But…" He left the sentence unfinished.

Star shook her head. "She was in here just two days ago taking out an ad for homes she was listing." They were silent for a moment. Then Star said, "I think I figured out the letter!"

He had momentarily forgotten the actual reason for his visit and felt a twinge of envy toward his fellow officers who, during this time of real crisis for the village, were out doing important work while he was wasting time with some eccentric's letter-writing game.

"Um, the one you read to me over the phone?"

She opened the file folder resting on the table in front of them, revealing the typed letter showing through a clear, plastic zipper bag. Several additional unbagged documents rested beneath it.

"The letter originally concerned me because of its vaguely threatening nature," said Star, who then quoted a line from the document. "*To those who wish to kill the village, it will respond in kind.*"

"But you printed it in Monday's paper," noted Nate.

"Well, yes. I had taken the words to mean the same sort of thing as when people say 'If we keep dumping crap in our rivers, we're all doing to die!' You said yourself that it wasn't really threatening anyone in particular."

"I couldn't help but notice that no one responded," said Nate. "To the riddle, I mean."

"That's right," said Star, pointing at another line in the letter. *"If the correct answer is printed in the Thursday edition of the same week, this will show an understanding of our shared heritage, and the soul of the village will be assuaged. But ignorance will only breed anger and death.* I guess the word 'death' should have been a tip off that this was going to be a bad idea."

It took a moment for her implication to become clear to Nate. "Wait. Are you suggesting that the letter and what happened last night are connected?" He suddenly wondered whether Star had lost more than just parts of her *physical* self in Iraq.

"There was no answer to the riddle. Now someone is dead."

Nate took a deep breath while deciding how to respond. "I don't know, Ms. Calloway."

"Star!"

"That seems to me like a pretty big stretch."

"Does it?" asked Star, her green eyes seeming to flash sparks. *"To those who wish to kill the village, it will respond in kind.* After I started hearing the rumors of who had died, that's when I really got scared! Sandy sold real estate. Some of those properties ended up being torn down, didn't they?"

"Well, sometimes, yes, but that all had to be approved by the village board."

"But it's not such a leap, is it, to think that someone might interpret what Sandy was doing as 'killing the village'? Someone who then responded in kind."

He was about to brush off her concern with a comment about coincidences when he remembered the photograph of the Caul house attached to the floating pinwheel that had marked Sandy's murky grave. Had Sandy sold that property, he wondered? Star saw the change in his expression.

"What?"

Nate held up a hand, his eyes somewhat glassy as he tried to piece together whether this was really significant. "I can't give out information about an ongoing investigation before it comes through the department. But..." He shook himself back into the moment and turned to Star before he said anything he shouldn't. "Was there anything else? About the letter? I notice you've got a few other things in your folder."

"Oh yes. Remember that the letter was signed Ho-ma-ba, which we suspected was a—"

"Pseudonym," said Nate, remembering the word.

Star seemed to suppress a slight smile. "Right. So I decided to do a little on-line search, and when I typed in that name, guess what came up?"

"I haven't the foggiest."

She pushed a printed document in front of him, a copy of an old newspaper article entitled "Mukwonago Legend and Lore: The Phantom of Phantom Lake".

"I've heard of this," said Nate, tapping the article with a finger. Most long-time residents of the village had. "I'm a little foggy on the details."

"It's obviously a myth," noted Star. "And its origin is dubious. The state historical society has a newspaper article on file that suggests it was told to a Mukwonago resident back in 1906 by an old trapper. Yeah, right. There are others who say it was just a tall tale dreamed up by a local businessman to drum up tourist traffic. Create a little Native American mystique for the area. I think that's where I'd put my money."

"What does it have to do with Ho-ma-ba?"

"In the legend, Ho-ma-ba is the name of a Native American who falls in love with I-wo-so. So does another young brave, Zi-ca-ho-ta. I-wo-so's father favored Zi-ca-ho-ta, and when Zi-ca-ho-ta and I-wo-so tried to sneak away in a canoe late one night, Ho-ma-ba, in a separate boat, confronted them in the middle of Phantom Lake. The two braves fought each other, eventually pulling I-wo-so under the water and drowning her."

"Jesus!" Nate ran a hand through his hair as he processed this horrifying revelation. "Sandy was drowned in a canoe!"

"And it fits with the riddle." Star produced a second sheet upon which only the original riddle had been copied and enlarged.

Five little hearts, all in a row.
The first one said, 'I love you so!'
The second one said, 'Pledge your love by these shores.'
The third one said, 'If you do, then it's war!'
The father said, 'Flee with your last breaths!'
The reaper said, ''Neath the waves, they met death.'

"Grim little ditty," grunted Nate.

"You don't recognize it?"

Nate shook his head.

"It's a traditional children's rhyme," said Star.

"If my mom had sung me that, I don't think I'd have closed my eyes all night."

Star rolled her eyes. "It's been altered." She went to her computer, tapped a few keys, and a moment later, the oversized monitor on one end of the meeting table blinked on, displaying the rhyme.

Five little hearts, all in a row.
The first one said, "I love you so!"
The second one said, "Will you be my Valentine?"

The third one said, "If you'll be mine!"
The fourth one said, "I'll always be your friend!"
The fifth one said, "We'll all be friends until the very end!"

"Yeah, that version is a little more kid friendly," said Nate.

"The letter writer chose something familiar. A Valentines rhyme for kids that's been around for decades. The first two lines are the same. Then it gets…creepy. But the altered version lines up with the phantom myth."

She went through it line by line as Nate looked on, fascinated.

"Okay, so the letter writer is trying to get us to guess which bit of local history the riddle refers to. Trying to point us to the phantom legend by dropping clues that refer to things we're maybe more familiar with. As I said, the first two lines haven't been changed from the original."

Five little hearts, all in a row.
The first one said, 'I love you so!'

"Still, it's obvious that the rhyme is steering us toward some sort of local event that could be regarded as a love story. And bingo, the next line makes a reference to the lake."

The second one said, 'Pledge your love by these shores.'

"Wait, it just says shores," interrupted Nate. "You can't throw a rock a hundred yards in any direction in Wisconsin without hitting water. That could mean anywhere."

"But it *could* mean the shores of Phantom Lake. Why would the writer refer to some other shore if he's trying to write a riddle about Mukwonago history? And if I'm right about this, the *first one* in the poem is I-wo-so, and the *second one*, asking her to pledge her love by these shores, is supposed to represent Zi-ca-ho-ta. Now, look at what comes next:"

The third one said, 'If you do, then it's war!'

"Just like in the legend! And I'll bet the *third one* represents Ho-ma-ba. The two braves went to war over I-wo-so. And if you read the article, you'll find that I-wo-so's father wanted her to hook up with Zi-ca-ho-ta."

The father said, 'Flee with your last breaths!'

"I didn't see in that article where the father told them to flee," said Nate.

"Well, it *does* say that the father favored Zi-ca-ho-ta, and it does say that Zi-ca-ho-ta and I-wo-so tried to flee. It's implied."

Nate scowled. "Sounds pretty shaky to me."

"It's meant to be a metaphor!" said Star impatiently. "The writer's not going to come right out and say it!"

"Save us a lot of time if he did."

Star sighed, pointed toward the final line. "Finally, the legend tells us that I-wo-so was pulled under the water and drowned."

The reaper said, 'Neath the waves, they met death.'

His head swam, trying to piece it all together. "All right, I'll give you that the last line is pretty creepy, considering what happened to Sandy. But this is just so...unreal. My brain is fried! But I guess I can see how you'd think this is connected to the murder."

Star looked at him accusingly. "Don't *you* think so?"

"I think there's a lot here that looks...interesting."

"That's your take on this? That it's 'interesting'? You really can't be serious!"

"Look, Ms.—"

"Star!"

He began again. "Look, Star, I don't make the decisions on whether things like this are worth investigating or not. I'll admit, there are a lot of coincidences."

"You can't be sure they're coincidences!"

"No, but you can't automatically assume they're not. Not without more evidence."

Star narrowed her gaze on him. "You want more evidence? Guess what showed up this morning?" She slid out a second plastic bag containing an envelope and typed letter, which she proceeded to read:

"To the Chief,

"How sad. Not even a single guess in your Thursday edition. Apparently no one has heard of the Phantom of Phantom Lake? The clues were so transparent! The reference to pledging love on the shores of the lake, the warring Indian braves, their deaths beneath the waves. In fact, it's one of the most popular local legends. I had hoped it would be an easy first puzzle and would prove me wrong. However, I'm beginning to think Mukwonago residents are indeed as ignorant of their community's history as I feared. And that can't be tolerated. The village is an entity that empowers those to act who truly love it.

"But I'm willing to give you all the benefit of a doubt. Perhaps it was a busy week, what with the end of the school year and such. Perhaps the 'intellectuals' had other items on their plates. So let's try again, shall we? It would be a shame if the entire summer passed without a winner.

"There was a crooked man, and he walked a crooked mile
"From Heaven to bet a crooked sixpence obtained through crooked smiles.

"And then he slipped away again, as crooked as a louse,

"All traces gone today, save for a crooked chameleon house."

The two sat silently for a moment, considering what had been read.

"I hope you don't mind if I take these to show Chief Beckman?" Nate finally asked.

Star shut the folder and pushed it toward Nate. "Please. It's signed Ho-ma-ba again. The letter. I put them in plastic to protect them in case there were fingerprints."

"Are you thinking that whoever wrote this is going to sink another body in a canoe if no one figures out the riddle?" asked Nate. "I mean, *if* the letters and the murder end up actually being connected?"

"I don't know," admitted Star. "But the first clue was about the Phantom of Phantom Lake, and the killer made sure that the murder was similar. If there really is another murder being planned, it wouldn't surprise me if it was connected to the answer to the second riddle."

"Oh God," winced Nate. "That can't happen. One murder is awful enough." Then another thought struck him: "That second letter with the second riddle. You're not going to print it in next Monday's paper, are you?"

Star rubbed her temples as she answered. "I've been struggling over that. My initial reaction was hell no. When the first letter showed up, there was no reason to believe it was a real threat to anyone. Now that we know it was—"

"Assume it was," interrupted Nate.

"*Know* it was," continued Star, "I don't want to play some demented killer's game. You don't know how badly I feel that I printed the first one! That young woman might still be alive!"

"You couldn't have known it would lead to that," said Nate. "I was just wondering...if the letter *hadn't* been in the paper, what do you think the killer would have done?"

Star shook her head. Then stopped, as if another thought had occurred to her. "This was obviously well planned out in advance. I doubt that the psycho would have called it off just because I didn't print the letter." She gave a grim chuckle. "Maybe he'd have even come after me."

"I can't say what would have happened either," observed Nate. "But if these letters are connected to the murder, this nutjob obviously has made some grandiose plans. I agree. I doubt your decision to not print would have stopped him from killing."

Star covered her eyes with a hand, then looked at Nate, seeming to come to a decision. "I'm not printing it. The second letter. I can't be a part of this."

Nate held up his palms in a surrender gesture. "You'll get no argument from me." He picked up the folder as he stood. Star rose as well. "Thank you for your help. We'll be in touch. But...is there anything else you can think of that might be relevant to all this craziness?"

"Just that today's letter arrived in a different way. I opened up the morning paper—not ours but the *Milwaukee Journal Sentinel*—which had been delivered, as usual, to our front desk, and the envelope fell out."

Seven

Chief Beckman was in his office, tapping away hunt-and-peck style on his computer. Nate could see him through the open door, balding head jutting forward toward the screen, shoulders hunched, fingers hovering, hesitating, stabbing. He guessed the Chief was trying to cobble together some sort of statement for the press. Nate had seen two choppers hovering over the lake while driving back to the station, presumably getting footage of the scene of the crime and the emergency vehicles on the ground. A news van with a large "12" on the side had zoomed past him in the opposite direction as well. Others were already at the scene based on the images on the television screen in the dispatcher's office, a sober reporter with microphone addressing the camera with Phantom Glen Park in the background—a different face but similar background on every channel. In Waukesha County, murders were still relatively rare. And in villages like Mukwonago, rarer yet. Unless someone set off a dirty bomb in Racine, this would be the big news of the day.

"Chief?"

He held up a puffy hand. "Give me a minute. I've gotta make sure whatever I say to the press doesn't make me look like Barney Fife."

Nate took a step back, turned, focused his attention on the television. A reporter was talking to a woman who lived on Andrews Street not far from Phantom Glen Park.

'Ma'am, you say you didn't notice anything out of the ordinary last night?'

The woman, probably in her sixties, shook her head, looking stunned. 'No, nothing. I've talked to my neighbors. None of us did. It was just an ordinary night!'

The reporter cast a meaningful glance at the camera before addressing the woman again. 'Yet, not so ordinary. Has this tragic turn of events made you feel less safe in your own neighborhood?'

Now the woman seemed to regain her focus, and the look on her face suggested that she found the reporter's question incredible. 'Why of course I feel less safe! Everyone feels less safe! A young woman was drowned! There's a killer loose out there! You'd have to be a fool to think we wouldn't feel less safe!'

Nate turned away and went to one of the three desk cubicles set aside where officers on duty could complete reports and do follow-up phone calls. As he sat, Beckman came out of his office, handed a printout to Carol, the dispatcher. "Let me know what you think." Then Beckman turned and approached Nate, pulling up a chair to sit next to him. "Carol's the sharpest tool in this shed. If I've screwed up, she'll let me know. So, you wanted to see me?"

Nate produced the folder given to him by Star. "I went to see the newspaper editor."

"Yeah, yeah," said Beckman, his mind clearly on other issues. "Star Calloway."

"She thinks the anonymous letters that are being sent to the *Chief* are from the same person that killed Sandy." He held one up in its plastic covering, but Beckman didn't take it.

"Letters?" he said as the message finally clicked.

"Star received a second one. Another riddle."

"So does Denzel Washington star in this movie?" asked Beckman wearily. "Jesus! Leave it to a Madison transplant to imagine the Zodiac killer is behind every small-town murder."

"I dunno, Chief. I'm not saying she's right, but you might want to take a look at these." He held out the file, but Beckman pushed it aside.

"Really? Do you think I have time for some hippie conspiracy theory with all this shit hitting the fan right now?" Beckman stood up. "Ten to one says it's the boyfriend. Some sort of jealousy thing. Or she was pregnant and he didn't want to be a daddy. It's always the boyfriend." Then he headed back to Carol to see whether she thought he was Barney Fife or John F. Kennedy.

After hearing Carol's assessment, he called back to Nate. "Janowsky! It's almost eleven and the vultures are starting to flock in the parking lot! Keep 'em out of the building!" Then, his head snapping in a different direction, he shouted, "Schnabell!" The two officers, who had just returned from Andrews Street, skidded to a halt. "Carry the department podium out to the sidewalk! And keep everyone out of the building unless they're wearin' a badge!"

Nate took his place outside in front of the door. The Mukwonago Village Police Department building faced east toward Rochester. Across the street, a retention pond and then the railroad tracks. The building itself was tan brick, single story, with a long bank of windows along the front and a garage for the police vehicles at the back. A good-sized parking area wrapped around the front and south sides of the building, but today, it was nowhere near big enough.

A few moments later, Schnell and Bell banged through the door with the podium and set it on the sidewalk facing Rochester Street. They set a couple of orange cones in the parking lot to create an open space in front of the podium. Two news trucks screamed in and, within minutes, a couple of techies were clamping microphones onto the podium. More cars arrived, parking in the remaining spaces on the south side of the lot. A few simply pulled over at the side of the street, probably figuring that the cops had better things to do this morning than give them tickets. Cameras were hoisted to shoulders and, at precisely eleven, Chief Beckman, wearing his hat and good jacket, stepped out of the building and behind the podium where he read from his prepared remarks.

"I will keep my remarks brief. We are in the midst of a very serious investigation, and I hope that you all will respect the need of our officers to do their jobs swiftly and efficiently. The best way to do that is to let them. All department communication should go through me. Please also respect the privacy of family members and other individuals related to the deceased.

"Here is what we know so far. This morning, a body was discovered in Phantom Lake in about twelve feet of water about one hundred feet offshore from Phantom Glen Park. Cause of death appears to be drowning. Time of death has not precisely been established, although we believe the deceased was in the water for twelve hours or less. We believe we know the identity of the deceased, but we will not be making an official statement until relatives have been notified. The condition of the body is consistent with homicide. The coroner will be supplying us with a detailed report as soon as possible.

"We have several persons of interest at this time. In the next twenty-four hours, we will be questioning a number of individuals who may have information helpful to the case. We do not, as yet, have a clear motive.

"Other details of the homicide will not be released at this time, so as to not compromise an ongoing investigation. This office will release more details as they become available and are relevant. Thank you."

A few reporters shouted questions.

"Is it true that the victim is a local woman?"

Beckman spoke, keeping his eyes on his script, although his reply was obviously not written there. "I won't be saying anything about the identity of the victim at this time."

"There are rumors that this was the result of a lovers' quarrel," said a second reporter.

"Any talk of motives at this early point in the investigation is merely speculation," said Beckman.

"Do you think the community is safe?" asked a third. "Are you concerned that there might be more killings?"

Beckman sighed, continued to speak in a tolerant monotone. "The officers serving the Village of Mukwonago have always done their best to make this a safe community, and our track record speaks for itself. The last murder was more than a decade ago. Our officers will bring this case to a close quickly. However, we do ask village residents to be vigilant, lock their doors, and come forward with any information that might be helpful."

The event wound down after that, and Schnabell wrestled the podium back inside the building. As Nate headed back toward the work cubicles, Carol called to him.

"Star Calloway wants you to call."

Nate sat, pecked out the number. Star quickly picked up."

"This is Officer Janowsky, returning your call."

"Thank you," said Star. "Just wanted to let you know that I've changed my mind. I've decided to print the letter."

Eight

When Nate arrived at the *Chief* offices, he found a small gathering in the lobby area. In addition to the receptionist, Judith Patrick—who remained seated behind her desk—there was a slim man, probably around thirty, who was unfamiliar to him, dark hair, neatly-trimmed beard, wearing a black Rolling Stones t-shirt and jeans. He held a tablet, pointing at the screen while talking with Sarah Cutler, slim, fifty-ish with silver-streaked cinnamon-colored hair that reached the middle of her back, owner of one of the village's growing number of coffee shops. Another woman, Grace Hall, tall, mid-thirties, a red bandana covering the top of her head since the start of her cancer treatments, owner of Grace's Gifts just across the street, chatted animatedly with Judith, her hands moving about like World War I airplanes in a dogfight, tears visible on her cheeks. Seated in one of the waiting area chairs was Craig LaForte, mid-forties, always dressed in sweatpants and an oversized team jersey, owner of Gordy's, a sports-themed burger bar whose softball team often won the city league—with Craig as its catcher. He also wrote the rather lengthy press releases for the league's weeky games, and it looked like he was waiting to turn one in now, listening intently to the general office hubbub. Why he didn't simply email them, Nate did not know.

Grace's voice rose above the rest. "How the hell? How the hell can something like this happen in Mukwonago, Wisconsin?" She wiped away tears with the back of a hand.

Judith shook her head sympathetically. "The world's getting worse, if you ask me."

"But," Grace continued, "Sandy? Why Sandy? What did she ever do to *anybody* in this town?"

"Maybe it wasn't somebody from here," said Craig, and both Judith and Grace turned toward him. "I mean, maybe it was some drifter. My money's on one of them carnies here for Summerfest in Field Park this weekend."

While he offered no comment to that effect, Nate doubted Craig's hypothesis. The murder had been too carefully planned to be the random act of some drifter.

Grace turned back to Judith. "I—I'm sorry. After I opened up the shop and people started coming in and I heard—" It took her a few moments before she could continue. "I just had to talk to someone...to see if it was true." She covered her face with her hands for a beat or two and shook almost feverishly. "And I'm just a little scared, you know? I don't know if I want to keep the shop open today. I mean, I'm sometimes in there all by myself."

Judith reached out, took one of her hands, patted it. "You just call if you need anything and I'll come right across the street. Or come back over here if you don't feel quite right."

Grace hurried out, Judith watching her go. "Poor thing. She's been through so much." Then she turned to Nate. "Officer Jan—"

She was interrupted by Craig who had popped out of his seat and was offering Judith his paperwork. "For Monday's sports section!" Then he turned to Nate. "They're still holding the carnival, right? They're not going to cancel the softball tournament, are they? I put up a lot of dough to sponsor those trophies! Which, I might add, I plan to get a few back!" He smiled, Nate thought, like a Hyena.

"I haven't heard anything about cancellations," said Nate.

Craig seemed satisfied, nodded, and headed for the door. "Ciao!"

Sarah seemed to have finished her business with the Rolling Stones t-shirt guy and now turned toward Nate. "I have to admit, I feel a lot like Grace," she said with a heavy sigh. "There are going to be times when that coffee shop isn't very busy, and I'm going to feel pretty spooked. I was kind of glad to have to come over here this morning to proof an ad with Kevin. Should we? Be worried, I mean?"

"I think we should all be concerned…and exercise a little more caution," said Nate. "But make no mistake, this is going to be our number one priority until we find who did it. And we will find him." He felt a little self-conscious, suspecting he sounded a lot like the scripted speech that Chief Beckman had recited. He hoped he wasn't spouting empty platitudes.

"Or her," said Sarah, who then headed out the door.

Nate watched her go, then turned back to Judith. "You can go back," she said, unsmiling.

Star met him at the wide table, shaking her head as if in disbelief.

"I should have stayed in Madison. It was less crazy!"

"So M—" He stopped himself before she could stop him. "So *Star*...What's going on? You said you were thinking about printing the second letter?"

"Hear me out," said Star, motioning for him to sit. "What happens if I *don't* print the letter."

Nate thought about it for a moment. "Maybe nothing. Chief Beckman thinks the letter writer is just some crackpot. Thinks the murder is completely unrelated."

Star's eyes bulged and her mouth dropped open. "Seriously? Did he even *look* at the folder I gave you?"

"Actually, no. When I explained what you had said, he just sort of waved it off. Called it..." Nate caught himself.

"Called it what?" asked Star.

"He called it a hippie conspiracy theory," said Nate sheepishly.

Star smirked. "Gotta love small towns. Anything else?"

"He said it's always the boyfriend."

Star sighed. "He could be right about that. But he needs to look at that folder. The murder is definitely connected to those letters."

"Then why do you want to print the second one?"

"Humor me for a second," said Star. "The murderer is the letter writer. The letter is printed, and we've got three days before the next edition of the paper. Three days where the killer expects people to try to figure out the clue."

"And if no one figures it out, he whacks another person."

"That seems to be the game," agreed Star. "But if I don't print the letter, will he just stop playing? Or will he go through with his plans for a second murder right away?"

"Right away?"

"I mean like, if the killer sees that the letter isn't in Monday's paper, will he get pissed and take someone out on Monday night? Or Tuesday?"

Nate turned the idea over in his head for a moment. "So you're thinking that printing the letter buys us a couple of days?"

"Right. At least until Thursday, when he sees there's no answer. That gives you guys more time to figure out who it is before he strikes again. And who knows? Maybe someone will figure out the second riddle, which buys us even more time." She passed a copy of the second letter to Nate. They looked at it again.

> *There was a crooked man, and he walked a crooked mile*
> *From Heaven to bet a crooked sixpence obtained through crooked smiles.*
> *And then he slipped away again, as crooked as a louse,*
> *All traces gone today, save for a crooked chameleon house.*"

She stepped to her desk, tapped a few keys and a text document appeared on the large monitor at the end of the table. "Again, it starts off like a common nursery rhyme, something almost everyone knows. Then the writer makes changes to feed us our clues."

There was a crooked man, and he walked a crooked mile,
He found a crooked sixpence against a crooked stile;
He bought a crooked cat which caught a crooked mouse,
And they all lived together in a little crooked house.

Rubbing his temples, Nate pushed the letter aside and squinted at Star. "I was hoping that when I looked at it a second time, it would seem easier. But I think this is worse than the first one."

"Don't say that," said Star. "You know this town much better than I do!"

"Grew up here."

"That's the thing. I didn't! When the writer mentions 'walking a mile from Heaven' or 'a chameleon house,' those phrases have to mean something! Somewhere there's a 'chameleon house' of some sort that he's talking about! I'm new here. I can't possibly be expected to make all of these connections! I don't know Mukwonago's forests and landmark buildings and parks and history! I need you to help! To think!"

He wanted nothing more than to be able to help Star. He admired the fact that she was a damned war hero. Yet she didn't act like it was any big deal or let her injuries bother her, or at least she did not show that side of herself to the public. And he admired the fact that, despite having lived in the community for only a few weeks, she seemed to really care about what happened to the people of the village. From all appearances, she wasn't out simply to get a story. She wanted to help.

And she was beautiful, the sort of woman who could have hosted her own talk show or maybe played the heroine in Hallmark movies if her life had played out differently. Yes, he would absolutely love to be able to help her, to see her smile at his ingenuity, at his capableness.

But he had nothing.

"Chameleon house," he said impotently. "Well...there are a lot of colorful houses."

The disappointment in her face almost killed him. "This psycho is obsessed with local history, so the chameleon house has to be some place where something historically significant happened."

Nate thought some more, trying to dredge up memories of houses in the village that were historically significant. He knew that the village had designated the neighborhood surrounding the Mukwonago Community Library as historic. The one that always came to his mind first was the Bissett home on the intersection of Pearl and Pleasant, not because it was particularly colorful, but because in 1897, the family had built a stone replica of the Blarney Castle they had seen at the Chicago World's Exposition—which still stood in their side yard. He doubted that was the house indicated in the rhyme, and his face burned in acknowledgement of his failure to contribute.

"I still...I...I got nothing."

Star exhaled loudly, recovered herself, smiled politely. "Keep thinking on it. And who knows, maybe a community member will get it if we don't."

"The word chameleon...they change colors, right? Maybe it's a place where a house used to stand, but now it's *changed*. I mean, they moved a house to build the first Wal-mart on 83 near the river. There's a church there now."

"Really? Down by the bridge over the Mukwonago River as you're heading out toward the freeway?"

Nate nodded. "And where the community library is…that's a big lot with a ball diamond on it. And a school used to stand there! And then there's the big intersection right in front of this building! It used to be a round-about with a bandstand in the center, but it changed! So maybe it's not colors. Maybe it's change!"

"That's good," said Star, a smile growing slowly from the corners of her mouth. "Your memories are going to be important if we're going to figure out what this letter means!"

A little spark of something ignited for an instant in Nate. It had sounded to him as if the two of them were working as a kind of team.

As Star moved to stand, Nate rose as well.

"There's one more thing," said Nate. "The last line of the letter before the poem."

It would be a shame if the entire summer passed without a winner.

"Yeah, that caught my attention too," said Star grimly. "It seems to suggest that we'd better find this schmuck, or Mukwonago's going to start feeling a lot more like Ramadi."

Nine

There would be a lot of overtime this weekend. No officer had objected to this announcement—at least out loud. They all knew the community was smothering under a thickening smog of fear. However, that didn't keep Nate from grumbling to himself on Friday evening, which was supposed to have been off, as was the whole day on Saturday. He would be doing security at Summerfest tonight, and would work noon until eight tomorrow.

While he could sleep in on Saturday, that would not begin to give him enough time to put a dent in his novel-length to-do list of everything from neglected laundry to getting the oil changed on his personal vehicle—a dark red 1988 Chevy Beretta that he referred to as "Higgins".

He took an hour for supper from five o'clock to six on Friday, stopping in at his condo to toss a Healthy & Happy entree into the microwave and wolfing it down while checking emails, throwing a load of towels into the wash, and taking out a long-overdue bag of kitchen trash. The hour passed quickly, and the tiny meal scarcely took the edge off his hunger. *But at least it was healthy.* If he didn't count the 1200 milligrams of sodium. And it definitely hadn't made him feel any happier.

After he brushed his teeth and washed his face, he was ready to head off to the park. As the garage door rose, he noticed Pete Moore—owner of the unit to his north, which shared walls with his own—in the common driveway. Pete wore plaid shorts and a pink polo as he washed his SUV with a bucket of soapy water, a chamois, and a garden hose. A computer programmer, Pete worked from home and pretty much set his own hours.

"Jesus, Pete, you've got the whole day tomorrow! You should be relaxing on a Friday night."

Pete, forty-eight with glasses and receding hair that made him look like George Costanza, shut off the hose, smiled back at his neighbor. "Emily wants me to drive her to an art show in Cedarburg tomorrow, so gotta sneak in a wash somewhere. I don't know why she goes to those things. She never buys anything. But I'm sure it'll be fun." He smiled as if he wasn't sure at all.

Nate nodded. "I'm jealous. More fun than my day will be."

"Yeah, what the hell, Nate. I'm sure you know more about it than I do. I just know what I heard on the news. But, wow! In Mukwonago?"

"The world is changing, I guess."

"Maybe time to find another world," said Pete, somberly. "Maybe Em and I will sign up for one of those one-way missions to start a Mars colony."

"You'd be an asset to the mission, Pete. Your grilling expertise would guarantee that no Mars colonist would starve."

"Speaking of which," said Pete, "We should be back from Cedarburg by mid-afternoon. If I'm lucky. I'm going to throw some brats and burgers on the coals around suppertime if you're interested."

"You know I'm interested, but I doubt I'll be off until late. You know they've got the carnival this weekend, so with that and the murder, we're all pulling extra duty."

Pete looked at the ground, shook his head. "For God's sake, Nate...you guys got any suspects?"

"It's early," explained Nate. "They took Sandy's body to Waukesha for autopsy. Other than the canoe, zip ties and duct tape, there wasn't much physical evidence. None of the neighbors noticed anything out of the ordinary."

"Wait. What?" Pete's eyes went wide. "Zip ties and duct tape? I just heard somebody got drowned!"

"Tied into a canoe," said Nate. "Just off shore from that park on Andrews Street. Unfortunately, there were no parking lot cameras, and the neighbors there don't have the doorbell cameras that might have captured something in the background. So nothing concrete yet. But like I said, it's still early. A lot more rocks to look under."

Glancing at his watch, Nate closed the door on the empty garage and slipped behind the wheel of his squad. *Higgins* was parked a mile and a half away at the police department. At the start of his shift, he would drive his personal vehicle to the station—like all of the other officers—and then switch to Squad 42, his usual ride, a black and white Ford Interceptor. The department had seven Interceptors, which were essentially small SUVs, plus an Expedition that the detectives and crime scene technitions used, and a Chevy Silverado for transporting large pieces of evidence.

"We'll now be having more intimate conversations with the people closest to Miss Sewell," Chief Beckman had said after the press conference earlier that day. "In cases of premeditated murder, that's often where the perp is going to be found. For most of us, though, our job is going to be keeping the rest of this community safe, making sure they feel like they're not in danger, and keeping the loose cannons who've had a few beers from forming vigilante groups and roaming the streets shooting stray cats or worse. The fact that the damned carnival is this weekend only complicates things."

Nate dreamed of getting an opportunity to participate in the questioning of suspects, but detective work was out of his lane, and some officers were needed to take care of the more routine and mundane business. So for him, it would be an evening in Field Park

The drive took less than two minutes. Shortly after that, Nate stood along the brightly lit midway at Mukwonago's Summerfest. Other members of the village police department circulated as well, along with a dozen citizens who had been deputized for the occasion. The idea: Be visible, keep moving, keep your eyes open.

The sun neared the horizon as Nate began his circuit once again. Bulbs that lined the fronts of midway games flashed frenetically as the carnies, with change making machines hooked to sagging beltlines, tried to convince passersby of the ease with which they could win a giant stuffed panda. The dull bell on the top of the high striker rang occasionally to signal that someone had passed the so-called "test of strength" with a sledge hammer. The air smelled of cotton candy and diesel.

The gruesome events of the morning did not seem to have discouraged folks, for Nate observed that the walking areas were well-populated. Not crushing crowds, but certainly not a ghost town. Perhaps, he thought, people needed to get out and behave normally as a way of dealing with the tragedy. It was reasonable to believe that this was better and healthier than surrendering to it behind closed doors.

Moving among the rides, the organ music from the carousel grew louder. There were also low "flying" airplanes and fire trucks whirling on circular platters for the littlest visitors. Farther along was the Tilt-a-whirl (which Nate recalled getting sick on when he was twelve), the Zipper, the Rock-o-plane (which had always seemed an inappropriate name, to Nate, for it did not look like a plane at all), and rising above it all, the Ferris wheel.

He took a turn past the beer tent, which was just now starting to fill up. He waved a finger toward a couple of deputies who were making it their business to keep an eagle-eye on the crowd there. Music from a country band boomed from inside the fenced off area, where an ID was required for admission.

Wandering father north, he found himself heading up and down the rows of cars parked on the grass. The pounding music from the beer tent was duller here and the carnival rides rose above the trees to the south like a bouquet of sparks. A few new cars wedged themselves into open spots as he toured the area, and an occasional couple, down for the count early, struggled to their cars, dragging small, vigorously protesting children after them. He passed Schnabell, the two officers heading in the opposite direction, pausing a moment to exchange comments on the ordinariness of the night.

It all looked so very much like a celebration in a small town where a murder had *not* occurred a mere twenty-for hours ago.

Now he walked down the park's main paved roadway, past the ball diamond where the softball tournament was being contested under lights atop high poles. Every once in awhile, renewed shouting erupted as a ball found the ground in the outfield and someone reached base.

After that, he was back at the Midway. He would linger here for a bit, breathing in the aroma of carnival food served from the side windows of white trucks—spicy and greasy food that seemed incompatible with the sorts of jarring carnival rides its consumers were likely to target afterwards—and then begin the circuit again.

A young boy passed with his parents. The corn dog he was holding, Nate realized, looked really good. It wasn't exactly on his diet—which wasn't exactly being followed to the letter anyway—but he was working overtime under extraordinary circumstances. Didn't that merit a little comfort food? He stepped to the window, coming away moments later with two battered dogs. Taking a bite, he closed his eyes. *Oh yeah.*

"You know, diet is the number one contributor to our well-being."

Swallowing quickly—and almost choking— Nate swung around in the direction of the voice to see Grace Hall regarding him with amusement.

"Sorry," he said, wiping the back of his hand across his mouth. Then he held up the remaining one and a half corndogs. "Yeah, probably not the best choice."

Grace wore another bright, red bandana atop her smooth head, perhaps a little flashier than the one he had seen this morning. Now, however, she also wore a loose-fitting, navy-blue summer dress covered in sunflowers. Nate thought she looked gorgeous.

"Nothing that's cooking in this park is 'the best choice'," said Grace with a slight smirk. "To boost my immune system, I'm on a super-antioxidant diet. Lots of oily fish, spinach, broccoli, blueberries..." She strode past him to the vending truck, came back a moment later with a corn dog of her own. "But sometimes, you just gotta go with the guilty pleasure! Oh, yum!"

Now it was Nate's turn to smile. She seemed to enjoy the first couple bites of her corndog more than he had.

"What a freakin' day," she said, between bites, her expression suddenly growing more sober. "It's still so hard to believe. We were friends." It looked for a moment like she might cry again, as she had earlier in the *Chief* office, but then took a huge bite of her corndog and seemed to focus on the act of chewing.

"It's been a day all right," said Nate. "You okay?"

She chewed a bit, swallowed. "No. But I'm not quite the mess I was this morning. Just sat in my store with the doors locked. Started to pull myself together later in the afternoon. Cleaned up. Decided to get out. Fresh air and all. And ended up here." She looked at the nearly naked stick in her hand. "Needing a corndog, I guess. God, these are good!"

No longer feeling self-conscious, Nate took another bite of his. "You walked. Weren't you scared? I mean, coming here by yourself?"

Grace laughed. "No, I drove. Windows down, of course. Was just going to drive out in the country. Wanted to get away from the village, you know? Because it made me think of…"

Nate nodded. "Yeah, I get it."

"But as I drove past the carnival, I thought the lights, the people, the noise…the food…" She held up the partially consumed corndog. "I thought it all might take my mind off things for awhile. And whataya know. Here I am, spending my evening talking about it."

"Well, we can't have that," said Nate. He had intended to follow up with some witty remark that would start a jaunty, upbeat conversation in a completely different direction. But he was suddenly at a loss. After a few moments, the silence got awkward. "So how are you feeling?" *God, what a dumb-ass question. Yeah, that'll lighten her mood. Change the subject from murder to cancer. Maybe next you can work the Hindenburg into the conversation.*

"You mean the treatments?" asked Grace, not seeming to mind. "They take a lot out of you. Sometimes I have to close the shop for a day or so. Hard to even move. But right now, I'm feeling good. Test results so far are promising."

She sighed, smiled again, a beautiful smile. Then the silence got too big.

"Well, I've got to make laps around the park tonight. Make sure everybody feels safe." Nate took half a step.

"I'm not here to ride the Tilt-a-whirl or win a big bear. Want some company?"

Of course he wanted some company. *Her* company. How often did beautiful women volunteer to accompany him anywhere?

"Suit yourself, but I'm not much of a tour guide."

Grace laughed. "Don't worry, I think I could give a pretty fair tour. I've lived here since I was five. Played in this park as a kid. There used to be several stone fireplaces scattered through here. Looked like they must have been built by the first settlers! We used to sneak over here with marshmallows and chocolate and make smores! I probably know this park better than you!"

They headed out into the rides.

"So you've really lived here almost all of your life?" he asked as they walked.

"Dad moved us here when I was in kindergarten. I was born in Fennimore. That's waaay over in the western part of the state."

"I kind of had a general idea."

"He got a better job," continued Grace. "I often wonder how things would have turned out if we'd stayed."

Nate suddenly remembered a terrible accident out on highway LO on a curvy section just west of where Rainbow Springs Resort had been. Head on collision. Parents both killed coming back from a night out at Sterlingworth Supper Club. Nate thought he must have been maybe thirteen at the time. Somewhere in the back of his mind he had known that Jerry and Evelyn Hall had left behind a daughter who had grown up with her aunt. This was the first time he had connected the dots to the adult Grace Hall.

"You were what, five years behind me in school?" asked Nate, clearing his throat. "I suppose that's why I don't ever remember seeing you as a kid."

"I wasn't much to see," said Grace. "Sort of kept to myself. Wore a lot of dark clothing. But I've always been a survivor. I crawled out of that hole."

The world got a bit quieter and darker as they entered the parking area. Colossus oaks, some of which had stood sentry over the area for more than a century, arched protectively above the silent vehicles. Their feet crunched sticks and acorns.

"So you're doing well now? Who's your doctor?"

"Dr. Susan Ayres."

Nate nodded. "She from the Mukwonago clinic?"

Grace shook her head. "Waukesha. You know, when you first hear it—that diagnosis—it's almost like you're hearing your own death sentence. I decided right there I was going to go big. That's why I chose Dr. Ayers. You know, she was named one of the Milwaukee Area's top 100 doctors last year? That was one of the things that caught my attention."

"You went big all right," said Nate.

Suddenly, Grace put her hands over her face and laughed. "Christ, why are we talking about medical issues on a beautiful summer night like tonight? We're not seventy!"

"Probably the corn dogs talking," said Nate, finishing the last bit of dog number two. "So much delicious nasty stuff in them that they probably immediately make you conscious of the health points you've lost."

"Tomorrow it's back to the antioxidants. So now you know about me. What kind of kid were you?"

"A big one."

"Come on. Seriously."

Nate thought about it for a moment. "I was a follower, not a leader. I had a group of three or four friends I hung around with, and I pretty much did whatever they did. Baseball, sledding, biking all the hell over the place. I was a free-range kid, I guess."

They turned a corner and headed down the paved roadway toward the ball diamond.

"What made you want to be a police officer?"

He shrugged. "Guess I like helping out people. You know...I guess especially the ones who really need protecting, who have a tough time helping themselves. Sounds pretty corny."

"Not at all," said Grace. "At least you can look at yourself in the mir—"

Angry shouts cut short their conversation and Nate's radio immediately crackled to life. "Nate, can I get you over at the ball field right now!"

It took him only a few hurried strides to reach the chain link fence. Slipping through, he noticed two men wrestling on the ground while Dick Andrews, a fellow officer, tried to break it up. A small crowd stood watching or trying to move in to help. Another man lay on the ground nearby, being attended to by several more. Nate barreled through the bodies like a warship, getting both hands on the man on top and pulling him off the other as if he were a rag doll. The man unleashed a string of obscenities, and Nate saw that it was Craig LaForte, wearing his team's green and gold jersey. Nate set him down, but Craig immediately started for the man on his back again. This time Nate roughly slammed him into the dusty third-base line, face down.

"Settle down, Craig!" said Nate, his voice booming. "What the hell!"

"Goddamn cheaters, that's what they are!" roared Craig, trying to get up, but held face-down by Nate.

"The guy's nuts!" said a paunchy man in a red and white Troy Tap jersey. "He almost killed Justin! Then he went after Mike!"

Nate looked toward the man who had been lying on his back when he arrived—Justin, apparently. He was now sitting up, working his jaw with a hand, his catcher's mask sitting in the dirt next to him. One of the men who had been looking after him jogged over.

"Looks like Justin is going to be okay. The mask took most of it." Then he pointed to Craig. "This asshole tried to kill him!"

Craig struggled under Nate's grip. "Goddamn cheaters!"

"Shut up!" Nate found Dick. "What the hell happened?"

Dick shook his head. "Craig's guys were losing by a run. He was the last up, last inning, tying run on third. Craig strikes out."

"It was a ball, a fu—"

"Shut up!" shouted Nate. "Go on."

"Craig swings the bat like he's chopping down a Sequoia—bam! The catcher goes down. The pitcher runs in, Craig takes a big swing at him, misses, then they're on the ground!"

Nate found his cuffs, snapped them onto Craig's wrists behind his back.

"Come on!" cried Craig, still struggling. "You've got to be kidding me!"

Nate pointed to the man in the red and white jersey he had first spoken to. "The rescue squad is parked over by the beer tent. Send someone over, get them to check out Justin, make sure he doesn't have a concussion or neck injury or something."

Then he turned to Dick. "Take Craig in. I'll stay here and take statements."

He pulled Craig to his feet, sent him off with Dick. Then he radioed Schnabell to come help with the paperwork.

Pat Wood, who had been umpiring the contest, stepped next to Nate, and they watched the two figures recede toward where Dick's cruiser was parked. "Stupid bastard."

Nate sighed. "Well, this murder thing has probably ratcheted up everybody's anxiety. People do things when they're afraid. Not very smart things, sometimes."

"Maybe," said Pat. "But Craig's always been a cruel bastard. Usually makes a joke out of it, and of course, he hangs with a group that tolerates it. I'm 74, and I remember that little prick as a kid. Lived just a few doors down. One time, he caught one of the neighborhood cats. Buried it up to its neck. Then fired up the lawnmower."

The story nauseated Nate.

"Yep," continued Pat. "When they start out that wrong, it makes you wonder what they'll do when they get to be adults."

Nate nodded, patted the older man on the shoulder. "Hang around if you would, Pat. You were right on top of things, so I'll get your statement in a sec." He moved back toward the chain link fence, craning his neck to see. However, there was no sign of Grace.

"Wow, the excitement never stops in Mukwonago."

He turned toward the sound of the new voice to see Star striding toward him from left field, an expensive-looking camera slung around her neck.

Fan of softball...or pro wrestling?" asked Nate.

"I was here taking photos for the *Chief* and heard the commotion."

"Yeah. The perfect end to the perfect day. And now I've got to go take statements."

"Sounds right up there on the fun scale with covering school board meetings for the paper," said Star. "Give any more thought to the latest riddle?"

"A little," he said, though he really hadn't.

"Me too. We should talk."

"We should. Right now, though..." He pointed towards the two teams milling about on the lighted diamond, their members waiting to give statements.

Star nodded. "Take your time. I'll wait."

#

By the time Nate was finished at the ball diamond, it was past eleven. The beer tent was closed and the stragglers were leaving the park. Nate felt beat, physically exhausted from having to deal with Craig LaForte, and emotionally spent from the punishing weight that homicide brings to a small town.

Star waited just outside the chain link fence.

"Police work. An hour and a half to collect evidence that a judge will skim in thirty seconds."

Star laughed. "The beer tent is closed, so I didn't have anything else to do."

"I don't take you for a heavy drinker anyway," said Nate.

"Oh, you should have seen me right after I got back from Iraq. Jack Daniels was my best friend. But he kept pissing me off because we'd just start to enjoy each other's company, and he'd disappear so quickly."

"I take it you ended the relationship?"

"It took sixteen years, getting fired and about six months of counseling." She forced a smile. "Been clean for a year. But days like today, it would sure feel good to invite Jack over for a visit."

Nate offered a sympathetic grunt. "You're better off without him. I'm a Spotted Cow man myself. But I try not to overdo it. Easy to get caught up in the drinking culture of America's Dairyland. So you said you'd given more thought to the riddle?"

They began to walk back toward the west side of the park where Nate's squad now rested mostly alone.

"I went to the Mukwonago Community Library, asked a few questions. The librarian there was very helpful. She directed me to a couple of books by a DeEstin Wright. I guess he was a middle school principal here back in the '60s who was really into local history. They say time stands still in little towns, but based on what I've read, there's not much that *hasn't* changed in Mukwonago over the years."

"So it was a dead end?"

"Not exactly," said Star. "I mean, I could be way off, but two things sort of jumped out at me."

Nate thought of the riddle again.

"There was a crooked man, and he walked a crooked mile

"From Heaven to bet a crooked sixpence obtained through crooked smiles.

"And then he slipped away again, as crooked as a louse,

"All traces gone today, save for a crooked chameleon house."

"Okay, I'm listening."

"The first is right at the center of the village near the *Chief* office. 110 Main. Around 1900, the basement of the building was a four-lane bowling alley. Pins were set by hand. The upstairs was a grocery store. But later, around 1960...well, you're not going to guess what it became."

"No, I'm not. Like you said, 110 Main has got to be somewhere near the downtown intersection, but I don't know exactly where."

"It became the *Mukwonago Chief* office—until the early '90s," said Star, beaming as if she'd just solved String Theory. "There would be some irony in our letter writer choosing that building and then having the letters published in the *Chief* in its new location."

Nate smiled. "That would be an interesting twist. And bowling alley to grocery store to newspaper office to antiques—that's what's in there now, right? Yeah, that's pretty chameleon-like."

Star nodded, smiling. "Just a theory. But I've got nothing on the rest of the rhyme. Who's the crooked man? What's a walk from heaven? Still drawing a blank on those."

"I don't know how you can think outside the lines like that," said Nate, shaking his head. "But you said *two* things jumped out at you?"

"Oh, right," said Star. "I was talking with Kevin. You know, the guy who does the ad layouts for the paper? Anyway, we were talking about how there was only one hotel in town, and he said that, according to his father there used to be one right on Rochester at MacArthur Drive—right across from Miller's pharmacy." She pointed in a south-easterly direction.

"Really? There's apartments there now, right?"

Star nodded. "This was back in the 1960s and earlier. It was called 'The Sunset Motel' or something of the sort, according to Kevin. It wasn't like a Holiday Inn or anything. It was a line of little individual cabins with a big old willow tree out front."

"Sounds cozy," said Nate drolly. "And yeah, it's quite different today."

"Right, but think about the name! 'Sunset Motel.' Sunsets can be very colorful—and different from one day to the next. How's that for chameleon-like?"

"Nice. But…"

"But?"

"The riddle says a chameleon house was left *behind*," stated Nate. "All of those little Sunset cabins are gone."

"True." Her smile evaporated. "And again, it doesn't address the *crooked man* or *heaven* components."

"Exactly. And it sort of illustrates a recurring problem."

"How so?" asked Star.

"I mean, you said it yourself before. So much in the village has changed. You could look at almost anything that isn't the same as it was a hundred years ago and say, 'Wow, chameleon-like! That must be it!'"

"I know," she said reluctantly. "Until we find a place that seems to fit *all* the clues in the rhyme, we're probably way off base."

Nate fell silent for a few moments. "Still, if you're planning on printing the letter, unless some reader comes up with a better theory, you should print any that you think of. There's always a chance you might be right, and then you'll buy some additional time. Theoretically."

"Way ahead of you." Then her tone became more serious. "I know you can't say too much. Ongoing investigation and all, But I heard you guys talked to the boyfriend today."

The high floodlights at the ball field blinked out so that only the glow from the carnie trailers, the streetlamps, and the grocery store across the street dimly filtered through the leaves.

"Rick Bryer," affirmed Nate, settling down onto the concrete step base of the park's flagpole. Star sat beside him. "You're right. I can't say much. I'll tell you this. Poor bastard cried his eyes out. Completely distraught. Don't know if I've ever seen anybody so wrecked."

"Overacting, you think?"

"I dunno," said Nate. "He had stuff coming out of his nose and I thought he was going to stop breathing a few times he was hyperventilating so badly. He's a big guy. A coach. If he was faking it, he deserves an Oscar."

Star nodded, then looked up at him. "Or he's a psychopath."

They sat silently for a minute.

"Better go," said Star, popping up suddenly. "I'll let you know if I think of anything else."

"Need a ride?" he asked.

She pointed to a blue Kia Forte only thirty feet from his squad. "I'm just over here!" Then she groaned. "Arg! I'm emotionally exhausted."

Nate got to his feet, watching her retreating into the shadows. "Then do me a favor, will you?"

She stopped, half turned. "What's that?"

"If your best friend Jack tries to stop by tonight, tell him to get the hell out!"

She smiled, found her car keys, and a few moments later, began rolling across acorns, twigs, and flattened grass toward the exit.

Eleven

Saturday was supposed to have been his day off, but murder in a small town changes the work schedule for cops. On the plus side, he did not have to come in until noon, and so *Higgins'* oil finally got changed. At the park, most of his afternoon was spent walking laps. Nate almost wished he had one of those fancy watches that counted steps so that you could hit 10,000 and have an extra light beer to celebrate.

Almost.

He was a little disappointed that he saw neither Grace nor Star during the day, as he instead had to settle for the homely mugs of Schnanell and Dick Andrews as he paced circles. On the plus side, the weather was 70s and dry, and he was able to knock off after the last softball game of the evening, which concluded at around eight, a couple hours earlier than planned, due to the disqualification of Gordy's from the consolation bracket. Craig LaForte had been given a citation for disorderly and released.

Nate went straight home to his condo located in The Glen of Mukwonago development on the village's north side. He showered, sat in a towel flipping through TV channels for ten minutes, decided to change into tan slacks and a navy polo and get out of there. He wanted a beer, wanted to feel life going on around him in defiance of the specter of murder that enveloped the village—but not the Technicolor chaos of Summerfest. That's where everyone would be tonight, he thought, and so he drove to Jay's Lanes.

Nate knew that there had once been another bowling alley on the site of the current Citizens Bank main location on Rochester and Lake Street, but that it had burned down around 1960, long before his time. And, of course, there had been the four-lane basement alleys that Star had mentioned. Jay's was the newest, and had been built on Atkinson Street just half a block from the center of town. Its first name had been Won-a-go Bowling. Eventually, Jerry Jay had acquired it, christening it with its current name. Nate bowled in a winter league at the lanes. It was a small house—just a dozen alleys—but it remained a popular gathering place with billiards, high tables at which groups could share drinks, and a wrap-around bar from which the bartender could survey every corner of the establishment.

As Nate had figured, there were only a handful of individuals in the place when he arrived. He ordered a tap beer and sat at the bar, no one on either side of him. About half the lanes were busy, and he watched them hypnotically. *I Walk the Line* played on the jukebox.

"So," said Skelly, the bartender, whose full name was Sinclair Kelly, a guy who had graduated with Nate, but whose huge beer gut, swollen nose, and heavily-lined face made him look like sixty. "No riots at the park tonight?"

Nate wasn't in the mood for conversation, but he did not want to appear rude. "There wasn't a riot last night. Just Craig LaForte taking the games a bit too seriously."

Skelly nodded as if he understood completely. "So..." Nate braced himself. "What do you think about this murder thing? I mean, wow, that never happens here! Right? You guys figure out who did it yet?"

"Everyone in the department's working on it, Skelly. Every waking hour."

"Well not you. You're here havin' a beer!" Skelly punctuated this with a raucous laugh to make sure the comment was perceived as a joke. Nate almost understood Craig LaForte's compulsion to beat the crap out of someone.

"Yup, I'm havin' a beer. Just me here, enjoyin' a beer. By myself." Jukebox music droned in the background.

> As sure as night is dark and day is light
> I keep you on my mind both day and night
> And happiness I've known proves that it's right
> Because you're mine, I walk the line

He thought about Grace. She was just being friendly, right? And maybe just a little bit scared. Sandy had been her friend. A little walk in the park with a cop...what could be safer than that? Fresh air and a man in uniform. If it hadn't been him, it would have been Dick or any of the deputies. He had just been in the right place at the right time.

But damn, he thought. She was an attractive woman, hair or no hair. He wondered how advanced her cancer really was. He thought back to their conversation from the previous night: *But right now, I'm feeling good. Test results so far are promising.* "Promising" could mean a lot of things.

Rather unexpectedly, Star popped into his mind as well. He had been struck by how attractive she was the first time he saw her. Seemed a little less vulnerable than Grace. At least on the surface. It had sounded like she had been through quite an ordeal. He couldn't imagine how shattering it would be to lose a part of yourself. And she had lost a job—been fired, more accurately. But it still had to have been traumatic and embarrassing. Plus, there was the Jack thing. *Been clean for a year*, she had mentioned last night. She had a bit of baggage, that was for sure.

"So..." began Skelly, interrupting Nate's thoughts again, causing him to clench his beer glass a little tighter. "What do you think? Was it the boyfriend?"

"We'll be checkin' into every lead, Skelly."

A new jukebox offering rose in the background.

Jolene, Jolene, Jolene, Jolene
I'm begging of you please don't take my man

"All I know is nobody better come prowlin' around my place," said Skelly. "I'll be sleepin' with ol' Mr. Glock under my pillow until whatever nutcase done it is dead or behind bars."

"Good for you, Skelly." Nate couldn't imagine a safer situation than four inches of goose down separating a loaded Glock pistol from the back of Skelly's head.

He wondered if Star was in the *Chief* office tonight, puzzling over the riddle.

Your beauty is beyond compare
With flaming locks of auburn hair
With ivory skin and eyes of emerald green
Your smile is like a breath of spring
Your voice is soft like summer rain
And I cannot compete with you
Jolene

"You want another beer, Nate?"

He watched a ten-year-old kid pick up a four-ten split. "Sure."

He drank slowly. The Brewers finished up a game on the big TV overhead. Looked like they were headed for another good season. Good enough to be not quite good enough. He ordered a twelve-inch pizza, which Skelly cooked in a small oven behind the bar. Nate had almost finished the pizza when he noticed that the bar had gotten quite a bit more crowded. His watch showed just past eleven. That meant the beer tent would have closed down, and since it was Saturday night, lots of folks who didn't want to head straight home and who very much wanted to keep on drinking would make their way to Jay's.

Time to get out of here.

Last thing he wanted to be was the cop in a room full of drunks. In fact, even if they had all been stone sober, he was in no mood to socialize. He had simply needed to go somewhere. Now he needed to go home.

He threw a fiver on the bar for a tip and stood up from his stool just as a new swarm burst through the front doors.

"Well, if it isn't the *big* man!"

Nate turned. Craig LaForte stood sneering at him, surrounded by whatever passed for the friends of such a lowlife.

"Have a safe evening, Craig," said Nate, who turned away to leave.

"What a goddamn loser," Craig said, just loud enough for Nate to hear. "Makes his living, sucking off the public tit, then arrests honest citizens who pay his salary when they're just trying to defend themselves!"

Nate wondered whether Craig was simply trying to paint a picture of himself as the hero of yesterday's episode for the benefit of his friends, or whether he had talked himself into really believing that was how it had come down last night. In any case, Nate knew better than to try and reason with fools whose only goal was to create greater discord. Without looking back, he took a step toward the door. Skelly reached a hand over the bar and caught Nate's arm.

"So...Nate buddy," he said in a voice low enough for only the two of them to register, "I wonder if maybe you'd stick around. Just for a few minutes, you know? This guy is poison. If he gets going in the wrong direction, there could be trouble. Maybe if he has a beer or two, starts talking about old times with his pals, maybe he'll get mellow, you know?"

Nate sighed, let his chin drop to his chest.

"Give me a ginger ale."

Skelly smiled, patted him on the shoulder. "On the house!"

He took the glass of fizz to a tall table near the front window where he drank alone. Most of the crowd sat at the bar or stood near it, chatting animatedly. He tried not to make his surveillance of Craig too obvious. He doubted that LaForte had noticed, since he hadn't stopped talking since arriving at Jay's. Five minutes passed slowly. Seeing no sign of an impending revolution, Nate downed the last of his ginger ale and made a beeline for the restroom prior to heading out. He was just toweling off his hands when the door opened and he recognized Mark Tasinski, who was an accountant or something of the sort.

"There you are! I was hoping you hadn't left!"

This can't be good.

"What can I do for you, Mark?"

Mark looked over his shoulder at the closed door, lowered his voice, which was completely unnecessary. "Why'd you let him out?"

"They just gave him a ticket for disorderly," said Nate matter-of-factly, figuring that Mark was referring to LaForte. "Not my call. Just a guy with anger issues. Not like he killed anybody."

"Maybe not yet," said Mark. "But he's been talking."

"Yeah, he's a talker all right."

"No, he's been trying to get people riled up to go over to where that teacher lives."

Nate's eyes snapped up. "What? Rick Bryer's house?"

Mark nodded.

"That's just nuts. What's he planning to do?"

"Nothing good, I'm sure," said Mark. "Hey, I just figured you should know. I've got to get back out there."

Nate thanked him and Mark left. Then Nate stood looking at his reflection in the mirror for a few moments. *You idiot. You should have stayed home tonight.*

When he re-entered the crowded bar area, it took him a moment to spot Craig. He walked over, set a hand on Craig's shoulder. "Could I have a word with you?"

Craig responded with a scowl. "Go to—"

Nate, who was a foot taller, tightened his grip on Craig's shoulder and pulled him backwards into a quiet corner. He spun the smaller man around, whose fists he saw were clenched, ready. Nate drilled him with a look that suggested this would be a horrible idea, and he could see the smaller man relax his grip slightly. He spoke in a lower voice so only the two of them could hear.

"Stay away from Rick Bryer."

"You can't tell me—"

"I *am* telling you. You got off easy with disorderly yesterday. Somebody cut you a break. If you go after a private citizen the day after, you're going to be looking at jail time."

Craig laughed a bitter pebble of laughter. "I got a good lawyer."

"You better have Clarence Darrow."

"Oh yeah? What firm's he with?"

Nate rolled his eyes. "I'm just saying, if you go after an innocent man, with your history, the only way your lawyer is going to get you out of a long jail term is by baking a file inside a cake."

"Innocent man!" snorted Craig. "He's guilty as hell! I'd be doing this town a favor! Anyway, we're just gonna persuade him to come clean!"

"Leave it to the cops, Craig."

"Oh, like you?" The look of dark hatred in LaForte's eyes was disturbing.

"Look," said Nate, his patience thinning, "no one needs more craziness right now. And you have a family to think about."

"I'm divorced, you asshole!"

Nate had not realized that. It had to have been recent. "But you've got a daughter, right? What is she, about seven?"

"Six," said Craig, and Nate realized he had found the man's vulnerable spot.

"You start pulling shit like this, you're going to lose custody and visitation."

"You'd do that?"

"Not me, Einstein! The courts would freeze you out!"

Craig looked like he wanted to say something, but for once, he had no words.

"People do stupid shit," said Nate more gently. "Stupid people *keep* doing stupid shit. Don't be stupid."

Then he left the lanes, not knowing whether anything he had said had really made a difference. He put in a call to have the officers on overnight duty take a few extra swings past Rick Bryer's house during the evening.

Breathing in the cool night air, he was surprised when his thoughts again went to Star Calloway. His watch read 11:48. Was she there in the office, trying to work out that riddle? Before heading to his car in the bowling alley parking lot, he walked the half block to the *Chief*.

The office was dark.

It surprised him again to discover the subtle disappointed this generated. He did an about face and headed back to Jay's. Five minutes later, he pulled into the driveway of his condo. He found Pete sitting in a folding deck chair on his front lawn, and when Nate exited his squad, Pete signaled him over.

"Sitting on your front lawn at midnight in a folding sports chair, Pete?" asked Nate with a smirk. "Some people would call that a bit eccentric."

Pete pointed toward the starry sky. "Supposed to be meteors. I haven't seen jack." Then he indicated Nate. "No uniform. Getting in from a date? You use that Tinder thing, don't you?"

"Tried it once. There should be laws against that level of false advertising. No date tonight. Just out having a beer at Jay's."

"I told you before, Emily says she can set you up on a date with her cousin Rachel."

"The one who's been through three divorces?"

113 / Rod Vick

Pete shrugged. "She's got a little baggage, but who doesn't? Then you could come over when I grill out for our family reunion."

"You always invite me to those things anyway," said Nate.

"Suit yourself," said Pete, then he patted the empty sports chair next to him. "Why don't you pull up a seat and watch some meteor showers without the meteors?"

"Thanks," said Nate, "but we've got a long day again tomorrow. Probably a lot of long days until this murder is solved."

Pete shook his head. "I don't know what's happening to this town."

"To be fair, almost any little town is going to have a murder eventually. It's not like we're Miami."

"It's not just that. I mean, are we really even a small town anymore? I remember when I was a kid and they first put in those stoplights next to the park! Now there are so many lights that it takes me as long to get to the Walmart in Mukwonago as to the one in Waukesha! And all those historic old buildings they've torn down in the name of 'progress'!" He made air quotes with his fingers. "The new ones they put up look like a salute to depressed architects!"

"Watch out, everyone. Pete Moore is on his soapbox."

"Damn right I'm on my soapbox. This town has a lot of great history and too much of it's being fed to the bulldozers!" He paused, gazed up at the stars for a few moments. "Still no meteors. You know, my dad lived here. All his life. Was born in a farmhouse out on 83 toward Genesee. The house isn't there anymore. He told me there was an old guy in town used to be named Pete Moore, only it was spelled Mohr."

"That who you're named after?"

"No, my mom's brother. Anyway, this Pete Mohr—his nickname was something like 'Hookum', don't know why—he owned the gas station downtown right across from Walgreens. Used to be a Standard Oil station. Forget what it is now. He and Dottie, his wife, lived upstairs. And they had a barn with horses right behind the station. Right behind it! And behind that, a pasture they could turn them loose into! Now whatta we got? Condos and parking lots and sandwich shops."

"Change is inevitable," said Nate.

Pete was silent for a few moments. "Maybe."

Nate raised his eyes to the heavens again. "Well, I hope you find your meteor. Goodnight." With a wave, he turned and headed back toward his unit.

"Yeah," said Pete, waving a hand while staring at the sky. "They're supposed to mean good luck."

Twelve

Mukwonago Summerfest ended on Sunday evening without further incident. Badger Burger won the men's softball tournament with Citizens Bank grabbing the women's division. There were no visits to Rick Bryer's house by vigilantes. By Monday afternoon, only two carnival trucks remained in the park, and the Boy Scouts had swept the area of litter. the *Chief* came out—with the second letter and a two-page spread of Summerfest photos. And there was Sandy Sewell's obituary. Her funeral would be Friday, visitation starting at 5:00.

With the carnival finished, most overtime was off the table, which was fine with Nate. He was pleased to receive a text from Star asking him to stop by the *Chief* office after work on Tuesday.

Everyone else had left the offices by the time Nate arrived. Star again met him at the long table.

"I wanted you to know that there were a couple of letters that I didn't publish in Monday's edition," began Star. She tossed two printed copies onto the table. "They came in electronically, but both had names that checked out. Unlike your police chief, the letter writers were true believers that the riddle was connected to the murder. In fact, they were so hysterical in tone, that I didn't print them for fear that they might start a riot."

"Okay," said Nate. "Anything else?"

"Yeah, as a matter of fact. Someone already emailed a solution to the riddle. A Trent Scheider."

Nate shook his head. "Name doesn't do anything for me."

"Address is Pickering out near Upper Phantom Lake," said Star. "He thinks it's the high school."

"You're kidding."

Star pushed another print-out toward him. "Read for yourself."

Dear Mukwonago Chief,

I don't exactly understand what you're doing here, but I'll play. I think the riddle refers to Mukwonago High School. Here's why.

A chameleon changes. Just look at the changes that school building has gone through over the years. It started out as a windowless box covered with rust-colored, corrugated metal. Then they covered that up with tan stucco. And now it's beautiful, modern reds and blues and grays. Even its shape has changed dramatically.

And as far as traveling from heaven, here's a little known fact about the school property. My grandfather said that years ago, the property on which the school now sits used to be a big flat field, and some people used to land airplanes on it!

But all traces of that are gone today..."save for a crooked (hard to get around in) chameleon house!"

So is there a prize, like a year's subscription or something?

Sincerely,
Trent Scheider

"Wow," said Nate, pushing the paper back to her. "This guy's got it all figured out. Or at least thinks he has. I'm impressed that he came up with something for the heaven clue."

"So you think it might be the right answer?" asked Star.

Nate laughed. "Every time I hear a new explanation for the riddle it sounds like the right answer to me. But this one worries me. What if this Trent character is right? Think about it. The first riddle referenced a myth relating to Phantom Lake, and that's where the murder occurred."

"Whoa!" Star exhaled slowly. "A murder at the high school?"

"And who says it would be just one person?"

"But," said Star, "it's summer break."

"Still plenty of people there during the day," noted Nate. "Summer school is going on. And summer sports camps. The band kids. Plus, there's the full-time administrative staff and custodians."

The two digested this silently for a few moments. Then Nate stood.

"I've got to go back to Chief Beckman and try to get him on board. We've got to get more cops up at that school. Jesus, we don't want another Columbine!"

"But," said Star, "if Trent's guess is correct, won't that satisfy whoever is writing the riddles?"

"Maybe," said Nate, "but I'm not about to put my trust in the hands of a psycho serial killer. What if he gets pissed that someone figured it out and decides to go ahead with his plan anyway? And some of these mass killers are megalomaniacs. Instead of keeping his word if we figure out the riddle, what if he can't handle it that he's not the smartest guy in the room anymore and goes on a shooting spree?"

Star stood as well. "Hell of a pep talk, coach."

"Sorry. It's hard not to be cynical with all that's going on."

She smiled. "I get it. Thanks for the help with this. And for the walk in the park Friday night. It took my mind off some of the craziness around here for a few minutes."

"Even though we mostly talked about the craziness around here."

"Not all of the time," she said with a grin. "And even when we were talking shop, it was more— relaxed. Don't tell me that our walk in the park was as intense as your little wrestling match with Craig LaForte."

"Craig LaForte is an ass. Don't quote me on that. The idiot wanted to storm the castle on Saturday night."

"Storm the castle?"

"He was trying to talk people into going over to Rick Bryer's house at about eleven. That wouldn't have ended well."

Star smirked. "I take it *you* talked him out of it?"

"You could say that. I just happened to be in the right place at the right time, having a beer at Jay's. It was almost midnight when I left."

"You should have stopped by the *Chief* offices here," said Star. "Would have been a nice break. I was working my ass off, trying to get things ready for the Monday edition."

Nate recalled that when he had looked toward the *Chief* building, all the lights had appeared to be off. However, it would not have been the first time someone working late had gotten the time wrong.

"I'll remember that next time."

*

Nate returned to the police station and found Chief Beckman in his office. Normally, the chief would have gone home by this time, but the murder was still far from solved.

"Got a minute, Chief?"

"For you, always," said Beckman, running a hand over his sagging face in a way that made Nate wish he hadn't asked.

"I thought maybe we could talk about those letters again."

Beckman sighed and grunted a response. "That nonsense."

"Here's my concern," said Nate, cutting to the chase. "The first riddle in the first letter was about the lake. And that's where the murder occurred."

"Coincidence."

"Maybe," said Nate, "but the second riddle might be indicating the high school as the target."

Suddenly Beckman was more attentive. "Aw Jesus! Are you kidding me?"

Nate dug out the copy of the email from Trent Scheider and went through it with him. "So do you think this Scheider is the killer?"

Nate blinked. "What? No, he was just responding to the riddle."

"Maybe he *wrote* the riddle," suggested Beckman, "and then wanted to look like the big hero by pretending to solve it."

Nate hadn't thought of that, though he found it unlikely.

"We're going to have someone talk to Scheider," said Beckman. "I guess that'll be you. And Christ sakes! When's this guy's answer supposed to be in the paper?"

"Thursday."

Beckman chewed on his lip. "How many kids gonna be there during the day this time of year?"

"Maybe a couple hundred with sports camps and marching band. Plus the secretaries, janitors, principals. And door security is lighter in the summer."

Beckman rolled his eyes. "What a shit-storm it'd be if something happened at the school after this letter comes out in the paper, and we didn't do anything. They'd ride me outta this town on a goddamn rail! I guess I'd better find a couple of guys to wander the hallways on Thursday and Friday during the day."

"Thanks, Chief."

"Don't thank me," said Beckman, making some notes on a yellow pad. "You're gonna be one of the guys! And I still think this letter stuff is some bullshit! But I can't risk my job on it!"

Thirteen

The interview with Trent Scheider had yielded little of value. At sixty-one years of age with emphysema—a portable oxygen pump and clear plastic tubing snaked into his nostrils—Scheider seemed like a poor candidate for leaping out of the bushes, overpowering a trained marathoner, tying her into a canoe, and filling it with heavy rocks.

Sandy's upcoming funeral seemed to be on everyone's minds, along with the fact that whoever had killed her was still out there. The Waukesha County Sheriff's Department was assisting with the investigation, but so far, the combined resources of the two departments had moved the case no closer to the finish line.

The Thursday edition of the *Chief* hit the stands, and Nate noticed that got people talking as well. Some in whispers. Some with expressions of unabashed incredulity. Some angrily. Most believed the author of the riddles was unbalanced and probably Sandy's killer. Many expressed confusion as to why the *Chief* was printing the riddles and the follow-up guesses. Was the *Chief* helping with the investigation?

Or enabling a murderer?

Mid-morning, he stopped at Sarah's shop to grab a mocha latte. *Corn dogs and Mocha Lattes. Good choices, Nate!* That thought did not keep him from leaving his squad, entering the shop, or eventually ordering a large latte—with a granola cookie.

Three other customers sat in comfortable chairs in an area that looked like a college student's living room, sipping their drinks, one reading a book, another a newspaper, while the third hunched over a laptop monitor. A high school-age girl, her long hair tied back with a purple bandana, filled one of the machines with whole beans. Sarah Cutler, the owner, stepped up to the counter.

"Iced vanilla!"

The bearded man who had been absorbed in his laptop sprang up, picked up the coffee, offered a cordial "Thank-you," and returned to his seat.

Sarah turned, smiled. "Hi, Nate! What can I get you, hon?"

"How about an all-inclusive vacation package to Barbados?" he said, sighing and stretching his arms toward the rafters simultaneously.

Sarah grunted good-naturedly. "Why Barbados?"

Nate let his arms drop to his sides. "Saw someone win a Barbados vacation on *Wheel of Fortune* last week. First thing to pop into my mind. Frankly, I'd take a ticket to anywhere else."

"Yeah, the energy in this town is pretty erratic these days," said Sarah. Then she pointed a finger at Nate. "But your energy is primo!"

"Must be the strong wi-fi signal in this place that you're sensing," said Nate. "I'm beat."

Sarah shook her head. "Don't undersell yourself, my friend Nate. Now let's get some caffeine in you so that you can get back out there and stop the ones with bad energy."

"Mocha latte," he said. "Small. No, large. That's it. Wait, these cookies look good."

Sarah rang him up and went to work on the drink.

"You said the ones with bad energy," said Nate as he munched on the cookie and she mixed the concoction. "Was that just a figure of speech, or do you think there's more than one with bad energy?"

"There's always more than one," said Sarah without looking away from her work. "There might be only one killer. But I heard you had a run-in with someone else on Friday night."

"Can't keep a secret in a small town."

"Between you and me, I'm glad he's not a coffee drinker," said Sarah. "How he stays in business is beyond me. Seems to cater to a certain crowd, if you know what I mean. The kind of guys who would laugh if the opposing quarterback in a high school football game broke his arm."

"A sad reflection on us, I suppose, that there are enough guys like that for him to be able to pay his rent," agreed Nate, finishing the last of the cookie. "But I heard he got divorced recently. Maybe that'll flip the switch. Shock to the system, so to speak. Send him in a better direction."

Sarah grunted her skepticism. "Don't bet your badge on it. You want this to go?"

"Please."

Out on the sidewalk, he decided to pay a visit to Grace's Gifts—just to check in, naturally, considering her departure had been so abrupt the previous Friday. He took a step toward his squad, then remembered the cookie and the latte in his hand, and decided it might be in his interests to walk the two blocks. That would work off at least a few of the extra calories.

A pleasant electronic tone sounded as Nate entered the gift shop, and Grace, who had been absorbed in something on the computer screen in front of her, closed her window, smiled and stood.

"Hey!"

She was definitely one of the most beautiful women he had ever seen. Not even the cancer had been able to alter her sufficiently to change that. Today, her head was covered by a green scarf bearing Celtic designs.

"Hey," he replied. "I remembered you had said that you sometimes felt a little creeped out when you were by yourself in the store, so I thought I'd stop by to see if you were okay. Plus, I didn't get a chance to thank you the other night for keeping me company for a lap."

"Oh yeah, that was nice," said Grace, and a little blush seemed to come into her pale cheeks. "I'm fine, I guess. Maybe starting to get used to being on edge, even when there's no customers. Which is a lot of the time." She gestured around the large room filled with collectibles, knick-knacks, games, and decorative accents perched on stark, white shelving.

"You obviously made it home safely," he said awkwardly.

"Once you got into it with Craig, I figured you were going to be busy for awhile."

"Police work," said Nate, smiling stiffly. "It's one percent protecting the public, ninety-nine percent paperwork."

"You put him down like he was a sack of flour."

"He's a sack of something all right," said Nate. "I was a wrestler in high school."

"Doesn't surprise me," said Grace, stepping from behind her small counter. "Hey, I've got some sparkling waters in a mini-fridge back here. Can I get you one?"

Nate raised a hand. "Thanks, but I can't stay. Plus..." He raised the other hand, which contained his mocha latte.

She nodded, seemed to search for something to prolong the conversation for a moment. "I heard you had another little meeting with Craig Saturday night."

"I think everyone in town must know that."

Grace's eyes darkened. "He's a vile little man."

Nate nodded. "He ever give you any trouble?"

Grace shook her head. "Well, not lately. Before I lost my hair, he used to stare, you know what I mean? The way creepy guys do. But after I started with the chemo, it's like I was some sort of freak, and he basically pretended I didn't exist."

"You're definitely not a freak," said Nate, hoping it didn't sound awkward. "But you're probably fortunate to be off his radar."

She nodded. "Poor Sandy wasn't as fortunate."

Nate took a couple of steps closer. "Sandy? What do you mean?"

"After Cookie divorced Craig, he stopped Sandy a couple of times in public, just making random conversation. Just talking about the weather and asking how the real estate business was going. It's not that people don't do that all the time, but he had never done it before with Sandy. And then he started showing up at her house. Like at midnight or one in the morning. How creepy is that?"

"Why didn't she report it?" asked Nate.

Grace smiled. "You know Sandy." Then the smile faded, and she put her hand over her mouth. "Knew." Nate took another step forward but stopped short, not knowing what was appropriate. Grace pulled herself together and continued. "She knew he had a little girl and didn't want to mess up his chances at custody. Even if he was a creep, he was still that little girl's dad. But she probably should have, because there were a couple more incidents after that where she swore someone was outside her house in the early hours of the morning, but she wasn't sure if it was Craig, you know?"

Nate's eyes glazed over for several moments as he considered the implications of this information.

"Grace, why didn't you say something? I mean, right after Sandy was killed. Didn't Sandy's allegations raise any red flags?"

"I did tell someone," said Grace. "I told Officer Andrews."

Fourteen

Friday morning, Nate arrived at Mukwonago High School feeling greater trepidation than he'd ever felt a quarter century earlier on an exam day. The *Chief* had come out Thursday, and Nate's stomach had been rolling all night as he worried that Friday morning might bring news of another murder. But there had been no bodies discovered anywhere in the village. He hoped that meant one of the answers published in the Thursday edition had hit the mark. He imagined that Star would be getting another letter from Ho-ma-ba confirming this.

However, it was possible that all of the guesses had been wrong and that the killer was simply waiting for the right moment to act. Consequently, Nate would be spending most of his day roaming the halls of Mukwonago High School.

It was not an unpleasant place to be. On the contrary, the building had undergone a relatively recent renovation transforming it from an uninspiring, beige box of mostly windowless classroom cubicles with all the charm of a Chuck E. Cheese, into a bright, clean, light-filled, highly functional work of art. The building had come a long way from its beginnings. Until the fall of 1972, the building that was now called Park View Middle School across from Field Park had been the community's high school. That autumn, the new high school building had opened on highway NN half a mile farther west. It was intended to be a cutting edge facility that would elevate Mukwonago's growing student population to the next level. From what Nate had heard, however, it had been mostly a nightmare.

There were old-timers who did recall some positives about the high school building of the '70s. The commons just inside the front doors was a useful gathering place for students. The auditorium, although rather small even for the 915 students that attended the school in 1972, was much nicer for student music and theatrical productions than setting up folding chairs in the gymnasium. There were collegiate-style large group classrooms with tiered seating where teachers could team-teach lessons. The gymnasium had been significantly larger, too.

However, the thin, fiberboard walls separating some classrooms created annoying and distracting teaching situations, as did the fact that many classrooms had only three walls, the place where one would expect a fourth wall left open to look out upon a shared learning space on the upper level. Wall-to-wall carpeting that deteriorated rapidly, leaky roofing, heating and cooling issues, and questionable decisions regarding scheduling and supervision left the community scrambling—and spending millions—

to repair and upgrade the facility. It took until the '90s for most of the wrongs to be righted, and then the massive renovations and additions of 2018 finally transformed it from "meh" to "marvelous". Classrooms were now large, bright, and filled with the latest useful technology. Three gymnasiums guaranteed practice space for all teams of the now more than 1600-student body, as well as seating for fans even in the most hotly contested Division I playoff games. And the new performing arts center was the crown jewel, offering more than twice the seating capacity of the old auditorium.

Nate had plenty of time to consider these amenities as he strolled dutifully around the building—which, he noted, took a long time.

In his first hour, he twice passed Jessica Duffy, one of the other officers assigned to patrol the building today, who circled in the opposite direction. Summer school classes droned on in several rooms, although the majority of classrooms were silent and illuminated only by natural light from windows or skylights. All visitors were screened through the main office, which required them to buzz in, sign in, and wear name badges. However, no one was pretending that there weren't other ways into the building. Even though most doors were locked, they were constantly opening and closing as athletes in summer programs bustled in or out of unsecured doors in the athletics areas. And the doors in the south gymnasium were actually propped open to take advantage of the gorgeous June weather.

Nate sighed. Short of putting a fifteen-foot-high, chain-link fence, topped with barbed-wire around the entire facility, with armed guards at a controlled entrance, Nate doubted whether a hundred police officers could stop a determined killer from getting into a school building.

On his third circuit, Nate encountered Dick Andrews, stopping him to make a bit of small talk about the Brewers. His real motive, however, was to follow up on what Grace had mentioned to him.

"Have you heard anything about Craig LaForte?" Nate asked innocuously once they had rehashed a few of the Brew Crew's recent performances.

Dick smiled. "Heard that you and him got into it the other night at Jay's."

"You heard why, right? He was going to get some hotheads together, go after Rick Bryer."

Dick snorted. "Craig's all talk."

"Maybe," replied Nate. "I heard he was stalking Sandy Sewell."

Dick shook his head. "Where'd you hear that?"

"From Grace Hall. She was a friend of Sandy's."

"Friends aren't always the most objective."

"Maybe not, but Grace said she told this to you," pressed Nate.

Dick's good-natured expression faltered. "What are you implying here?"

"I'm not implying anything," replied Nate, who felt the conversation slipping out of control. "Just saying that sounds like a pretty relevant detail in a murder investigation with no suspect."

"Did you come up with that idea on your own, or did your girlfriend think of it for you?" Dick snarled.

"My what?" Nate felt his ears burning. "That's not the way it is."

"Sure," said Dick skeptically. "I saw you walking in the park. Out of your league, pal."

Nate felt his anger growing. "Jesus, we were only talking! And I'm just saying if a guy's stalking someone and that person ends up dead, that's something that needs to be checked out! Which makes me wonder why *you* didn't pass that information on to Beckman!"

"I did, dumbass!" Dick declared triumphantly.

Stunned, Nate swallowed the next words he had planned to say. "You did?"

"Of course!" said Dick.

Nate pondered this for a moment. "Sorry then. But...why, then, aren't we camped out on Craig's doorstep?"

"You're asking the wrong guy," said Dick, resuming his walk. "The call on that would be Beckman's."

Fifteen

Carl Mullenberg opened his eyes, as if from a pleasant nap. But this was not his usual napping spot, a puffy brown sofa in the den, where he would nod off on Saturday afternoons while watching PGA golf. And his wife, Vicky, was not gently shaking him awake, bringing him a plate of meatloaf, sitting down on the sofa next to him so that they could switch to a romcom on Netflix.

As his eyes focused, Carl realized that he was in a very unlikely napping spot. It was dimly lit, but enough illumination filtered in through a small window that he knew he was in the storage shack at Kiwanis Park, known throughout the village because of the colorful mural painted on its outside, first in the early 1980s, and then occasionally refreshed and modified in the decades since. As a Kiwanis member, Carl typically volunteered to keep the grass cut in Kiwanis Park, which was on the northwest corner of the intersection of Rochester Street and Veterans Way. The park was often used for Maxwell Street Days parking and other events. During December, Christmas trees were sold there.

Instead of a sofa, he currently sat atop the riding lawnmower that was kept in the shed. He realized that he had been leaning forward, his head resting uncomfortably on the tractor's steering wheel.

What a fool I am to doze off like this.

But as his mind began to clear, the picture made less and less sense. He remembered driving to the park, pulling his car near the shed. Although late in the afternoon, it had been early enough, he had hoped, to allow him to finish mowing and then head over to the funeral home to pay his respects to Sandy Sewell's family. An awful situation. Chilling to think that such a thing could happen in Mukwonago.

He had left his insulated coffee mug just inside the shed's larger door so that he could circle back occasionally and get a sip or two. He recalled making a few trips around the park, and then, nothing. It was a blank, until he woke up moments ago, inside the shed, its doors closed.

Other alarming elements now asserted themselves. He could only breathe through his nose. Something—tape perhaps—held his mouth shut. His wrists were zip-tied to the steering wheel of the tractor. When he tried to move his feet, he realized that his ankles had been secured to something as well.

What the hell!

This had to be someone's idea of a joke. Carl was known for pulling practical jokes of his own, and he was aware that there were others in the Kiwanis who had creative senses of humor and who had threatened good-natured "revenge". Had someone put something in his coffee while he was on the far side of the park? But such a thing seemed way over-the-top, way beyond what was acceptable for a good-natured practical joke.

Then he thought of Sandy Sewell, the circumstances of her death, the letters in the *Chief*, and a surge of panic hit him.

Calm down! It's going to be okay! You're just tied to a tractor.

He willed himself to breathe slowly, and after a few moments, he felt less anxious.

That was when he heard it. Outside the shed somewhere. A motor was running. A car engine.

His car.

Carl whipped around as far as he was able, and after a moment, he saw that a small pane of the window had been broken and a black hose dangled through the opening. Rags had been bunched up to fill the gaps. Without seeing the other end of the hose, Carl knew it led to the exhaust pipe on his car.

And the wave of panic returned, multiplied a hundredfold.

He struggled against the zip-ties, but he had no way to create leverage, nothing sharp enough to rub against, and so they simply dug into his wrists and ankles. Although his eyes bulged with the exertion, he knew his attempts to cry out were almost completely stifled.

Had the motor been running when he first woke? He could not remember, although he knew it would not take long for a lethal quantity of carbon monoxide to fill the small shed. Even as he thought these things, he perceived a bit of darkness at the edges, his vision, the room seeming to narrow. He felt afraid, but this lasted only a few seconds. Suddenly it was hard to focus. He had to get out. Get up. It was time to go. In a minute now he would stand up and open the doors. And have Vicky get him something to eat.

But so hard to keep his eyes open.

First, just a little nap.

Sixteen

In a herringbone sport coat over a navy dress shirt with no tie, Nate stepped into the funeral home. Almost immediately, he wished he had arrived earlier than 6:30, for the place was packed. No way he would make it through the long line leading to Sandy's parents and siblings before the funeral began at 7:00.

His day monitoring the school had been uneventful, except for the conversation with Dick Andrews, and for that, Nate was grateful. He dared to hope that the killer had decided he had bitten off more than he could chew, that the threatened murder spree would be a one-and-done.

Since he had not known Sandy as well as many dozens in the room, he loitered near the back, eyeballing a chair in the last row. If he were lucky, he could sort of blend in, avoiding conversation.

A good crowd had been expected, and Nate had to admit that this was one of the largest he had seen in the new funeral home, built just a few years ago after operating for a seeming eternity just two blocks away from the Rochester and Main intersection. Scanning the crowd, he recognized dozens of familiar faces, some smiling as they pointed to the posters bearing photographs of Sandy as a first-grader or at the junior prom or on the tubing trip down the Wolf River last summer. Others wiping away tears or talking somberly. Some chatting animatedly in that way people do when they want to convey the impression that everything is normal and they're okay — but, of course, they are not.

Schnell and Bell — Schnabell — from the force were also there in civilian clothes, as was the boyfriend Rick Bryer, though Nate noticed a few individuals giving him the stink-eye, no doubt due to suspicions that still lingered in the absence of a suspect in custody — or even on the radar. Skelly from Jay's lanes was in line, as were Sarah Cutler and Albert Sutherland, who Nate knew felt terrible that his canoe had been used in the commission of the murder. Most of the downtown business owners were milling about or in line, as well as a hundred others that Nate did not recognize.

He craned his neck, trying to spot Grace in the crowd. She had been good friends with Sandy, and Nate had expected to see her somewhere near the front of the viewing room, but she was nowhere in sight. He also did not see Chief Beckman, who he had expected would put in an appearance as a way of assuring the community that he was a caring public servant who was doing everything in his power to make sure Sandy's killer was brought to justice. He might, of course, have come earlier.

Craig LaForte seemed to be absent as well, although that was probably a blessing, for Nate could envision a potential confrontation between LaForte and Rick Bryer that would be, at best, awkward, and at worst, an embarrassing public brawl.

And Star was not in the throng. That did not surprise him too much, for she was new in town and had not known Sandy beyond a brief stop-in or two at the *Chief* for business. However, Nate was hoping she might have put in an appearance just to be the good neighbor, to show that, despite being the newbie, she cared — and felt their grief.

"Nate!"

He turned to his left and saw Emily Moore smile, change direction and head over to him. She gave him a hug, though it seemed she was the one who needed it.

"Oh, I still can't believe it!" she said breathlessly, releasing him and bringing a tissue to her eyes. "This isn't what our little town is about! Oh, that poor young girl!"

Emily seemed, from one moment to the next, angry or on the verge of collapsing into tears.

"It's awful, Em," agreed Nate. "Pete here?"

She shook her head. "Visitation started at 5:30. I was helping out at Mount Olive. That's where Sandy attended. We've got a little reception there after the service. Pete will probably be there. I think he came early to the visitation."

"I'll see him there, then," said Nate, and Emily, with a parting wave, drifted off like a lost boat in a rough sea.

Fifteen minutes before the start of the funeral service, Nate saw Grace cross the front of the room, coming in through a side door. As there were several rooms where individuals might gather, he guessed she might have been here for some time. She wore a somber black blouse and pants. He watched her for a solid minute, and then was embarrassed when she looked in his direction. However, she simply smiled, raised her hand at the wrist in a subdued wave of acknowledgement, and began making her way through the mob toward him. Arriving, she gently touched his forearm in what he thought was a pleasantly familiar way.

"Hi. It's all so very sad, isn't it?"

Nate nodded. "I've been to my share of funerals. It's sad enough when someone dies in their seventies or eighties. But someone this young. It feels so wrong. And the circumstances make it ten times worse."

Grace sighed, hugged herself. "Lately, everything about this town feels wrong."

"I know what you mean," said Nate, his eyes traveling around the room before resting comfortably back on her. "Ever since this damned murder, I've started second-guessing everyone. People I thought were friends, innocent neighbors, now I wonder what secret grudges or dark motives they might have.

Which one of them might be walking among us showing smiles and tears, but thinking murder?"

She now patted his hand softly, and he felt himself begin to perspire.

"You're different. Than the other officers, I mean. They seem to simply go through the motions. You really seem to care about the people of Mukwonago."

"I grew up here," said Nate by way of explanation. "How can you not care about your home?" Then his expression hardened. "Damn it!"

"What is it?"

"Craig LaForte just walked in."

LaForte wore dress slacks and a short-sleeved dress shirt with no tie. He breezed into the large viewing room as if he were arriving at league bowling night, laughing about something with an acquaintance. His demeanor turned dark, however, once he spotted Ricky. But, Nate was pleased to note, he did not approach the younger man, and in fact found a seat on the opposite side of the room.

"He's got a lot of nerve," said Grace. "Coming to the funeral of a woman he stalked."

"He's probably not smart enough to realize he's tactless," said Nate.

Grace surveyed the room. "There's so many people. That's good, but it's also so sad. Oh, there's Allie Crossman up by the family! She and Sandy were best friends in high school. She must be devastated!"

The funeral director's voice interrupted them. "Ladies and gentlemen, the memorial service for Sandra Sewell will be starting in just a few minutes. Please begin making your way to the seating if you plan on staying for the service. I've also been asked to tell everyone that there will be a reception following the service at Mount Olive Church just down the street. You are welcome to stop by for refreshments and conversation whether or not you attend the service."

Nate straightened, prepared to step toward the chairs.

"Do you mind if I sit with you?" asked Grace.

Nate felt a little flutter in his chest. "Not at all. As long as you don't mind sitting near the back."

"No, I'd prefer that. Just be aware, there are probably going to be some tears shed."

"By you and everyone in the room," said Nate, moving behind her to the back row, where they found two seats. An instant after he was seated, his phone pinged. A message from Star.

NEED TO SEE YOU. ANOTHER LETTER.

Before he could respond, he felt a hand on his shoulder. Turning, he saw Dick Andrews in uniform, motioning him toward the lobby. He excused himself and followed.

"You're back on the clock, Romeo," said Dick once they were in the lobby and able to speak freely.

"My next shift doesn't start until eight in the morning," said Nate.

"Beckman is calling in everyone," said Dick. "There's been another murder."

Seventeen

While Nate knew his first stop should have been Kiwanis Park, where the alleged murder had taken place, the text from Star was too intriguing—and potentially important—to ignore. The *Chief* offices were on the way, and he planned to not stay long.

The *Chief* office was empty except for Star, who was already at the meeting table with her file folder in front of her.

"You're not in uniform," Star observed.

"Was at Sandy's funeral when I got the news."

"I heard it on the scanner," said Star soberly. "And I was shocked, because there was no letter earlier. But right afterwards, I rushed out to the front. Judith was long gone. But there was another letter, sitting right in the middle of her desk." She pushed a new letter in plastic across the table toward him.

To the Chief,

Well, you get an E for effort. A big improvement over last week. Three guesses published in your Thursday edition. But still not much participation from the community. Two of the guesses were supplied by the newspaper. It's like the community doesn't even care. We'll see if they care by this time next week. I'll try and make the new riddle a little easier, since we seem to be slow learners. But first, the previous riddle:

> *There was a crooked man, and he walked a crooked mile*
> *From Heaven to bet a crooked sixpence obtained through crooked smiles.*
> *And then he slipped away again, as crooked as a louse,*
> *All traces gone today, save for a crooked chameleon house."*

By this time, you know the location that answers the second riddle: the brightly-painted shed in Kiwanis Park. And you'll note that the building has been painted with many different designs over the years, making it chameleon-like.

What many may not know is that the shack long ago served as a storage area for tack for horse races that were held in the Field Park. You may also not realize that gangsters from Chicago came to Mukwonago to stay at the hotel at Heaven City. Some of those 'crooked men' made side trips from "Heaven" City to Field Park to bet their 'crooked sixpence' on those horse races. Of course they're long gone now, but the shed—the chameleon-like house— remains.

Until the community takes its history more seriously, I'm afraid I'll be writing many more verses. Perhaps you'll have better luck with this one.

Yankee Doodle came to town
Astride an iron pony
To earn a feather for his cap,
The eighteenth of his cronies.

Yankee Doodle, what was that?
Exploding myths and more!
Love the U.S. as they did
More than a century yore.

"This is nuts," said Nate. "How's that supposed to be easier?"

"We just have to connect the dots," said Star. "Any ideas?"

Nate glanced at his watch. "I don't have time for ideas. I have to get to the park. I can't take the letter now."

"Meet me later," said Star. "Text me once you get done tonight."

"*If* I get done tonight."

"Text me."

He hurried off, not bothering to change into his uniform before pulling into the park where flashing lights from at least six emergency vehicles gave the twilight an unsettling quality.

"Nice jacket," said Beckman as Nate arrived at the shed near the park's north end. "Where the hell have you been?"

"Got a call," replied Nate, breathless after the brief jog from his car. "Another letter sent to the *Chief*. It directly references this killing."

Beckman stared at him. Nate expected another crack about the hippie journalist from Madison, but Beckman refrained. "Tell her no more letters."

"Sir?"

"Nada. She doesn't print them. Is that clear? Jesus, she's going to get even more people killed."

"We don't know whether not printing the letters will make any difference," said Nate. "We thought it would buy us some time to—"

"We?" shouted Beckman. "Are you working with her or with us? I just told you what's going to happen. She's not to print any more letters. If she does, I'll come in there and shut her down. You make sure she gets that message, understood?"

Nate nodded.

Beckman jabbed a thumb to where Schnell and Bell were standing. "Schnabell can fill you in on what happened. Then help with crowd control."

"I-I'm not in uniform," said Nate, indicating his civilian clothing.

"For Christ sakes, Janowsky, everyone in this damn town knows you're a cop! Now go. I'm up to my eyeballs in this." He started to turn away.

"Sir?"

"Jesus, Janowsky! What?"

"Who was the victim?"

"Carl Mullenberg," said Beckman.

"Oh my God!" Carl had been Nate's Boy Scout leader years ago. Beckman made his escape and Nate walked over to Bell and Schnell, who filled him in.

Carl had been found zip-tied to the lawn tractor—same kind of zip-ties used with Sandy. Someone had run a hose stored in the shed from Carl's exhaust pipe to a window.

"They closed the door, started the car with his own keys, and it didn't take long for the carbon monoxide to kill him," said Bell. "At least that's what it looks like."

"How did the killer zip-tie Carl?" asked Nate. "He would have fought that."

"Not sure yet," said Schnell. "Maybe someone knocked him out when he came back to the shed. Maybe they had a gun and threatened to shoot him. Maybe he was drugged. Hopefully we'll know more after the autopsy and toxicology reports. They did find an insulated coffee mug in the shed that they believe was Carl's. Would have been easy for somebody to slip him something, have him drink it when he takes a break from mowing."

"Aw geez," said Nate, his face contorted in barely controlled grief. "Aw geez." He had liked Carl. The old scoutmaster had made meetings and campouts fun. He'd had a million stories, almost all of them funny and barely believable, though Carl had sworn that all were true. On outings, Carl would find coins, odd or colorful rocks, even little bits of junk that other people wouldn't notice. Many community members knew Carl simply as "that old guy in Field Park," which was where he would be seen a couple of times a week with a metal detector. Everything was a treasure to Carl. Even a quarter century after his Scouting days, when he had seen Carl in the store or at a community event, he always greeted Nate with a wide smile and a new story—which, despite its quirkiness, Carl swore by.

Nate thanked Schnabell and made his way to the tape line that had been erected along the pedestrian path on the west side of highway 83. The gawkers on foot were actually few in number, certainly less than one hundred. Not the easiest place to pull off a car. He noticed traffic on 83 and Veterans was pretty thick. A lot of people were curious.

And a lot of people were probably just plain scared.

Nate was one of them.

Eighteen

The crime scene was finally scoured and secured by 10:30, and although Nate was exhausted, he made good on his promise to text Star.

Not at the office. I'm at home. Stop by.

She texted her address, which was an upstairs apartment overlooking the Main and Rochester intersection in the center of town. All she had to do to get to work was walk across the street.

He parked in the municipal lot behind the east side shops and pushed the buzzer at the door to the stairs. He heard her footsteps, heard the sliding of the deadbolt, and then she ushered him inside. As she climbed ahead of him, he got his first good look at her left leg prosthesis, for she was wearing shorts and a gray, crew neck sweat top. As she had explained, it looked like it could be fitted with a running blade, although a more conventional-looking foot with some sort of flex action was currently attached. She moved so smoothly up the steep stairway that had she been wearing pants, he would have scarcely imagined her injury.

"Nice jacket," she said, looking over her shoulder as she climbed, though unlike Chief Beckman, when she said it, it seemed to Nate that the words had the sound of an actual compliment. "I hope this isn't inappropriate. Us meeting here, I mean. It's just that I've been in that damn office ALL day. I had to get out of there. This new killing…it was sort of the final straw."

"I know the feeling," said Nate as they mounted the landing and made a right turn through a second doorway and into a small kitchen. "I haven't had a chance to sit down all day. Except for about ten seconds at Sandy Sewell's funeral. And the crime scene at Kiwanis Park was a zoo, especially after the news crews arrived. I swear that there were three times as many reporters as with Sandy's murder."

"Welcome to Casa Calloway." She swept a hand around the room, smiled wearily. "Decorated in modern American rummage with a touch of indifference."

A door opened off the kitchen on the right to what appeared to be a bathroom. Straight ahead through a wide opening was the living room, and a closed door off it to the right of this was presumably a bedroom. The furniture looked puffy, worn, and 50 years out of vogue. The wallpaper, the vinyl flooring, the ceiling paint—everything—seemed to radiate a brown mustard color scheme that Nate's mother had used to refer to as "baby shit yellow". Unpacked boxes sat here and there, as did piles of paperwork, unshelved stacks of books, and several vanilla-scented candles, lit.

"The candles are a nice touch," said Nate, pointing to one on the mustard-yellow kitchen counter.

"On the plus side, the place was furnished, so I didn't have to move a lot of big stuff," said Star. "On the negative side, the place was furnished. Can I get you something to drink? A beer?"

Nate raised his eyebrows. "You've got beer?" After what she had told him of her issues with drinking, this surprised him. And she had implied that she hadn't had alcohol for a year.

"I keep it for company. I'm drinking LaCroix."

"Props to you for willpower. If you've got beer, I'll have four."

"One at a time, cowboy," she said, moving to the avocado-colored refrigerator. "Spotted Cow okay?"

"Perfect."

Beer and sparkling water in hand, they moved into the living room to a sofa that rested against the far wall, partially blocking one of two street-facing windows in the room. Nate snuck a peek before sitting and registered a view of the town's central intersection, quiet at this hour.

In front of him was a coffee table onto which he placed his beer as he sat. Star's file folder rested in the middle.

"I told Chief Beckman about the new letter."

"And?"

"He says if you publish it, he'll shut down the paper."

She shook her head, smiling humorlessly. "He can't do that."

"Don't shoot the messenger."

"Don't worry," she said, settling beside him. "I'm conflicted about it, too. I don't know if printing the damn letters is helping or hurting. And now I've got another one on my conscience. I heard it was..." She consulted a note in her folder. "Carl Mullenberg? Don't think I'd met him."

"Good guy," said Nate, studying the label on his beer. "Was my scoutmaster."

"I'm so sorry." She pretended to look for something in her folder for a few moments. "So you were at the park?"

"What a circus."

"That was last weekend. What can you tell me?"

Nate considered this. Star would get most of the details anyway, and he was sure he could trust her to be discreet. "Beckman will release a statement tomorrow. I'm sure Carl's name will be in it. Most of the town probably knows by now. You're going to get the official details eventually, but only mention what's in the release. What probably won't be in the first report is that he was zip-tied to a garden tractor in that painted shed up in Kiwanis Park."

"Oh God! Zip ties! Like Sandy!"

"The sicko ran a hose from Carl's car, pumped carbon monoxide into the shack. Looks like that's what killed him. Again, we have to wait for the post mortem. They're not sure how the killer got the drop on Carl. Knocked him out. Could be chloroform. Put something in his coffee. Tricked him. We're just guessing until we get the labs."

Star rubbed her temples. "Ugh! What a nightmare!"

"My guess is there won't be many clues," suggested Nate. "No security cameras in the park. Maybe they'll get lucky and a parking lot camera from the grocery store across the street will show something, but I'm doubting it. This guy is sick, but he's smart."

Flipping open her folder once again, Star removed a photocopy of the most recent letter. "Look, whether I publish it or not, I think we should try and figure out the riddle. Chief Beckman didn't say anything about not publishing a solution to the riddle. Or you could just give the answer to Beckman. I just don't want the body count to keep increasing. I want to do *something*."

She centered the page between them and they examined the rhyme again.

> *Yankee Doodle came to town*
> *Astride an iron pony*
> *To earn a feather for his cap,*
> *The eighteenth of his cronies.*

Yankee Doodle, what was that?
Exploding myths and more!
Love the U.S. as they did
More than a century yore.

"I hate these stupid riddles," said Nate after a few moments. "It's like when I was in high school, trying to figure out the symbolism in *The Old Man and the Sea*. Whatever my interpretation was, it was always wrong."

"Well, we know whatever the verse is referring to happened more than a century ago," said Star. "That seems pretty literal."

Nate reluctantly took another look at the verse. "Okay, 'love the U.S.' sounds like it must be some big patriotic event. Maybe the anniversary of Wisconsin's statehood. When was that, I wonder? 1840s?"

"People go to Google, not me, for the answer to questions like that," said Star. "There's the word 'exploding'. When it's used with 'myths,' that usually means disproving a myth or legend. But I suppose it could also mean a literal explosion. Maybe something blew up."

"And 'earn a feather for his cap'. Maybe that refers to Indian tribes in the area. Didn't they wear feathered headpieces? I'm ashamed to say that I know zero about that part of our village history."

Star laughed. "So we're looking at a major historical event in Mukwonago that involved Indians, explosions, and patriotism. That should be easy."

"If it has to do with Native American lore, that's the sort of thing that I'd have to look up in the history books. Maybe I'll stop at the library tomorrow." Then another thought came to him. "Or the Red Brick Museum. I think that's open this weekend. There's a couple of folks that volunteer there that know everything. Or it seems like it anyway. Maybe this will make sense to them. May I?"

He indicated the photocopy, and Star nodded. He folded it into a jacket pocket, noticed his beer was empty.

"Get you another?"

He was about to say no, politely excuse himself, head home, get out of the monkey suit, but the beer had tasted good. The apartment, though small, was quiet and smelled like warm vanilla cookies. And having settled on his next course of action, he was just starting to relax a little. Another beer would taste damn good.

"Sure."

A minute later, she returned with a second bottle.

"So," began Nate as she settled back onto the sofa, "I have a rather personal question to ask."

"Is it 'Do you ever fall over in the shower?'"

Nate's mouth fell open. "Excuse me? No!"

She laughed. "Relax. An actual question a third-grader asked me when I was doing a school visit in Madison to talk about how newspapers work."

Nate smiled hesitantly. "Madison is kind of where my question was headed."

Star closed her eyes, but only for a moment. "So you want to know how I got from there to here."

"Only if you want to talk about it," said Nate. "In fact, forget it. It's really none of my business. I let my curiosity get control of my big mouth. You're here, and that's great. Really great."

She stared at the floor, nodding gently. "I've heard all sorts of rumors about me. Some of them are so nicely embellished, I wonder whether they know the correct version of events and I'm the one who is misinformed." She smiled, looked up at Nate. "It's really pretty simple. I got fired for letting my emotions override my common sense."

"That sounds pretty...human."

"What it sounded like to my publisher was unethical," said Star. "And I would agree. One hundred percent."

"Well...it's not like you killed someone." He paused. "Did you?"

"For a journalist, worse, just the opposite. I created someone. In fact, I created several someones."

"I'm a cop, not a journalist," said Nate. "But even I know that's bad."

"Bad doesn't begin to cover it."

"I suppose this is going to sound cliché," said Nate, "but I'm sure you had a good reason."

"Oh, I had great reasons." She took a sip of her LaCroix. "I was the news editor. The one who's supposed to know better than those wet-behind-the-ears twenty-somethings just out of journalism school, kids just itching to smooth out that line in the sand that separates what they *know*, from what they *believe*, in order to get that first big story into print. I was supposed to be the one who kept re-drawing that line, the one who made sure they kept their asses on the right side of it."

"That's a lot of responsibility," observed Nate.

"For which I get paid big bucks." A pause. "*Got* paid big bucks. We had this newbie. Twenty-three. Nothing but A's all through school. You could tell right from interview one that she's thinking Pulitzer in a year. Two, tops. Fairly full of herself, too. Reminded me of a young me."

"I think I prefer the now you," said Nate.

"The young me, for all her flaws, never got sacked. That didn't happen until I was the mature forty-one-year-old me."

"So what exactly happened?"

A long sip before she continued. "There was this big landscaping company in Madison. They were into all sorts of illegal shit. Stole heavy equipment, filed off the serial numbers, then reported the numbers for equipment that had been taken out of service so no one was the wiser. Laundered some drug money. But the worst of it was that they were into human trafficking."

"Are we talking…kids?" asked Nate.

"Kids, adults—mostly young, though," explained Star. "Disgusting sons of bitches. Through the grapevine, we'd heard they had a pretty refined system that operated below the radar and didn't leave a lot of loose ends. Had a lot of illegals working for them, paying them peanuts, of course. They'd tell them they had work for their daughters, but they'd have to travel. The fathers would get a bonus in their pay envelope, and the daughters would go off to work in Arizona or Florida or somewhere like that supposedly. Most times, that was the last they'd see of them."

"Oh my God!"

"And who are you going to complain to? You're a freakin' illegal. At the very least, you're going to lose your job, as shitty as it may be. At worst, deported or jail. So we had the newbie—Kristal— working on the story for months. I figured it was going to be one of the biggest things we'd ever printed—bust up the trafficking ring and put these criminals in prison. But when Kristal turns the story in, it's shit."

"Seriously?"

"The research is so thin that it's going to look like a bad Yelp review. Of course, Kristal thinks it's Woodward and Bernstein good. But it's so lacking in hard evidence that it's unusable. I'm facing deadline, so I tell her that I've got a few sources on the story as well, and I'm going to add a bit of depth, which isn't uncommon for an editor to do. She's not happy about it, but that's life in the news business."

Nate felt he was getting the idea. "I take it your sources—"

"Were bogus," said Star. "The finished story had Kristal's framework, which told the basic details of corruption. And it was interspersed with haunting stories from victims, supposedly being quoted under assumed names. Horrible stories of cruelties and family separations and sexual bondage. Stories that made you want to get a hundred friends with pitchforks and torches and go after the bastards who were exploiting children and their families."

"And all of it fake."

"Oh, it was really happening," said Star. "It's just that we had no convenient way of interviewing the real victims, particularly before deadline. So I created fictional victims to tell their stories."

"Without letting readers know they were fictional."

Star nodded. "'Marucha', age nine, who hadn't seen her parents in two months, who lived with a woman she called 'Aunt Paula', though she had never seen the woman before Marucha had been whisked away from Madison in a panel van with two other children, and who slept on a bare mattress in an always-locked room of 'Aunt Paula's' house until she was 'needed'. 'Juan,' who was thirteen, and who had managed to escape from his handlers at a gas station in southern Illinois, and who was afraid to go home because the bad men would just take him again and force him to do things. 'Jasmine,' age fourteen, whose mother ran off with her before she could be sold into slavery, and who was able to describe the whole process."

"Wow." Nate found that the second beer was gone. "You have one hell of an imagination."

"These things almost always unravel," continued Star. "I knew that. It was stupid. But I was so angry, so wrapped up in the story and the *need* to see the evil bastards in prison that I convinced myself that the end justified the means. That's self-righteous bullshit, of course, but I couldn't bear the thought of more kids being sexually exploited. So I printed the story. We were heroes for about twenty-four hours. Then people in the know started noticing cracks in the foundation of the piece. It didn't take long before the whole dam burst. Lost my job. Actually spent a day in jail for contempt when I initially refused to talk about my sources. Word got around and nobody wanted to hire me. And the worst part was that my shoddy reporting allowed the bastards to get off without any sort of consequences. The story gave them a blueprint for covering their tracks."

"So you left Madison then."

"What does a journalist do when no paper will hire her?" asked Star rhetorically. "She starts her own paper. Or, more accurately in this case, re-starts one.

163 / Rod Vick

It took awhile. I lived on some savings and waitressed a little, a hell which by itself should absolve me of my sins. Eventually, I was able to work out the details and ended up here."

"Man, you jumped from one hot mess to another," said Nate.

She noticed his empty second beer, got up to get a third. "I hadn't realized I was stepping into the murder capital of rural Wisconsin. I thought this was going to be a nice, quiet little gig. Next time I'll know better and open an Etsy shop."

"I heard some of those ladies are pretty cutthroat," he said, reaching out for the third beer as she brought it.

"All right, I've laid bare my soul. What about you?"

He shrugged. "Not much to tell. Mukwonago born and raised. Well, actually, the born part was in Waukesha. But I've lived here all my life."

"Parents?"

"Yeah. Had some."

Star rolled her eyes. "They still here?"

"Orlando," replied Nate. "For the last five years. Retired. They love it. Dad's become a golf fanatic. They've got Disney season passes."

"Married?"

"Yeah, my parents were sort of old-fashioned about that."

"Dumb ass!" laughed Star. "*You*. Ever been?"

Nate sighed. "Not that I recall. You?"

"Surprising the number of guys who aren't comfortable with a girl who's missing parts."

He took another sip. "But you're beautiful."

Had he actually said that out loud? Had to have been the beer. It felt as though someone had suddenly turned up the thermostat about thirty degrees.

After a moment of awkward silence, Star replied, "Well thanks. I was hoping you'd be impressed with my mind."

"Well yeah, that's pretty nice, too."

And then, someone kissed someone else, or perhaps they simply kissed each other. He was never able to recall the exact details afterwards.

He did recall making awkward conversation in the aftermath, making an excuse about the lateness of the hour and the craziness that was sure to come with the next day's continuation of the murder investigations, and then he was out in the parking lot, the cool air chilling his suddenly sweaty body.

What just happened?

He headed to his car, feeling like a seventeen-year-old again—that same feeling of semi-euphoria that comes with a first kiss, and the same feeling of self-loathing over his bungled response to it.

Nineteen

He arrived at the Red Brick Museum in the center of the village at one o'clock sharp on Sunday afternoon, just as Ellie Patterson was unlocking the front door. Just a few feet behind the two of them was Vern Haug. Both were members of the Mukwonago Historical Society, Ellie its president. He had known both for years, not as close friends, but well enough to say hi and exchange pleasantries when they met on the street or in the grocery store. The two were in their mid-seventies.

"Might rain," said Vern, glancing sideways at the mostly cloudy sky before ascending the stoop and stepping inside.

"You might be right," said Ellie. "Well, we need it."

"Mr. Nate!" said Vern good-naturedly. "So you decided to come learn a little bit more about your home town, did you?"

"You could say that," said Nate. He had been in the museum before, but it never failed to amaze and impress him. The Red Brick Museum was the first brick house built in Waukesha County, and the interior had been lovingly restored to what it had probably looked like around the time it was constructed in 1842. Entry was blocked to two rooms by waist-high plexi-glass panels, and these rooms were filled with furniture and myriad artifacts that gave visitors the impression that they'd stepped right out of a time machine and into the 1850s. Guests were free to wander through other rooms, including a later addition to the building that housed an enormous collection of Native American items and displays, donated by Arthur Grutzmacher.

Nate pulled out a scrap of paper onto which he had copied the most recent verse. "I was hoping you could help me with something."

"Sit. Sit." Vern ushered him over to a wooden table that took up most of the north end of the kitchen, plopping Nate down onto a painted wooden chair.

"Okay, someone has been sending odd letters to the Mukwonago Chief," he began, tapping the paper in front of him with an index finger. "We think they may be connected to the murders."

"Horrible!" said Vern. "Just horrible! I can't believe it! Who would do such a thing?"

"It's awful," agreed Ellie, moving to the table but remaining standing. "That poor young girl. And now Carl. He used to help out here as well, you know."

"He was a good guy," said Nate.

"He had one of those metal detector things," explained Ellie. "After every Maxwell Street Days or big event up at Field Park, he'd be out there the next day, looking for coins that people had dropped. Sometimes he'd find car keys, too, and help get them back to their rightful owners. Other times he'd find an old thing, an antique ring or belt buckle, and he'd donate it to the museum. Once he found a railroad spike that looked to be from the 1880s. Imagine that! I have no idea how it ended up in Field Park!"

Nate offered a quiet smile. "We're going to find out who's responsible," he finally said. "And we hope that figuring out this riddle will help point us in the right direction." He smoothed the paper onto the table so that both Ellie and Vern could see.

Yankee Doodle came to town
Astride an iron pony
To earn a feather for his cap,
The eighteenth of his cronies.

Yankee Doodle, what was that?,
Exploding myths and more!
Love the U.S. as they did
More than a century yore.

"Like I said, it's a riddle," explained Nate. "The writer never comes right out and says what he's talking about. It's supposed to be a clue. It might point us to an event or a location. And it has to do with local history."

"Local history?" asked Ellie, turning toward him.

"Mukwonago history," clarified Nate. "Please, take a look, let me know if any ideas come to you."

Vern and Ellie read silently. A minute passed.

When they still hadn't said anything after a second minute, Nate decided to try and prime the pump.

"We were wondering whether it had something to do with Native Americans. You can see they wrote about a feather in his cap. And loving the U.S. Maybe some big patriotic event years ago."

Vern shrugged. "Could mean a lot of things."

Nate sighed. "Yeah. Unfortunately, that's the way it is with these damn riddles."

"We have a whole wing of Native American artifacts," said Vern. "Maybe we could go poke around. But I don't recall anything that really deals with patriotism in there. There's certainly plenty that reflects Native American pride, though."

Ellie bit her lip. "Maybe…"

Nate turned to her. "Maybe what?"

"Well, I was just thinking. What about the number? Someone came to town and he was 'The eighteenth of his cronies'."

"Cronies are what?" asked Nate. "Like friends?"

"Or colleagues, associates," said Vern.

"So are we talking about the eighteenth settler in the village?" asked Nate. "You don't have records of something like that, do you?"

"I wasn't thinking that," said Ellie. "I was thinking that maybe the rhyme is talking about him being the eighteenth of his companions, and he's coming to town here."

"Like a congressman?" asked Nate.

"Or a president," guessed Vern. "Didn't we have a couple presidents visit Mukwonago over a hundred years ago? Lincoln? And Grant?"

"I think so," nodded Ellie. "Let's see, who was the eighteenth?"

Nate already had his phone out and was tapping away. "It...was...almost there...Grant! Grant was the eighteenth president!"

"Why, that fits the rhyme!" said Vern. "Ulysses S. Grant—U.S. Grant! Love the U.S.!"

Love the U.S. as they did more than a century yore.

"That's amazing!" said Nate, shaking Vern's hand and giving Ellie a quick hug.

"Lincoln came too," added Vern as an afterthought. "Not at the same time as Grant, of course. Honest Abe stayed at the inn at the intersection of Front Street and Main, right along the Mukwonago River. It's just someone's house now, but thirty years ago, it used to be a tavern and served the best fish fry in the area."

Nate thought about it. "But when Grant came to Mukwonago, were there any explosions or fireworks or anything? The rhyme talks about 'exploding myths,' and I don't know if 'exploding' is being used in the literal or figurative sense."

Ellie shook her head. "Nothing comes to mind. But we could give it a bit of thought if you'd like. Maybe poke around here."

"That would be great!" said Nate. He then rose, shook both their hands and turned toward the door, turning back at the last moment. "Thank you, really! You've been a great help!"

Then he was out.

Vern called after him. "You're welcome! But don't you want to tour the exhibits?"

*

He sprinted across the street to the *Chief* office. Locked. No surprise, since it was Sunday, although he knew Star often set odd hours for herself. Then he crossed Main Street, rang the buzzer for Star's apartment. It seemed that no one was home, and he was disappointed on two fronts. First, he had desperately wanted to share with her that Vern and Ellie had pointed them in an intriguing new direction. Second, he had wanted to see where things stood after the unexpected "moment" that had occurred Friday night.

Instead, he headed back to his car. Nate was ninety-nine percent sure that Chief Beckman would be in his office. And he was one hundred percent certain the Chief would want to hear about this latest development.

Twenty

As expected, Beckman was in his office. He invited Nate to sit without looking the least bit happy about it.

"This is the latest letter to the *Chief*," said Nate, sliding the plastic sleeve across the desktop to Beckman. He read it while Nate explained. "The previous riddle all matches up with the location we found Carl. And this new letter arrived before anyone else knew of Carl's death."

Beckman finished, tossed the letter onto the center of his desk as if it were something evil. "Did you tell the hip—" He seemed less angry than he had been at the crime scene and caught himself. "Did you tell Ms. Calloway that I'd shut her down if she printed it?"

"I told her," said Nate.

"And?"

"I think she'll cooperate."

Beckman's eyes, which had been gazing at the desktop, snapped up to laser focus on Nate. "You *think*?"

"She's conflicted about it," explained Nate. "Doesn't know if it's helping. Says Carl's death is a weight on her conscience."

"Her poor conscience," said Beckman with a sneer. "People's lives are at stake! Maybe I'll have to pay a visit to her office."

Nate could only imagine what a love fest that meeting would be. "The riddle," he said, pointing again to the letter. "We were way off on the second one. But I got some help from Vern and Ellie over at the museum on the new one."

He explained what he had learned at the Red Brick Museum.

"If we print the correct answer in the paper, that may satisfy Ho-ma-ba," said Nate, "and no one will die."

Beckman grabbed the letter again, read the riddle over and over, moving his lips as he did so. He stared at the page quietly. Then he seemed to come to a decision, his anger and frustration bursting forth again.

"No correct answer in the paper. No letter. Nothing. You tell the publisher of the Hippie Herald that she puts anything in that rag, and I'll have her behind bars before she can say pica!"

Nate started to protest, but Beckman cut him off.

"We're still stumbling around in the dark! You think you have a theory? Great. I'll bet a hundred different people could come up with a hundred different theories about that crazy riddle. You come back to me and say, 'Chief Beckman, I'm 100% sure this is what the riddle means,' then I'll get excited. Until then, I'm fed up with all this Indiana-goddamn-Jones figure-out-the-clues bullshit!"

"Yes sir."

"And who the hell made you the goddamn lead investigator on this case?" asked Beckman. "From what I recall of the duty roster, your job is to make rounds, keep an eye on things, make your traffic contacts, your non-traffic contacts! I've got guys on this case working their asses off with a shitload more experience than you!"

"I was the one who took the call from Star— Ms. Calloway—about the first letter. I just thought it would be appropriate to follow up."

"Well, I'll tell you how you can follow up. Just make sure she doesn't print anything. And for God's sake, not a word about this third letter! 'For Sale' signs will be popping up all over town!"

Nate felt that the prudent course would be for him to retreat at this point. But something hadn't been sitting quite right, had been bothering him for days. "One more thing. It's about Craig LaForte."

"What about him?"

"Well, Grace Hall was a friend of Sandy Sewell's, and she said Craig had stalked Sandy. I would think that a guy who has stalked someone who ends up murdered should be a suspect."

Beckman shook his head. "Man, you've really got it out for LaForte, don't you?"

Nate felt intimidated, felt the sweat coming again. "It just makes sense that he would be on our short list."

"Of course he's a suspect," said Beckman. "Everybody's a suspect. You don't see anybody sitting in jail yet writing up his confession, do you?"

"No, it's just with LaForte's stalking history, I'm surprised no one has questioned him."

"He's been questioned," said Beckman resolutely.

"Who questioned him?"

Beckman's scowl darkened. "Not that it's any of your business, but it was Dick Andrews!"

Twenty-one

Although Nate could not tell if Star was in the *Chief* newspaper office, he pulled his car into a spot nearby, exited, tried the front door and found it unlocked.

"Hello?"

He stepped inside and around the divider, saw that lights were on in the back and that Star was hunched over her desk. A part of him had wanted the door to be locked, which would have delayed whatever awkward fallout there might be from their moment of intimacy the other night. On the other hand, he was curious to see what her reaction would be to the event after having had a day or two to think about it. He was not certain how he felt about it himself. Or at least not ready to admit to himself how he felt about it.

"Come on back!"

He reached her work area in several long strides and stood over her desk.

"Just about ready to hit the submit key," she reported without looking away from her screen. "Giving the pages a final look. Years ago, we had to set up pages on light boards, by hand, then physically take them to the printer, where they were photographed and made into plates. Now, a touch of the button, and they go from my screen to the printer in less than a second. Plates are produced within an hour, and a truck delivers the finished papers early tomorrow morning."

Nate had never thought about the process before, and he found her explanation of it fascinating. "That's pretty cool."

"Not cool enough," she replied with an ironic smile. "We print papers are still getting our asses kicked by the online publications."

It seemed to him that if she felt funny about things, she was masking it pretty well. "Speaking of asses getting kicked," said Nate, remembering suddenly, "that's what will happen to mine if I don't relay a message to you from Chief Beckman."

"Don't worry," said Star. "Based on our talk the other day, I figured he would go full-Gestapo."

There was an unexpected pause as if both of them, in hearing the words "our talk the other day," had been reminded that the "talk" had led to more than talk. Or perhaps Nate only imagined this. A moment later, she hurried on.

"And like I said, I've been feeling pretty guilty about printing them anyway."

"So you left the letter out?"

Star nodded. "I could have pushed the issue. Got a lawyer. Got led out of the office in cuffs, I suppose. But after you've allowed your ego to destroy your own career once, you sort of lose your taste for it. Any new leads?"

"Well, I think I have a pretty good lead on the latest clue."

"Really?" said Star, taking her eyes off the monitor for the first time to glance at him, but only for an instant. "Hang on, let me hit the button...there!" She turned toward him, indicated the seat near her desk for him to take.

"Actually, Vern and Ellie over at the Red Brick Museum did most of the figuring," he confessed, lowering himself into the chair.

Star rotated her main monitor so they both could see it. On the screen, in enlarged, bold letters was the latest riddle.

**Yankee Doodle came to town
Astride an iron pony
To earn a feather for his cap,
The eighteenth of his cronies.**

**Yankee Doodle, what was that?
Exploding myths and more!
Love the U.S. as they did
More than a century yore.**

"Lay it on me," said Star.

"It's Ulysses S. Grant," said Nate. "The president."

"I know he was the president!" said Star testily.

"U.S. Grant," continued Nate. "U.S., like in 'love the U.S. as they did more than a century yore.' And Grant was the eighteenth president."

"And he visited Mukwonago?" asked Star.

Nate nodded.

"I admit, I hadn't thought of that," said Star. "But how does all that other stuff fit in? I mean, in the previous two riddles, everything was a symbol. So what about the 'exploding myths'? And the 'iron pony'? And the 'feather'?"

"I don't know," said Nate. "Maybe the townspeople lit off fireworks."

"Do they have some record of the fireworks occurring?"

"Maybe it'll come up. Ellie and Vern said they were going to do some more looking."

"Ellie and Vern?" She shook her head. "Still a lot of holes. And the U.S. Grant thing? That's all we've got. And is it just me, or did figuring that part out seem too easy?"

"Didn't Ho-ma-ba say that this riddle was going to be less challenging?" asked Nate.

"Yeah," admitted Star, "but...I dunno. Just doesn't sound right."

This seemed like an odd response, he thought. Almost as if she were being argumentative just for the sake of creating an argument. The Grant interpretation sounded solid to him.

"What exactly is it that doesn't sound right? The eighteenth president. U.S. Grant. That's the most spot-on answer we've come up with so far, right?"

His question seemed to make her impatient. "Come on, Nate, don't you see it? The other two riddles were really nuanced. I think you're biting on the easy solution, a possible red herring, just because a couple of nice old-timers happen to have the words 'museum volunteer' in their resumes."

"I'm just saying it's a starting point."

"And I'm saying maybe you should get a second or third opinion on that theory. I just think it sounds a little thin."

"Yeah," said Nate. "I'll do that." The silence then grew uncomfortable, and not in the way it had the other night when it had seemed to invite closeness. In this silence, he could almost feel a wall being built.

Out on the sidewalk a minute later, a headache forming, a big heap of heavy something in his chest, he considered his next move. Perhaps getting another perspective on the riddle would not be a bad idea. But who else knew enough about Mukwonago and its history to be able to contribute a worthwhile response?

He was surprised at how quickly an answer popped into his head. Mr. Duminski, his U.S. history teacher had also been the high school's history club adviser. They had done all sorts of activities and community service projects that dealt with the village's heritage. Tomorrow, he would stop by the school and see if Duminski—or as some students called him behind his back, Doctor Doom—was teaching summer school. If not, the office secretary would have his summer address.

Nate massaged his temples to try and take the edge off his headache, gave a wistful glance back at the front door of the newspaper office, and then headed to his car, trying to replay every line of his conversation with Star, wondering what he might have said that cooled things so abruptly.

And wondering whether the apparent change had been his fault at all.

Twenty-two

Monday morning, Nate sat in his squad on highway 83 just south of Wolf Run, clocking speeds on vehicles zooming over the final hill before the highway divided and the limit plunged to 40 miles per hour as vehicles entered the village. He was required to make two traffic contacts per day. That didn't mean writing speeding tickets. If he pulled over someone for a broken taillight and wrote them a notification to get it fixed, that counted, as did warning tickets—or even pulling over and putting on his flashers to provide a safer situation for a guy changing his tire. Unfortunately, any type of traffic stop seemed to give the public the impression that he and his fellow patrolmen were writing twenty or thirty tickets per day. He sighed. Perception versus reality.

Today, he wasn't thrilled with the duty himself, because it had nothing to do with the investigation of the two homicides. Other officers were out questioning people, looking at security camera footage from nearby businesses, and running down leads. The only real tasks that had ever been assigned to him relating to the murder were crowd control and telling Star not to print the letter. He wondered whether it might be time to freshen up the resume, look for a job in a department elsewhere. Beckman didn't seem to take him very seriously. He wasn't getting the promotions.

Time to move on.

A bit after 11:00, he pulled into one of the downtown municipal lots and took a walk over to Grace's Gifts. Just to see whether she had any new thoughts on Sandy or on Craig LaForte or on anything else connected to the murders, of course. After that, he would head up to Mukwonago High School.

Entering the shop, he did not see Grace behind the counter, which was where she frequently perched. He glanced around the large main room, stepping behind some of the free-standing shelves to see if she was arranging merchandise on display or adjusting price stickers. However, she was nowhere in sight.

"Hello?"

He said it loudly enough, he thought, to be heard in the small back room where she kept boxes, supplies, and unshelved merchandise, but he stepped down the short hallway to have a look anyway. Again, no sign of her. The fact that she seemed to have gone away and left the store wide open worried him.

His throat tightened. Two people had already died. And now Grace was gone, her shop empty, in the middle of a business day.

Then he noticed the closed door on the other side of the short hallway and heard a sound like someone coughing, followed by gagging. Nate was about to say something through the door when it occurred to him that it might be embarrassing for whomever was inside—he assumed it was Grace—to feel like they were being listened to by someone outside. Instead, he treaded lightly back into the main room and waited.

After another few minutes, he heard the turn of the latch and the restroom door opened. Grace emerged, walking unsteadily, her face damp, her eyes half shut. She reached out for the counter as she entered the main room, steadying herself.

"My God, Grace," said Nate, moving a step closer in case she fell. "You look…"

He didn't want to say awful, but the fact was, it would have fit.

She wore bib overalls with a yellow long-sleeve shirt underneath, and dragged one of the sleeves across her mouth before she spoke, finishing his sentence for him. "Shitty? I feel shitty. It's the chemo."

Nate stepped even closer, helped her to the stool behind the counter. "Is there anything I can do?"

Grace shook her head. "Shoot me?" She leaned forward, crossed her arms on the countertop and rested the side of her head on them. "Sometimes you don't feel much of anything. Other times, maybe a little nausea. Then there can be days like this." Her eyes bulged and she raised her head. "I think you'd better get me to the bathroom again."

Nate quickly helped her from the stool, guided her down the hall and she dove into the little restroom, closing the door behind her. Nate heard the sounds of retching again and felt his heart breaking for her.

Goddamn cancer. No one deserves that shit.

He heard the flush of the toilet, and a minute later, she reappeared.

"I think I'd better close up the shop for today. I thought I could soldier through. But I don't have the strength to sit upright on that stool for more than a minute. And I'd probably be in the bathroom puking most of the time anyway. Not exactly conducive to big sales."

"I think that's wise," said Nate. "I'll help you. Do you need a ride?"

She shook her head. "No." Then, a moment later: "Maybe. Yeah, that's probably good."

He helped her lock up, and then he guided her out to his squad.

"Try not to throw up in here," he said, attempting to lighten the mood as he helped her with the seat belt. "I'm already low man on the department totem pole." As soon as he said it, though, he wished he hadn't, for it was clear that if she did throw up, it wouldn't be for lack of trying not to.

He drove to her small house about halfway between her shop and the lake. Nate imagined that on a normal day, she would probably walk to and from the shop. Today, however, she seemed so fatigued and nauseous that it would have been callous for him to just drop her at the end of her driveway, as he had intended, and so he parked and helped her into the house.

"Thank you," she said, a tear sliding down her slack cheek. "I just feel like I want to die."

"That's no way to talk," said Nate, getting a cup from the cupboard and drawing her some water. "This isn't going to last. You'll feel better tomorrow."

"I feel awful now." She took a small sip, set the cup aside. "I need to lay down."

"Sofa?" he asked.

"Bed," she replied, pointing down a short hallway.

The home really was quite tiny, Nate noticed as he guided her to the first door on the right. Small kitchen that transitioned into a small living room—no kitchen table. Two bedrooms just big enough for a full bed and a dresser in each. Bathroom across the hall, just big enough to stand at the sink. Everything painted either white or pale yellow. Grace attempted to climb onto the bed, but succeeded only in pulling the bedspread toward her. Nate lifted her with both arms and gently lowered her into the middle, although in doing so, he found himself sitting on the bed, reclining against the headboard, with his left arm pinned beneath Grace's neck.

"Thank you again," she said hoarsely, without opening her eyes.

"Don't mention it." He would wait until she was asleep to gently extricate his arm. It would surely not take long.

"You can almost fool yourself into thinking everything is okay, that you're normal, just like everyone else," she said dreamily, eyes still shut. "You laugh. You do things you've always done. Then you have a day like this and it scares the hell out of you again. You wonder if there are worse days coming, and if eventually, that's all there will be."

"You've got a great spirit," said Nate. "You'll beat this. There'll be lots of good days."

She did not respond to this and was quiet for awhile. Nate let his eyes travel the room, neat as can be except for the top of the dresser where there were several running trophies and medals, a runner's bib number with the words EAST TROY RUN DOWN CANCER, and a framed photograph of Grace along with two other bandana-clad women in WALK TO END CANCER t-shirts.

He thought for a moment that she had fallen asleep, but then she spoke again.

"Do you like my little house?"

"It's very nice," he said.

"It used to be bigger. Not this one, but the one I lived in before. I was married. My husband died."

He had heard that somewhere. She went on.

"And I had a hard time with that. I lived on Grand Avenue at the time. The big house with the stone porch and the turret."

"The old Emerson House," said Nate softly. "Yeah, I remember. Beautiful place. When I was a kid, we used to say it was haunted."

"I loved that house," said Grace. "But Bob died, and then I was out of work, and I couldn't make the mortgage. The bank sold it to a developer. And he bulldozed it. Most beautiful house in the village and he bulldozed it."

"I remember it. It was amazing."

"So now this is home." Her voice was becoming more dreamy now. "It's very pretty, don't you think?"

He looked at her. Even as sick as she was, he had scarcely ever seen a woman as beautiful.

"Very pretty."

Shortly, her features relaxed, her breathing slowed and became regular. Nate gently slid his arm from beneath her head, and without a word, she rolled onto her side and continued to sleep. Finding the edge of the bedspread, he carefully drew it over her, and then he padded softly out of the house, locking the door behind him.

Stop thinking about her, he told himself as he pulled out of the driveway. *Do you think she's going to give you the time of day once she's well again? Hell no. She'll be looking for a guy whose abs are six-packs, not garbage sacks. And what if she doesn't get well?* He didn't want to let his mind go there, and so he wheeled toward Mukwonago High School and focused on the task he hoped to accomplish there.

Cherry Landsburg performed a number of office duties in the summer, and today she sat behind the attendance counter.

"Oh-oh, here comes trouble," she said with a smile as Nate sauntered through the entrance. "Make any arrests yet? I'm getting tired of packin' heat!" Cherry, who was in her sixties, had red hair that embodied her name piled high on her head. As thin and nimble as an Olympic beach volleyball player, she gave everyone a bit of sass.

"If you're packin' heat in this building, you're damn right I'll be making an arrest," replied Nate, giving her a wink. "Hey, do you know if Doctor Doom teaches summer school?"

Cherry frowned. "Who now?"

"Mr. Duminski. History teacher."

Cherry thought for a second. "Donovan Duminski?"

"Yeah," said Nate. "When I was a student, he used to advise the history club."

She shook her head. "Donovan Duminski is history all right. Ancient history. He hasn't worked here for more than ten years, I'd say."

"Oh no," said Nate, his high spirits suddenly plunging. "He didn't pass away, did he?"

Cherry took a deep breath, drawing her closed mouth into a straight line. "I imagine a few people wish he had."

"What do you mean?"

"I really don't know how much I should say," she said.

"Cherry, if you can't trust me, who can you trust?"

She gave him a sideways glance. "I remember you as a student, Nate Janowsky, and I don't recall 'trustworthy' as one of the words anybody used to describe you."

"Hey, but I'm a cop now. And I know you're dying to tell me anyway."

She looked from side to side to assure that they were not overheard, and she leaned a little closer over the counter. "He got fired."

"No way! He was a great teacher."

"That may be," said Cherry knowingly, "but he didn't get fired over his teaching."

"What then?" asked Nate, completely off balance as a result of this new information.

"Inappropriate relationship," said Cherry. "With a student. One of the young girls in that history club he was advising."

Nate shook his head. "Doctor Doom had sex with a student?"

"Keep your voice down! I don't think it went that far. I think he made some inappropriate advances. The young lady was horrified, from what I remember. Immediately told her parents who informed school officials. And they bounced him. There were no criminal charges, I guess, and so they kept it pretty quiet at the time. But his wife divorced him. He couldn't get another job teaching. No one would hire him. Still lives here in town, I think."

"Wow," said Nate. "And I thought I knew everything there was to know about this town. Then in the last couple of weeks, I find out it's got more secrets than the freaking CIA."

"Sweetie, you don't know the half of it!" said Cherry, breaking into a laugh at her own joke. "But it was just very sad at the time. It really upset the poor girl. She was supposed to be the Homecoming queen, had gotten way more votes than anyone else. But then she couldn't come to school for a couple of weeks, she was so out of sorts. They had to crown the couple with the second-most votes. Julie Mixon and Brent Olivetti. I never liked either of them."

"Who's the current adviser to the history club?" asked Nate.

"That would be Zenner. Carla Zenner. She does teach summer school, but she's only here until noon. I can give you her number, or you can stop back tomorrow."

"I'll stop back," said Nate.

"Kind of spooky, though, isn't it?" asked Cherry.

Nate had been preparing to go, but stopped to address her question. "What's do you mean?"

Cherry rolled her eyes. "That's right, you didn't realize that Duminski had been fired. So you wouldn't know."

"Wouldn't know what?"

"Well, in light of what happened. The first murder. Sandy Sewell. She and Roger Bach were supposed to be king and queen. She was the one."

Nate's eyes widened. "You mean with Duminski?"

Cherry nodded. "She was the one who got him fired."

193 / Rod Vick

Twenty-two

When Nate visited with Carla Zenner during a break between summer school classes the next day, she was able to shed little additional light on the latest verse. Zenner, around fifty, who had purple highlights in her hair and wore knee-high, high-heeled boots, was unable to even hazard a guess, despite an apparently impressive knowledge of area history. However, she did add a few details about Doctor Doom.

"Donovan came off as kind of a prick," said Karla. "He knew his stuff, yeah. In fact, he was never wrong about anything. According to him."

Nate nodded. "Arrogant, huh?" He thought back to when he had been in Doctor Doom's class. The man had been a taskmaster whose word on every aspect of history was regarded as Gospel. He had seemed to be well-liked, but woe to the student who questioned either his knowledge or authority. At the time, it had felt right to have an unimpeachable rock of certainty into whose hands one's young mind could be entrusted and molded. Now, Nate could see how others might have viewed Duminski in a less positive light.

"He got reprimanded one time for tearing up a valedictorian's paper in front of the class and telling him he should probably consider enrolling in a junior college," said Carla. "I mean, it wasn't like he was fined or suspended or anything. Just a letter in his personnel file, critical of how he handled the situation. But he never forgot about that letter. Found excuses to bring it up all the time to give the impression that he was being persecuted."

"Sounds like he held grudges," noted Nate.

"Same thing when he got fired," continued Carla. "Make no mistake, it was all him. The poor girl didn't do a damn thing. She was mortified! But do you think that the bastard ever apologized or took any personal responsibility for it? No, according to him it was the school board out to get him. I'm glad they yanked his ass out of here the day after it all came out. With his combination of bitterness, arrogance and paranoia, I always pegged him for the kind of guy who'd bring an assault rifle to work and start gunning people down."

Nate wondered if he had really been this blind to Doctor Doom's character flaws. He concluded that he probably had. As a general rule, teenagers, he had observed during his adult life in law enforcement, were not exactly poster children for wise judgment. "But Duminski really knew his stuff. Was he pretty well-versed in local history, too?"

"I think so," said Carla. "I remember he used to take the history club kids on a walking tour of the village's historical sites. It was a great tour, designed by an MHS grad, if you'd like to see a copy."

Hoping that it might shed more light on the community's mysterious past, Nate said that he would. Carla dug in a filing cabinet for a few moments before emerging with a book entitled *From Mequanego to Mukwonago: Four Walking Tours* by Kathryn Bergmann. She pointed to the title. "That's the village's original spelling. I guess in retrospect, Duminski did some cool things. But he was still pretty creepy."

Nate took a moment to process this information. "I heard he still lives around here. Wonder where he works?"

"Don't really know, don't care," said Carla. "I heard he was cutting grass for a living."

On his way back to his squad, Nate's thoughts went to Grace, and he wondered whether he should stop back at her house and check in on her. Since he had locked the door behind him when he left, however, he would either have to ring the bell and wake her up, or she would be up already and would not need checking on. He forced his thoughts back to a much less appealing subject, which was Doctor Doom.

A few inquiries informed him that Duminski apparently was mowing grass at one of the local independent living facilities for elderly adults. Five minutes later, he was pulling up to the main entrance. A woman inside at the front desk told him that

Duminski was probably out on the riding mower, seeing as it wasn't raining at the moment and was a Tuesday. Nate took a walk outside around toward the back of the building where he heard the buzz of the mower and smelled the freshly cut grass.

The mower was heading toward the far hedge when he first spotted it, but he guessed the operator would eventually swing around. Nate waited, and a minute later, the mower trundled back toward him. He flagged it down.

The driver brought the machine to a stop, switched the key into the off position, took off his ear guards. Donovan "Doctor Doom" Duminski looked to have gained a few pounds. His hair, which had been a neatly oiled inch twenty years ago, was now about four inches longer, significantly grayer, and significantly less combed. He wore a tattered Milton College sweatshirt.

"Mr. Duminski, I was hoping you might have a minute to talk."

Donovan Duminski had at first looked concerned, maybe even a little frightened, but now he seemed merely irritated. "Is this going to take long?"

"I don't think so, sir," said Nate, wondering if his former teacher recognized that he was talking to a former student. Nate recalled getting a C+ in Duminski's class, not exactly the sort of academic prowess that makes a student stand out.

Nate thought the man might get off the tractor, but Duminski just sat there. Nate took a step closer.

"What's this about?" snarled Duminski. "My car registration or some nonsense?"

"No, sir," said Nate, feeling the same tightness in his throat that he had felt as a junior in Duminski's class when a question about the reading assignment—the smart money would have said he hadn't completed it—was directed his way. "This is about something else. I'm sure you're as concerned as everyone else in the community about the recent homicides."

"Those murders?" Duminski's eyes widened. "What does that business have to do with me?"

"We're casting a very wide net in this investigation, sir," Nate explained. "As a result, we may question individuals whose connections to the victims or their families were very slight, just to make sure we haven't missed a tiny detail that could end up making a big difference."

"That sounds like a bullshit answer, if you'll excuse my French," said Duminski, glaring at Nate.

"Sandra Sewell was a student of yours."

Duminski shook his head. "Complete and utter bullshit!"

"Sir, I'm going to ask you to calm down," said Nate, his own voice betraying just the slightest tremor.

"Or what? You'll cuff me and take me in? Listen, I had nothing to do with what happened!"

"There was an incident a few years ago."

"Twelve!" shouted Duminski. "Twelve goddamn years ago! You know what I did? Nothing! I hear people talking all the time. They think I'm not listening. 'He's the guy who raped that high school girl and got fired.' There was no rape! There was no sex! She stayed after all the time, working on history club projects. Lots of times we were the only ones. She'd laugh and talk about her family and ask me about my life, what I did in my spare time. Always the little flirt. So many nights, staying late."

Nate felt his initial anxiety fading. Duminski's unrepentant arrogance made him feel angry. He suddenly wanted to piss this guy off. "I looked up the old report yesterday," said Nate, which was a lie. "It didn't sound like 'nothing'."

"For *one* kiss! One little kiss! And for that tiny indiscretion, I lost my job, my teaching license, my wife, my home, my friends!"

"The way she told it, your tongue was halfway to her gallbladder," said Nate, still making it up, hoping that something of the sort had either been reported or had actually occurred. "And she said you touched her."

Duminski's face had grown beet-red during this exchange. "Her memory of events and mine were quite different."

"That may be so," said Nate. "But I hope, sir, that you can see how we might want to ask just a couple of questions of someone whose life was turned completely upside down and who might, consequently, have reason to hold a bit of a grudge."

"That's ridiculous!" roared Duminski. "I'd never do something like that!"

"Just like you'd never put your tongue down a sixteen-year-old's throat?"

Duminski's jaw clenched and a vein on the right side of his head throbbed noticeably. "There were two murders, weren't there? That lawnmower guy…"

"Carl Mullenberg."

"Why would I kill him? There's no motive, is there?" He straightened himself in the tractor seat, triumphant, like an attorney who had delivered his closing statement.

"I never said you killed anybody, sir. I just said that since you had a connection, I wanted to ask you some questions."

"I know what you wanted! There was a time when things were different in this community. I was treated with respect! Police did their jobs! Developers didn't come in and bulldoze all the old landmarks so they could put up chain stores! People respected traditions!"

Sounds like he's delivering a sermon.

Nate pulled a paper from his pocket. "I'm going to read something to you, sir, and I want you to tell me if it makes any sense to you. *Yankee Doodle came to town astride an iron pony to earn a feather for his cap, the eighteenth of his cronies. Yankee Doodle, what was that? Exploding myths and more! Love the U.S. as they did more than a century yore."*

He fell silent and looked toward Duminski.

"Sounds like gibberish," said Duminski.

"It doesn't make you think of anything that relates to Mukwonago's history?"

"Really?" Duminski's lip curled. "I'm supposed to get something about Mukwonago out of that mess?"

Nate nodded. "Mr. Duminski, thank you for your time. We'll be in touch."

He turned to go, but almost immediately, Duminsky shouted "Wait!", and Nate turned back.

"You look familiar. Were you one of my students?"

"Little over twenty years ago."

Duminsky regarded him silently for a moment, his expression seeming to soften a bit. Then he said, "You didn't do very well, did you?"

Nate shrugged. "I got by."

Duminsky nodded. "You know your life is shit when you've fallen to the point where your success or failure is in the hands of former C students."

Then he fired up the tractor and headed back off toward the far hedge.

Twenty-three

News vans from the TV stations in Milwaukee were a regular occurrence during the week, most setting up near one of the two murder sites or in front of the police department, a clean-looking reporter giving the recap, updates, and adding just enough adjectives to create an element of intrigue and make it all sound like the teaser for the next episode of CSI. If there was nothing new to report, they often concluded with an ominous statement of some variety that inferred that the entire community might be doomed.

Also in town, Nate noticed, were more Waukesha County squads, since the county sheriff's office was providing additional manpower where the investigation wore the local resources thin. While life went on, it seemed to him that neither the news vans nor the county squads did anything to comfort village residents. No matter where in Mukwonago one went, conversations almost always included some reference to the murders and how the little town had been changed.

He had not seen Star since their rather cold exchange on Sunday, and it was now Wednesday. If she had come up with a better theory on what the most recent verse meant, she had not shared it with him. He thought of Grace as well, and would have called or texted her, except that he did not have her number. Mid-morning, he stopped in at the gift shop, which he was pleased to see was open for business.

As soon as he stepped in the front door, she came out from behind the counter where she had been sitting, crossed the room, and threw her arms around him, giving him a heartfelt hug. "Thank you so much for yesterday! Oh, God, I think you saved my life!"

She released him then, seemed to feel a little embarrassed by the greeting, and stepped back.

"Happy to be able to help," said Nate, clearing his throat. "Looks like you're doing better today."

"Much," she said, putting a hand on her forehead. "I think I lost ten pounds yesterday! Couldn't keep anything down." Then she looked at him and smiled. "Too much information, huh?"

"No, I get it," he said. "I give you props. I'm sure I'd be in bed for weeks."

She shook her head. "I don't think there's much that could keep you from doing the right thing. Did I tell you my life story or did I imagine that?"

"You mostly just fell asleep," said Nate. "You needed it."

A smile. "You are too kind. Look, it's not very busy right now. Can I take you over to Sarah's, buy you a cup of coffee?"

Nate shook his head. "On the job. Just stopped by to see how you were doing."

Her eyes twinkled. "Do all citizens get this kind of personal treatment from Nate Janowsky?"

"When most citizens see Nate Janowsky, they just hope he doesn't have the radar gun pointed in their direction. And they're happy if he completely ignores them."

She laughed. "Well, I'm glad you don't ignore me." Then she quickly hugged him again before stepping back. "Okay, don't get too crazy with that radar gun."

He started toward the door. "Maybe I can take a rain check on that coffee." She nodded and then he was out on the sidewalk.

Twenty-four

The Phantom had to be careful. The first time, no one had expected it. That had been easy. People who lived in small towns were so trusting. Too trusting for their own good.

Carl Mullenberg had posed more of a challenge. Getting the drug cocktail just right—to knock him out quickly, but not for too long. People needed to know that Carl had been awake, had been afraid before he died. That would make the community more afraid too, desperate, on edge, ready to lash out. That would come in handy later when widespread panic would be another asset.

Despite the need to be careful, the Phantom enjoyed challenges. One could find the recipe for any poison if one was perseverant and sufficiently inquisitive. And if one knew how to navigate the Dark Web using a false identity and a digital tablet that would disappear without a trace after all of this was over.

Getting to and from the shed in Kiwanis Park had been a challenge, and had involved some risk. But it had worked out perfectly. The Phantom had hidden in the back of Carl's van, which Carl had parked right next to the shed. After Carl had been dealt with, the Phantom had waited for a lull in traffic and had hopped onto the pedestrian path in sweat pants and a hoodie—a little much for a June evening in the low 70s, but effective at camouflaging one's identity—clothing which had been discarded along the Vernon Marsh access road at the north end of town where a parked car had been waiting.

Tonight, Thursday, Corrine Barker had posed several challenges as well. But Corrine's habits had rendered her vulnerable, and the Phantom knew those habits well from weeks of observation.

Poor, lonely Corrine.

She came off as a tough but fair, tell-it-like-it-is, middle-aged woman who suffered no nonsense and kept her emotions under control. In reality, the Phantom's meticulous scrutiny indicated that Corrine had been hurt badly by the divorce three years earlier. Now, at age forty-nine, with a still pleasant-looking face, Corrine had grown a little thick around the middle, had streaks of gray hair, and puffiness in the jowls and under the eyes, At times, she seemed to barely conceal an anxiousness over the possibility that she might be alone for the rest of her life.

Her night life, on weekdays, consisted of supper between 6:00 and 7:00, work in her garage until nine, and then falling asleep on the living room sofa.

Her garage work did not involve cars. Corrine's sat in the driveway, twenty-four/seven, rain or shine. Her garage was filled with junk, although Corrine referred to much of the stuff as "antiques" or "collectables." Folding tables displayed ceramic knick-knacks, hand-painted dinner plates, dolls in elaborate dresses and costumes, sewing boxes, care-worn boxes containing old board games, gaudy table lamps, and more. Some of the merchandise was packed away in large cardboard containers tucked beneath the folding tables or stacked along the wall closest to the house. She kept a U-shaped pathway through the garage and added to her treasure storehouse frequently.

Every night, she came to the garage, without fail, opening the garage door so that the whole world knew she was out there in her own personal museum. She cleaned, polished, and repaired recently acquired items. She unpacked some, packed others away. Each night, she decided on a couple of new items to try and sell online, and these she photographed. Every Thursday, Friday, and Saturday, the "GARAGE SALE" sign went up on her lawn. Sometimes, people even stopped by and inquired about items they had spotted from the road or wondered if a late-in-the-day rummage sale was in progress. And so it really did not surprise Corrine when the Phantom slipped out of the shadows at about 8:45. Of course, Corrine had not known that it was the Phantom, had in fact recognized the visitor as a familiar face, although not exactly a friend. And so it had been easy for the Phantom to ask a question about one of the items, and when Corrine had turned away and begun her explanation, she had been surprised when a sweet-smelling rag had been pressed over her nose and mouth by someone behind her.

Her surprise had lasted only a few moments.

The Phantom had then shut the garage door, grabbed the keys for Corrine's car out of the house, and now, the Phantom and Corrine were behind the feed mill. They were several hundred feet north of Oakland Avenue along the railroad tracks that cut a swath through the village. No light from houses or streetlamps reached them here, although the Phantom's eyes had adjusted nicely to the darkness by this time.

The Phantom stood next to the tracks, looking down at Corrine who was just now regaining consciousness. Duct tape covered Corrine's mouth, and she was tied to the tracks. Naturally, she did not understand where she was at first.

"You're actually near the site of a rather historic event," said the Phantom as Corrine became suddenly more aware of her surroundings and began to make muted but confused noises. It was clear to the Phantom that Corrine did not yet realize the terrible danger she was in.

"Oh, don't struggle," said the Phantom. "Just try to relax, although I know this isn't the most comfortable place to lie down. A few feet south of where we are right now, there used to be a train station. A passenger station. Can you imagine? Like all of the historically significant things in this town, the rubes destroyed it. Torn down years ago."

Corrine now made angry sounds, and the Phantom was glad the woman was securely tied. But the Phantom also knew that there was far more terror than anger in Corrine, and this became apparent as the angry grunting quickly gave way to muffled sobs.

"And there was apparently a big event here a little more than 150 years ago," continued the Phantom, heedless of Corrine's suffering. "Ulysses S. Grant, hero of the Civil War for the North, arrived in Mukwonago by train to give a rousing speech. You see, Mukwonago's citizens, back during the Civil War days, were staunch abolitionists. They provided a stop on the Underground Railroad, smuggling fleeing slaves in hay wagons. So after the war, Grant came here. They say that the speech was so good, virtually everyone in town voted for him in the presidential election."

Corrine suddenly became more animated, as if she had detected something that disturbed her greatly, although her increased protestations could generate no more volume or success than before.

"You used to be able to take the train to Waukesha. Or Burlington. Lots of other places along the line, I suppose. It was before my time. Now it's just freight trains."

A rumble, so faint that one might suspect they had imagined it, seemed to drift in from a great distance and continue like a prolonged dream.

"The freight trains used to sound their horns when they came through town," said the Phantom. "That doesn't happen anymore, either. I suppose I can see the point, particularly at night time. But between you and me, I've always enjoyed the sound of train whistles!"

The rumbling ebbed slightly louder now, rolling in from the north. Corrine's body heaved and twisted as far as it was able, although her wrists and ankles remained firmly bound to the tracks.

"It always seems like the trains are going so fast, doesn't it? But in reality, they rarely exceed forty miles an hour when they pass through town. That's interesting, isn't it? And many of them have more than one hundred and fifty cars. I've counted."

Corrine made tortured animal sounds, increasingly desperate, but still futile.

"I'm going to leave you now. I won't be too far away. I have to stay close so that no one accidentally happens by and releases you. But I'll be hidden in the trees so that the engineer won't be able to see me."

The Phantom moved off to the brush, a spot that had been spotted during daylight reconnaissance weeks ago. The rumbling was very noticeable now, and Corrine's body jerked around as if she had brushed against a power line supplying juice to an entire neighborhood. The Phantom actually found it comical and had to suppress a laugh.

Now the ground began to shake, and the light on the front of the train lit the tracks. And something happened that surprised the Phantom. One of Corrine's hands shot up in the air. Somehow, perhaps a superhuman feat of strength magnified tenfold by adrenaline, she had broken the zip tie loops securing her right hand. She clawed at the zip ties securing her left, realized that her time was running perilously short, tore the duct tape from her mouth and uttered a heart-shattering scream. The engineer, of course, could not hear it, although as the Phantom had expected, he certainly must have seen Corrine tied — or partially tied — to the tracks and applied the brakes, and so the train sent out a piercing, metallic scream of its own. But there was no circumstance, even in full daylight, where the train would have been able to bring 150 cars to a stop in time. Corrine's cry was abruptly overwhelmed by the much louder cries of the slowing train. And at almost the same moment, Corrine herself disappeared beneath its wheels.

Twenty-five

Two murders had changed the mood of the village dramatically. By the Monday following the third murder, even the look of Mukwonago had been altered.

Previously, news vans from the stations in Milwaukee could be seen in town for a half hour here and there, giving updates which consisted mostly of repeating that the police were still searching for leads and questioning suspects. The backdrop for these reports changed occasionally, sometimes featuring the reporter standing in front of the police station, sometimes at the gate to Field Park, sometimes with Phantom Lake as the background, or sometimes just somewhere in the downtown area to give the report a Mukwonago "feel".

By Monday, it was no longer just Milwaukee news vans. The national networks arrived, setting up virtual camps. It appeared to Nate that most were set to stay for the long haul. In some respects, it felt as if it were the week before Summerfest once again, as if the carnival had come to town.

However, the increased presence of the media was not the only change in the look of the village. The

FBI had set up a field office consisting of a forty-foot-long trailer on a flatbed truck in the parking lot of the Mukwonago Village Police Station, a pulling of rank that had made Chief Beckman about as angry as a high school football star whose homecoming date ran off behind the bleachers with the captain of the chess squad. In addition to making their presence known, the feds had called dibs on several aspects of the investigation that had been handled exclusively by the Mukwonago officers up to that point. Beckman seethed. Nate was certain the air temperature surrounding Beckman's office was ten degrees higher than anywhere else in the building.

There seemed to be more traffic through the village, too, particularly at times when traffic should have been a little lighter. Nate wondered whether people from surrounding communities were doing drive-bys, as if while cruising down Rochester Street, they might suddenly spot a guy who was instantly identifiable as the serial killer. Or perhaps identify some flaw in the community's human architecture that would explain why murders were committed here and not in their own towns. Some business owners weren't altogether displeased with this development, as it led to greater traffic through the village's restaurants, convenience stores, and especially liquor stores.

Connie Barker's grisly death had prompted these changes, which Nate felt was completely understandable. He had not been part of the crew that responded to the scene after the train had run her over, and he was rather glad of that. The officers who had been there still turned pale when asked about it.

Beckman had addressed his on-duty crew this morning, giving them all the updates. Yes, Corrine had been tied to the tracks. Yes, they believed this was the work of the same individual who had committed the previous two murders. No, there were no suspects. Or more precisely, no new evidence had been uncovered that pointed toward a specific person of interest.

"Her car was found nearby," Beckman had reported. "We're not sure why she would have driven to that location, or whether she might have been forced to drive. This thing just keeps getting weirder and weirder."

Nate agreed with the "weirder and weirder" assessment. Recalling the most recent riddle, he was sure that some historic event must have occurred near the site of Corrine's death, and was hoping that Vern and Ellie could provide some insight.

Beckman had been adamant that the local officers needed to do a better job of keeping eyes on the community. "This sick creep isn't invisible! He has to move around somehow! And when people sneak around, they're taking a chance at being spotted! We've got to be vigilant, and we've got to get lucky! No way are we going to let the FIBBIES come in here like they own the place and grab all the credit! Think about it! Three people are murdered on our watch, and we've got squat! Then the Feds come in and solve the case! How is that going to make us look? Like a big, fat waste of community resources, that's how!"

But how do you catch a phantom? wondered Nate. Where does one begin? When the phantom is making up the rules and knows the path, how do you ever catch up?

As Nate pulled into the Kwik Trip on the north side of town to grab a therapeutic crème-filled chocolate doughnut, his cell pinged and he saw that it was a message from Star.

Can you come right now?

He had not seen her in days. Had been mystified and — if he were honest — a little annoyed by her tepid response to him. He guessed that he had misread things. Well, it wasn't like that had been the first time. His record as a Romeo was about equal to the Minnesota Vikings' record in Super Bowls. Heck, his record as a Romeo had very few participation trophies.

Reluctantly, he left the doughnut for later, returned to his squad and drove to the *Chief* office. When he arrived, he found the place pretty busy. An unmarked van was parked out front as well as a black SUV, the vehicle of choice of FBI road trips. Two suits stood by the front door.

"Shop's closed," said Suit One as Nate neared the front door.

"What do you mean, 'Shop's closed'?"

Both suits laughed. "I can see why you guys haven't caught this creep yet!" said Suit One. "You see, 'closed' means a place isn't open for business."

"Did Ms. Calloway close it?" asked Nate.

"I'm sure Miss Calloway understands the situation."

"That sounds like a hard no," said Nate. "You know, there's a little thing called the First Amendment. I can see that you guys haven't passed Basic Civics 101 yet. But I'm not here to buy a newspaper. I'm here at the request of Ms. Calloway. Is she under arrest?"

The two suits said nothing.

Nate plunged between them. "If she's not under arrest, you can stop wasting my time. You guys and us...we're on the same side!"

Inside the building, he couldn't resist a smile.

That felt kind of bad-ass.

Toward the back of the room, Nate found Star seated at the meeting table with three more male suits, one of whom was standing, and a woman. Star stood when she saw Nate come around the divider.

"Looks like a party," said Nate, stepping to within a few feet of the table.

"They shut me down," said Star, her voice shaking. "Completely. They won't let any of the papers go out for distribution. They think I've got something to do with the murders."

Nate looked around at the suits. "You guys are kidding, right?"

One of the suits at the table rose, though he did not approach Nate to introduce himself or shake hands. "My name's Agent Daniels," said the man, who gave the impression that he was in charge of all the suits. "What's your business here, officer?"

"My name's Janowsky," said Nate, who felt like Daniels' introduction had established a precedent. "Ms. Calloway asked me to be here."

"And how did she do that?" asked Daniels.

"Text message, sir."

Daniels cast a quick glance in Star's direction. "We're not here to create conflict with the local police force," Daniels assured him. "Ultimately, our job is to provide you with another agency to collect evidence and follow up on leads. We both have the same goals."

"And you think Ms. Calloway killed these people?" asked Nate.

"She's a person of interest to us," said Daniels. "As I'm sure she is with your force."

"Because?"

"She's the one who's been receiving the letters. But there's no evidence to show how they're being delivered. They magically end up here. Could be a very clever murderer. Could be an inside job?"

"Seriously?"

"Ms. Calloway's reputation regarding the truth is certainly a factor here," explained Daniels. "As is her record of criminal violence."

"Criminal—?" He looked to Star, but her eyes were focused on the table in front of her.

"Assaulted a former coworker with a shovel," stated Daniels. "Due to her lack of a record, she pleaded to a misdemeanor and community service."

"That's not exactly the same thing as murdering three people with whom you have no history," said Nate. "And why stop publication?"

"We're confiscating anything that might encourage the killer—assuming the killer's not Ms. Calloway," said Daniels. "We have another letter allegedly received by Ms. Calloway on Friday." He held up an envelope in a clear evidence bag. "This isn't getting out."

"The new letter wasn't printed in today's Chief," said Star between gritted teeth. "The third letter wasn't printed in LAST week's Chief. There's no reason to stop publication!"

"We've got to cover all our bases here," said Daniels. "Maybe the fact that the letters aren't being printed is enraging this maniac. Maybe Ms. Calloway is working secretly with the killer, sending coded signals through the paper."

Nate emitted a bitter laugh. "That's nuts."

"Is it? Psychopaths don't think like normal people. If there's no paper published this week, will that change the way the killer does things, get him to do something careless? If we take away the game board, will the killer make a fatal mistake? Try to contact the community another way to keep the game going? Put himself at risk? He's been used to calling the shots. We're calling them now."

Nate glanced at Star. "Is Ms. Calloway under arrest?"

Daniels shook his head. "We're simply questioning her. And letting her know what her role is going to be moving forward."

"And the confiscated newspapers? You're not concerned about the ACLU slapping you with a lawsuit somewhere down the line?"

"We have the authority to confiscated evidence that is material to an ongoing investigation," said Daniels. "That includes those newspapers. And the fourth letter."

"I wonder if a judge would see it that way," said Nate.

"I'm willing to take that chance," said Daniels. "And you surprise me, Officer Jasinsky."

"Janowsky."

"Remember, officer: We're on the same side. But you don't seem to be acting like it."

"No disrespect intended, sir," replied Nate.

"If you have no further business here, officer…"

Nate looked to Star, hoping to get some sign from her as to how he should proceed, but her eyes had dropped to the table again.

"I'll be in touch," said Nate, turning to head back toward the front of the building. He did not know what else to say, and in the end, his message had been intended just as much for Star as for Daniels.

As he came alongside the front desk, Judith Patrick, the receptionist, held up a plain, business-sized envelope. "From Ms. Calloway." After Nate took it, she returned to her business at her monitor.

Nate opened the envelope and was stunned by what he found: a photocopy of the fourth letter and verse.

Daniels and his group certainly had not intended for this to make its way into Nate's hands. What he should do, he knew, was take this back to Daniels and let him know what had occurred.

Instead, he pocketed the letter and walked out.

Twenty-six

In his squad, Nate removed the letter from the envelope and read it in its entirety:

Have you given up? Conceded? Is that what you're admitting by not publishing my letter to the Mukwonago Chief last week? If so, it only underscores how pathetic you are. Unable to solve my simple riddles, even with the fate of your community on the line. Thinking that you will somehow be spared if you do nothing. The only thing more deplorable than a community that is ignorant of its heritage is a community that will do nothing to save itself.

But perhaps redemption is still possible. In the interest of leveling the playing field, I'll make this fourth riddle simpler still. Solve it. Publish it. Save yourselves.

This old man, he played dead.
Yearly rituals above his head
With a knick-knack paddywack
His name doth chill the bones.
This old man owns many stones.

Ho-ma-ba

How was anybody supposed to figure these things out, Nate wondered? According to Ho-ma-ba, the letter writer, this one was supposed to be easier, yet, to Nate, it seemed as enigmatic as the others.

He would have liked to sit down and discussed the riddle with Star, but the feds had her occupied at the moment. Glancing over his shoulder at the Red Brick Museum, he wondered whether any of the volunteers were at work tidying things up after yesterday's tours. Exiting the squad, he made his way across the street and found the front door unlocked. Vern Haug was changing a light bulb in the kitchen when Nate entered.

"You're becoming one of our most frequent visitors, Mr. Nate!" said Vern good-naturedly. "Working on another puzzle?"

"As a matter of fact, I am," said Nate with a smile.

Ellie came out of the side room that served as an office. "Ooh, another riddle! Is this one about Mukwonago too?"

Nate nodded. "It is. But you both have to promise me something. You can't tell anyone I shared this riddle with you. And you can't reveal any of the details. It's very important."

"Police business, eh?" grunted Vern. "More of that murder stuff, I suppose."

"Don't you worry, Nate," said Ellie, patting his forearm. "We won't tell a soul. Will we Vern?"

"No one talks to me anyway," said Vern.

Nate read the poem to them.

This old man, he played dead.
Yearly rituals above his head
With a knick-knack paddywack
His name doth chill the bones.
This old man owns many stones.

After he was done, neither Vern nor Ellie said anything for a long moment. Ellie breathed a deep sigh as she stared at her hands, her brow furrowed in thought. Vern scratched the side of his head. Nate finally broke the silence.

"I was thinking maybe it had something to do with the Blarney Castle," said Nate, glad to finally be able to use the unusual structure on Pleasant Street as a potential clue. "The man who built it is dead. And he must have owned many stones to build it. It's made of thousands."

"Well, that's true," noted Ellie tentatively.

"Lot of stones, that's for sure," added Vern. "But that's not it."

The certainty with which Vern had shot down the idea stunned Nate. "How can you be so sure?"

Ellie shook her head, looked at Vern. "Blood?"

Vern nodded. "Yes, that's what I was thinking."

Nate wondered if he had misheard. "Excuse me? You said…"

"Blood," said Ellie, following this with a cheery smile.

"'This old man, he played dead,'" repeated Vern. "Well, Blood is dead."

"If we're talking about a person, so are 10,000 other former village residents," protested Nate. "Who's Blood anyway?"

"There's a Blood Street in Mukwonago," said Ellie. "It's named after Ira Blood."

"I knew that," said Nate. "That there's a Blood Street. Just a block north of Andrews, isn't there?"

Ellie nodded. "Ira Blood surveyed some of the earliest plots of land in the village. He came here in the 1830s."

"1837," offered Vern authoritatively.

"Yes, 1837," she continued. "And he's buried up in Oak Knoll Cemetery."

Vern repeated the next line from the rhyme. "'Yearly rituals above his head.'"

"That's right," said Ellie. "Every Halloween, people—teenagers, mostly—go to Oak Knoll Cemetery to see whether the book will bleed."

Nate's mouth dropped open for a moment. "I'm lost."

"Half-assed nonsense," said Vern. "Local legend. There are several Blood tombstones in a plot."

"'This old man owns many stones'," interrupted Ellie.

Vern continued. "And right in the middle is a stone pedestal made to look like a tree stump, probably three foot high, with a stone book top of the stump. Word 'BLOOD' is on the cover. Legend says if you go to the cemetery on midnight on Halloween, the book will open and bleed."

"But nobody's ever seen it…"

"No dear," said Ellie. "No one's ever actually seen it bleed. To our knowledge."

"I can't even imagine how creepy it would be to have Blood as your family name," he said, and immediately thought of the remaining line of the rhyme. *His name doth chill the bones.*

It seemed to fit perfectly. He stood to go, shaking their hands. "Thank you so much. Again!" Then he headed for the door, but stopped short when Ellie spoke.

"We're sorry we weren't more help with the previous riddle."

"You helped a lot," said Nate. "We just didn't quite figure out where it was all going to happen."

"You mean near where the old railway station was?" asked Ellie.

Nate nodded.

"When Grant came to visit, he came by train, and they wanted to give him a salute by firing off a cannon, but the cannon exploded," said Vern.

"'Exploding myths and more'," whispered Nate, quoting the previous rhyme.

"We didn't know about that until we did a little research after you left," said Ellie. "But we assumed you knew that it had something to do with the train that came through Mukwonago."

"Why would you assume that?" asked Nate.

"That was the easiest part of the rhyme!" said Vern. "'Yankee Doodle came to town astride an iron pony'! 'Iron pony!' You know? A pony is a *horse!*"

Nate closed his eyes, cursed himself. How could they have missed it? Was it just too obvious? Had they been looking for something much more complicated and looked right past it?

How could they not have registered that an "iron horse" was another word, popularized in the 19th century, for *train*?

Twenty-seven

Nate had Monday evening off, but he knew the rest of the week would be long hours. He showered and changed at home, then drove back to the center of town. He wanted to meet with Star if she was home, but he did not want to call or text. If the FBI considered her a person of interest, he didn't want to have his number coming up in her phone records at the wrong times.

As he drove past on Rochester, he saw that lights were on in her flat, which suggested that Daniels hadn't taken into custody. Or maybe she was just a slouch when it came to energy conservation.

He was relieved when it turned out to be the former.

"That was quite a little stunt, having your receptionist slip me a copy of the latest letter," said Nate as he reached the landing and stepped into her flat.

"Hello to you too," said Star, shutting the door behind him.

"I mean, you really took a chance there. I appreciate it. But wow, stickin' it to the FBI! Damn, I hope this place isn't bugged!"

"I had a feeling they might play hardball, so I made a photocopy and told Judith what to do," said Star. "But I trust you didn't do anything stupid, like telling anyone. Beer?"

"Thank you," said Nate, stepping through the kitchen and settling on the living room sofa—where things had gotten awkward during his last visit. "You realize I'm going to have to show the letter to Chief Beckman. If I don't, I could lose my job. And probably worse."

"I figured as much," said Star, depositing one of the Spotted Cows on a coaster on the coffee table in front of him, then taking her seat with a cup of tea for herself. "Maybe you could be kind of vague about how you came into possession of it."

He nodded. "I'll think of something. And I just wanted to say…I'm sorry."

Star squinted her eyebrows into a V. "What are you sorry about?"

"I don't know," said Nate with a shrug, avoiding eye contact. "Whatever I did to piss you off the other day. It was my fault, I guess. I misread things. I—"

"Shut up."

Now Nate looked at her, surprised. "W-what?"

"Shut up!" she repeated. "You didn't do anything wrong."

"But…you were obviously upset about s—"

"Did you ever think that it wasn't you that was the problem? That maybe it was me?" She took a long drink, set the can down hard. "I felt good…afraid…confused…angry…"

"Angry?"

"With myself," said Star. "I wasn't sure I should be crossing that line with you. I didn't want it to be the wrong thing for you."

Nate wasn't sure what to say. After a few moments he offered a suggestion. "Why don't we just put that whole thing off the table for right now, since neither of us knows what to do with it. And right now, we need each other's help."

Star nodded. "Yeah. We'll give that a try. We'll give that a goddamn try. I think we need some chips and salsa."

She stood up, headed toward the kitchen. A few moments later, came back with the chips in a plastic bowl, setting a jar of salsa next to it. "Help yourself. So what are your thoughts on the letter?"

"Well," said Nate, leaning forward, "I think I might have figured it out."

Stars eyes widened. "Seriously? But we've thought that before, and now we've got a pile of corpses."

"But this time, it really seems to fit. And Ellie and Vern both agree—"

"Wait!" interrupted Star. "You showed the letter to Ellie and Vern? Shit!"

"No, it's okay," said Nate. "I made them promise to keep it zipped."

Star rolled her eyes. "Oh, that makes me feel so much better. Did you make them pinkie swear? Are you effing crazy?"

"Telling Ellie and Vern is like telling your grandparents!"

"My grandfather went to jail for tax fraud."

"Hear me out," said Nate, a bit annoyed at her impatience and paranoia. "I think they're on to something. And I would have never figured it out on my own."

She sighed. "All right. I'm intrigued. What did 'Ellie and Vern' have to say?"

Nate pulled out the copy of the letter, smoothed it onto the table, and explained.

"Really?" She wrinkled her nose in disgust when Nate had finished. "That's a real thing? A family named Blood?"

"Apparently one of the village's early movers and shakers." He repeated as much of the family's backstory as he could remember.

Star's irritation seemed to melt away as he narrated the details. "It really does seem to fit. But dang! A family named Blood! Their kids must have either been the punching bags for every bully in school, or the biggest bad-asses in the county."

Nate nodded. "Crazy, isn't it? Teenagers visit the grave on Halloween hoping to see blood flowing out of the monument. I guess it's a stone book."

"I think I would have liked this family," said Star. "So what's next?"

"I've got to tell Beckman," said Nate. "But I don't want to get you in trouble. I suppose I can make up some story about the letter just ending up on my doorstep."

"Oh, right, you're such a convincing liar." She rolled her eyes again. "Plus, who besides me would possibly have put it there?"

"I'll think of something," said Nate. "Beckman is so pissed about the FBI possibly getting the credit for catching the killer that he might be okay with not asking too many questions about where the letter came from."

Star smirked. "Who says there's no upside to petty, small-town rivalries? What do you think Beckman will do?"

Nate considered this for a moment. "Well, both he and the Fibbies will have the letter. But with Ellie and Vern's analysis, Beckman will have a piece of the puzzle that the FBI doesn't. I suppose it's possible that they'll ask around and come up with the same answer."

"What are the chances that they'll talk to Ellie and Vern?" asked Star.

Nate shook his head. "Don't know. They hadn't talked to them yet when I was at the Red Brick Museum earlier today. And I just ran into them by accident. They just happened to be in there doing a little...whatever the hell it is they do in museums on off days. I suppose if it occurred to the FBI to contact someone from the Historical Society, they might track

Vern and Ellie down at home. But then again, they might end up talking to some other members of the Society. Maybe ones that wouldn't come up with the same answer that Vern and Ellie did. Plus, I told them not to say anything about the letter, so even if the Fibbies did talk to them, they might play dumb."

"A lot of 'ifs' and 'mights'," noted Star. "Regardless, Beckman's going to want to use the information to catch the killer. So he'll probably plan some sort of surveillance of the cemetery on Thursday. A stake-out?"

"I can't really comment on what I think is going to happen," said Nate. "All I can say is keep whatever you're thinking to yourself. The more people who get wind of any of this, the less successful we're likely to be."

"Hey, you're the one who's been flapping his gums to all the village's senior citizens," said Star.

Nate smiled.

Twenty-eight

As expected, Chief Beckman was happy to get the letter and content to not ask too many questions about its origin. Nate could almost see the gears turning, Beckman analyzing how he could use this information to outshine the FBI. Once he had heard Ellie and Vern's analysis of the verse, he almost smiled—something Nate had not seen him do, except sarcastically, since well before the first murder.

"You said the first riddle was about the phantom in Phantom Lake...and that's where the murder occurred," said Beckman. "The second was about the shed in the park. Again, that's where the murder occurred. The third?"

"Apparently a reference to Ulysses S. Grant arriving by train," said Nate.

Beckman nodded. "And the third murder occurred on the train tracks. Now this one mentions the tombstone of Ira Blood." He tapped the photocopy of the letter with a middle finger. "I'd bet your next week's salary that's where the next murder is supposed to be! Only we'll be staking it out. We'll catch that son of a bitch red-handed!"

"How's that going to work?" asked Nate. "I mean, how do we stake out the cemetery without anyone noticing? This creep seems to know this town pretty well and moves about like a ghost."

"You let me worry about that," said Beckman. "And not a word! I'll brief the squad once I get all the details worked out! Damn, I would give anything to see the look on that bastard Daniels' face when we make the collar! Little hick-town police force sticks it to the Feds!"

Nate nodded. Since Beckman seemed to be in a good mood, he decided to ask about something that had been bothering him. He knew it was foolish to ask, since it would obliterate Beckman's sunny disposition and he would revert to his default setting of angry martinet.

"Chief, I have a question about Craig LaForte."

Beckman's face immediately darkened. "What about him now?"

Nate took a deep breath to steady himself. "Well...it's just that I got conflicting stories from you and Dick Andrews about whether he was being investigated in Sandy Sewell's death because of his history stalking her."

Beckman frowned. "Andrews is a putz!"

"No argument, sir. But...Chief, LaForte isn't a suspect, is he? And that doesn't make sense to me."

For a moment, it looked to Nate like Beckman was about to tear him a new one. Then the chief seemed to soften.

"Look, this is between us, okay?"

Nate nodded.

Beckman folded his hands on his desktop, looked at them as he began. "LaForte has freakin' issues, okay?"

"Don't all psychopaths?"

"LaForte's not a psychopath," said Beckman. "Not yet, anyway. He's just broken. Poor sonofabitch."

"From what I understand, that poor sonofabitch was stalking Sandy Sewell. Was outside her house several times in the middle of the night."

"What you understand isn't always the whole truth," said Beckman. "You probably heard that LaForte and his wife divorced. Do you know why?"

"I had assumed because he was an asshole."

"Yeah, he's an asshole sometimes. Aren't we all? But there's a bit more to it than that. LaForte has a six-year-old daughter. Everything was fine with the kid the first four years, then she starts having problems. They diagnose this degenerative neuro-muscular disease...I forget the exact name. In less than a year, she's in a wheelchair and needs around-the-clock care, so the medical bills are through the roof. Family isn't rich by any stretch. But they make too much to qualify for Medicaid. So..."

It took Nate a few moments to connect the dots. "Are you saying they were forced to divorce to get healthcare?"

"So they could qualify for health care for their daughter without going bankrupt," affirmed Beckman.

"Yeah, that puts a new spin on things."

Beckman smiled wryly. "Nice world we live in, isn't it?"

"But that doesn't explain why he was wandering around outside of Sandy's house."

"I'll admit that LaForte has had a little trouble keeping it on the rails since his daughter's diagnosis and the forced divorce. He's in a support group, believe it or not. But once in awhile, he'll do stupid shit. Like visiting Sandy's house in the middle of the night. Only it wasn't to see Sandy. You see, that's where he and his wife lived before the divorce. He'd go over there and just sit there staring at it, remembering how happy they had all been back when they were living there."

"Jesus! That's the saddest thing I ever heard. But..."

"But what?"

Nate chose his words carefully. "You said he had a tough time keeping it on the rails. How do you know he didn't lose it? Start raging. Go after the young woman who was occupying the house he felt should be his?"

"He was with me that night," said Beckman.

"You?"

"I'm the guy who tries to keep him on the rails. Craig and I were football teammates in high school.

He was having a tough time, so we went out, shot some darts. And let's be honest here. Does LaForte really strike you as sophisticated enough to have written all these poems or to know all this village history? He can remember the batting average of every member of the Milwaukee Brewers, but that's about the extent of his genius."

Twenty-nine

Since he was already downtown, he walked over to the Red Brick Museum and was fortunate to find Ellie and Vern at work again. Chief Beckman was going all-in on the theory that the riddle was a reference to Ira Blood. If this were not the case, Beckman was going to look rather foolish, particularly if the FBI boys came up with the correct interpretation. And since Nate had supplied him with the Ira Blood theory, Nate suspected it would not go well for him, either. Thus, he wanted to touch base with his friends at the museum to see whether a different interpretation had occurred to them since they had last talked.

"Do you two live here?" Nate asked, only half-joking, as he entered the museum kitchen through the front door.

"Fourth of July coming up soon!" said Vern.

"We'll have special hours, some patriotic displays," added Ellie. "And we'll be open after the salute at the library."

"And to tell the truth," said Vern, "there's always something to keep us busy here."

Ellie nodded. "We've got boxes of old photos and clippings," she explained, pointing to a mess of pictures and yellowed paper on the table. "Little by little, I'm trying to go through, get the ones worth saving into albums or presentations."

Nate was impressed by the massive amount of artifacts that the museum contained. He had been in the basement once, which was off limits to regular museum visitors. It was filled with shelves containing special displays, collections of clippings, and items that might be put out to commemorate anniversaries or holidays. There was more than enough for an entire separate museum.

However, Ellie had not given the riddle any additional thought.

"Ira Blood still seems to make the most sense," she said. "Though if you ask me, this riddle business seems so foolish."

"An evil kind of foolish," agreed Nate. "If you're really sold on the idea that the riddle is related to Ira Blood, do you have any information on the Blood family that I could look at? It's probably a long shot, but maybe there's something that'll help us out."

"We do, I think," said Ellie, motioning him into the next room, where they crossed to a door that led to the basement stairs. She switched on the light and they descended. The walls were thickly-mortared round stone, most of which were obscured by shelving upon which neatly-labeled boxes were stacked. They moved past dozens of boxes with labels like BASEBALL STATE CHAMPIONSHIP, OLD GRADE SCHOOL, and SESQUICENTENNIAL before stopping at a shelving unit set against the far wall. She dragged a finger over boxes near the top of the unit, moving down, stopping suddenly about halfway through the pile. She carefully removed the several boxes on top of her target, then pulled it out. "I think there's a small packet in here. Some of our earliest settlers."

She removed the top, searched for a moment, pulled out a manila envelope. A white sticker label on the envelope read BLOOD FAMILY.

"You can take this with you if you promise to bring everything back."

"I will," said Nate, raising his right hand in a Boy Scout salute. As she returned the other boxes to the shelf, he noticed one marked HEAVEN CITY/CHICAGO GANGSTERS. "That's interesting," he said, pointing to the box. "Heaven City and gangsters who bet on horse races in Field Park were part of the second riddle."

"Al Capone was one of them who visited," said Ellie. She opened the box, which contained a single, large, manila envelope. "Take this too, if you want."

"Capone? Wow!" Nate tucked it under his arm with the other. He wasn't sure he actually needed it or would even have the time to look at it, but it did sound interesting, and he didn't want to be perceived as impolite if he refused.

Ellie nodded. "All of those hoodlums seemed to love the food at Heaven City. And the girls." She gave him a knowing look to suggest she knew exactly what kinds of girls had enticed the gangsters to come to Heaven City. "He liked betting on the horses, too. A very strange man, in some ways."

"Well, he *was* a mobster, a murderer," noted Nate.

"He was strange in other ways, though. They say he didn't trust the economy. You see, he ran his criminal empire during the Great Depression. Very paranoid. Thought there was a chance that the banks would eventually collapse and U.S. money would be worthless. So he began converting portions of his ill-gotten wealth to gold."

"Like gold jewelry?" asked Nate.

"And gold coins. And gold bars. And diamonds, too. He figured gold and precious gems would retain their value no matter what. Like I said, he was pretty paranoid. It was probably the Syphilis."

Nate's mouth dropped open a bit. "Excuse me?"

"They say it affects the brain. Rots it away. He was apparently quite a vile man, Mr. Capone was." She made an injured face. "The Syph—the disease probably made him act a little eccentrically, like with all that betting."

"Wasn't betting on horse races pretty common back then?" asked Nate.

"Not with gold."

"Gold? Instead of cash?"

Ellie nodded. "It's all in here, though a lot of it is hearsay. He placed his bets using gold and gems. That is, he did until one of the jockeys stole his loot one time. I think after that, he stopped coming. At least that's how the story goes."

Nate chuckled. "I see why you enjoy volunteering here. These are fascinating stories."

Ellie shook her head. "If people knew only half of them, we'd be busier than Starbucks!"

Thirty

Thursday morning, Chief Beckman dispatched three pairs of officers to stake-out locations adjacent to Oak Knoll Cemetery. One team occupied a house on Eagle Lake Avenue just to the south of the cemetery, separated from it by only an old wire fence. And fewer than one hundred feet inside the fence was the family plot of the Bloods.

A second team occupied an apartment in Ashlyn Village, an apartment complex overlooking the cemetery from the north. A final team was sequestered in a home across Rochester Street. Arrangements had been made with the owners of the residences, and the officers had arrived on foot by 6:00 a.m., in plain clothes, unlikely to command anyone's attention. "This will assure that no one, the remainder of the day, will observe any unusual comings or goings in the neighborhood, and that no unusual vehicles will be parked in the area that might raise the suspicions of our perp," Chief Beckman had stated. "Our teams will surveil the Blood family graves from those three vantage points, and our squads will remain a respectful distance from the cemetery, giving the impression that they are going

243 / Rod Vick

about their rounds in other neighborhoods. If our teams observe unusual activity, they will respond immediately, and squad backup should be able to arrive rapidly. A fourth surveillance site of one officer will be positioned inside a house at the intersection of Eagle Lake Avenue and Gibson Street, which will be out of the sight line of the Blood family plot, but which will allow us to monitor comings and goings at the cemetery's south entrance."

Naturally, Nate did not make the cut for one of the four surveillance teams. He was instructed to cruise the subdivision to the west and southwest of Field Park, and if backup was requested, to approach from Oak Knoll Drive on the west side, cutting off retreat in that direction. This portion of his day began at six p.m., although the general belief was that if something was going to happen at the Blood family site, it would probably not be until after dark.

At the start of his rounds, he phone ordered a steak sandwich with fries from Fork in the Road restaurant, stopping briefly to pick it up. If he was going to sit in his car for hours, cruising the streets of the same neighborhood over and over, at least he was going to eat well.

The Thursday edition of the Mukwonago Chief had not been printed this week under orders from the FBI. The psychopath had no doubt noticed that his vehicle for game play had been quashed. The theory was that this would compel him to act, although one could never be certain how psychopaths would react.

And there was no guarantee that the reaction—if any—would occur on Thursday evening. Carl Mullenberg had been killed on a Friday. That meant Nate would probably be driving around the neighborhood for hours again tomorrow night. Maybe he'd try one of the fish fries. There were lots of good ones in the area. He could eat that in the squad. Yes, that would be nice.

He glanced hungrily at the bag on the seat beside him, his stomach growling at the thought of the good food. The Blood family packet from the Red Brick Museum sat beside the bag containing his steak sandwich. Unfortunately, the information had not seemed to provide any additional help. Aside from their unfortunate name and the unusual design of the tree stump monument resting in the center of their memorial plot, the Bloods had been no more unusual or eccentric than any other early settlers. Ira Blood had served terms as Waukesha County surveyor, and had helped lay out the lots and streets of the village of Mukwonago. He returned to his native Vermont briefly in 1939 to marry Esther Jordan, but then returned to the Mukwonago area where, in 1859, he was elected to the state assembly as a Republican. Blood was apparently a staunch supporter of the temperance movement of the time, which Nate mused would probably not have earned him a great many friends in the current day. Articulate and vocal, he gave numerous speeches in support of the cause. None of these details, however, seemed to provide a clue that would point toward a 21st century killer or the method he might use to kill.

His radio and phone had remained silent during the evening except for the usual police business. Until there was activity in the cemetery, there was to be no mention of the surveillance in case the perp somehow possessed the capability to listen in, even on restricted access channels. In fact, since listening in on police channels was so common these days, most communication was done by cell phone.

By seven-thirty, the steak sandwich was gone, and Nate wished that he had ordered two. However, in the last couple of weeks, he had also thought more seriously about starting some sort of exercise program, maybe improving his diet.

Maybe I should pack a salad for tomorrow night rather than the fish fry.

On the other hand, it was more difficult to eat a salad while driving, whereas he could easily reach over and snag a fry or breaded piece of fish. Heck, he could always start the diet on Saturday. Or Sunday. Or Monday. Yes, a fresh start at the start of a fresh week, that sounded about right.

However, instead of ordering a second sandwich, he pulled into a convenience store on the north side of town and bought a Diet Coke. And a peanut-chocolate protein bar.

After eight, it began to get dusky, and despite the long hours of repetitive driving, he felt himself growing more alert. It still wouldn't be dark until after nine, however, and so he figured he had at least an hour before there was a real likelihood of activity at the plot. This made him anxious for two reasons. First, the thought of encountering a murderer who had lived like a phantom alongside his friends and neighbors in the village, the same friends and neighbors who would become his victims, was simultaneously thrilling, sickening, and incomprehensible. Second, the theory about the Blood family and its relationship to the verse had been presented to the chief by Nate himself. If it ended up being wrong, and a murder was committed at some other location in the village, at the very least, Nate would become the punchline for an entire community—and someone would surely die.

His eyes lit upon the second packet in the passenger seat, the Heaven City and gangster history packet, which he had found even more interesting than the Blood family background.

As Ellie had promised, there had been lots of Capone information, and a few items in particular had jumped out at Nate. He had learned that Capone was born in 1899 and, as a teenager, became a bouncer at various illegal establishments. He moved up in the world of organized crime to become a bodyguard, and at the tender age of 26, became the head of a criminal network that supplied illegal booze to speakeasies and brothels. As revenue increased, he morphed into a ruthless and feared crime boss, and survived a number of attempts on his life. This led to

Capone and his closest associates taking trips by train or car to "get away" from it all, traveling and booking hotels under assumed names.

Although they frequented Kansas City, Cleveland, and other Midwest destinations, Capone also traveled to Mukwonago, where he and his entourage would stay at the Heaven City Hotel. The hotel, Nate learned, had an interesting history of its own. The fifty acres on which it stood, just across the Fox River on the north side of National Avenue, was purchased by A.J. Moore in 1934 to start a utopian city. Moore, who like Capone was from Chicago, built a hotel, a school, a dance hall, a church, a restaurant, and even an airstrip—in addition to a number of small houses. It had truly been a community unto itself. The destination soon began attracting residents and visitors, including Chicago gangsters, which may not have been part of its utopian dream.

Nate learned that Capone had rarely traveled inside the Mukwonago village limits, except on the occasions when horses raced in Field Park. There was a story that Capone had cultivated a rather intense rivalry with another crime boss, and that the two had bet heavily on an upcoming race. By this point—the summer of 1940—Capone was not the man he had once been, although still relatively young and still a powerful figure in the Chicago underworld. However, he had served time in Alcatraz between 1932 and 1939, where he had survived a stabbing. His body had been wracked by syphilis and gonorrhea, and the diseases had begun to affect his brain, heightening his paranoia and dulling his decision making abilities. While his lieutenants in the Chicago Outfit—the name of his crime empire in the Windy City—ran the day-to-day "business", Capone made his last trip to Wisconsin. He would spend the final six years of his life mostly in his mansion at Palm Island, Florida, his health continuing to deteriorate, until he died of a stroke and heart failure.

But in 1940, his last hurrah in the Dairy State, Capone had wanted to make a big, showy score and rub it in the face of the rival boss. The bet had been a cool $2 million each, with Capone's portion mostly in gold coins and diamonds, due to his distrust of the government monetary system that the Great Depression had wrought. However, on the day of the race, Capone's loot was stolen. Suspicion fell on one of the jockeys, Eddie Glynch, who it was said thought Capone's mental capacities had diminished to those of a twelve-year-old, and who would thus be an easy mark. Unfortunately, Eddie was not the sharpest tool in the shed, either, and had underestimated both the amount of suspicion that would fall on him in the clumsy commission of his crime, and of the ruthlessness with which Capone's thugs would respond.

Eddie fled. The race was never held. Capone's men caught up to him in Peshtigo, Wisconsin, where Eddie Glynch met an unpleasant end outside a tavern. However, Capone's gold was not found on

Eddie, nor at any of the stops he had allegedly made on his way north.

As Nate recalled these details from the packet, he wondered whether anyone had ever dug beneath the shed in Kiwanis Park looking for the gold. Ellie had mentioned that was where jockeys had at one time stored equipment. He imagined they must have, for the structure had been moved. The shed currently sat at the north end of Kiwanis Park. At one time, he recalled, it had sat at the south end, not far from the highway 83 and highway NN intersection.

He thought of Carl Mullenberg, who had died recently in that shed.

A seed of an idea had begun to form after Nate had read the Capone clippings. Two million dollars in gold and diamonds, it seemed to Nate, was a far stronger motive for murder than a bit of crankiness over a community's ignorance of history. What if Carl had been killed so that the murderer could search beneath the shed?

But that made no sense. As Nate had already observed, the shed had been moved from its original location. And Carl would have eventually left the park, once he finished mowing. There was no need to kill him. Or either of the other two victims.

He was letting his imagination run away with him.

Nate drove west down MacArthur Drive. The sun was setting.

He wondered whether the phantom would be on the move.

Thirty-one

The Phantom hovered in the shadows near the cemetery. Few people were out at night lately. As a result, one had to take even greater care to avoid being noticed. That was all right, and expected. The Phantom was always very careful.

The Chief of Police, Beckman, could have declared a village emergency and imposed an earlier curfew, forbidding anyone from being out after sundown. Instead, he had set it at eleven. The Phantom knew that the whims of local tavern owners and restaurateurs had figured into the decision. But it was likely that the police also hoped that having people out and about—even in smaller numbers— would give them a better chance of catching The Phantom than if the streets were deserted. There had to be cheese with which to bait the trap. Perhaps the appearance of the FBI on the scene had helped as well. The Phantom smiled. Had Beckman's widely-known desire to prove his local force superior to the "Fibbies" made him more willing to take chances?

On three sides, the cemetery was quiet. Most homes along Eagle Lake Avenue to the south showed a light or two in the windows. Same with the apartments to the north. The "newer" section of the cemetery rolled away to the west and northwest, and beyond it, another neighborhood. The only noise and significant light came from Rochester Street on the east, with its streetlights and residual traffic. A busy avenue during the day, traffic sometimes was backed up from the stoplight at Eagle Lake Avenue to well north of the cemetery. But now, things were quieting down.

They would not be quiet for long.

The people of the little community, the Phantom observed, really were quite naïve and simple. So little sense of their own history. And so easy to manipulate. It saddened the Phantom—just a bit—that more people had not chosen to play the game, to embrace solving the riddles. There were so many community resources that they might have drawn upon to access this history—the library, the Internet, the local museum and historical society. It probably came down to laziness, apathy. In the long run, however, that was unimportant. These sad souls would serve the Phantom's purpose. And in the end, it would all be worth it. All the suffering, the unfairness, the intolerable pompousness and ignorance. In the end, justice would be done.

A stillness greater than before seemed to descend on the graveyard. This seemed, to the Phantom, a sign that the stars were almost aligned. And sure enough, the Phantom's quarry approached.

It was time.

Thirty-two

His police radio buzzed to life at 9:16.

"Janowsky! Woman down in the cemetery! Suspect heading west toward you!"

Nate flipped his lights on, the siren blared, and he accelerated rapidly toward Oak Knoll, just half a block away on the cemetery's west side. He pulled onto the cemetery access road, activating his spotlight and sweeping it across the dark grave sites. Movement on the right caught his eye. A running figure along the north side of the tree and intermittent fence line that separated the cemetery from the homes along Eagle Lake Avenue. Nate hit the speaker button.

"Stop! Stay where you are! Keep your hands in plain sight!"

The figure halted, seemed indecisive for a moment, then rounded the west end of the last of the tree line and headed across the mowed cemetery property that extended toward Eagle Lake Avenue. Sirens suddenly wailed from that direction along with the pulse of flashing lights, and the figure changed directions again, heading north and darting across the access road ahead of Nate, racing between the neat rows of headstones.

The space between stones was too narrow for the squad, and so Nate slammed the vehicle into reverse, squealed back fifty meters, then drove across the taller grass on the cemetery's undeveloped west end. As Nate rounded the last of the graves, he caught sight of the figure again, loping wildly through the knee-high weeds toward the Field Park subdivision. His quarry, dressed completely in dark clothing, seemed to be wearing down.

I've got you, you son of a bitch!

A thrill of adrenaline coursed through Nate as he closed in, and he even dared to think of the accolades that might come his way for apprehending the killer. This might be his ticket to doing something more than just writing tickets to speeders or working crowd control. His key to being taken seriously. To making detective.

Suddenly, the front of his squad plunged down a foot or so, dirt flew up in a cloud and Nate was hurled forward into his airbag.

"Shit!"

His ribs hurt from the seatbelt, but he was out of the squad in seconds, grabbing the flashlight, spotting his quarry a bit farther ahead now, darting between two houses on the south side of MacArthur Drive.

He activated his phone and ran. "Pursuing north on foot across 200 block of MacArthur!"

255 / Rod Vick

Whatever had happened with his vehicle would have to wait. He followed the path the figure had taken between the homes, saw him ahead passing between two houses on the north side of the street. Nate shot across MacArthur. He was not much of a runner, had once thrown up after a 100-meter dash race. However, his quarry, who had run at least ten times as far, seemed to be losing steam even faster than he was.

"Heading toward Field Park!" Nate reported between gasps. The sirens that had been wailing in the distance seemed to be getting closer.

The figure scrambled onto the chain link fence that ran along the south border of the park. Nate, drawing deep, painful breaths, knew he would never make it over the fence, and so he headed for the open pedestrian gate a little farther to the east. His quarry struggled with the fence, but made it over. While Nate had covered more ground to go through the gate, he had actually made up time, since the fence itself had not slowed him at all.

"Police!" he shouted, although he had so little wind that it barely carried. He tried again, and this time, mustered sufficient volume. "Police! Stop or I'll have to shoot!"

As he ran, he unclipped the safety strap from his revolver. He was now barely fifty feet away.

"This is your last warning!"

He stopped to steady himself, removed the revolver. All of a sudden, his stomach lurched and a wave of exercise-induced nausea swept over him.

No! No!

But there was no stopping it. Up came the steak sandwich, the fries, the peanut-chocolate protein bar. He tried to shake it off and continue his pursuit, but he heaved again, this second round bringing him to his hands and knees in the grass near the park playground.

The park then exploded in light as squads poured in to both vehicle entrances. Nate now straightened, wiped his mouth with a sleeve, continued at barely a jog in the direction in which he had seen the figure running last. Shouts and commotion on the darkened ball diamond drew his attention, and Nate limped over there. Half a dozen officers had guns drawn, and it looked like they had someone down on the ground. A voice cried, "We got him!"

Nate was drenched in sweat, panting, and realized he smelled faintly of vomit, but he pushed in among the others. The figure, who wore a black hoodie, was face-down, hands cuffed behind his back.

"Nice job, Rob," said one of the men to Officer Salazar, who had apparently chased down the suspect in the outfield.

"Who?" gasped Nate. "Who is it?"

"Duminski!" said Dick Andrews.

"Doctor Fucking Doom!" shouted another voice.

Salazar now hoisted Duminski to his feet, and Nate saw the look of white-hot terror on his dirty face along with tears streaming down his cheeks.

"I didn't do anything!"

"You cry your heart out, sweetheart," said Andrews. "I just wish Wisconsin had the freakin' death penalty!"

Salazar began walking Duminski toward the parked squads while reading him his rights.

Nate stopped Andrews. "Who did he kill tonight? The fourth victim?"

"No clue," said Andrews. "Man, you look like shit!"

"Can you give me a lift?"

"No way, man! You smell like shit, too!"

Nate turned and headed back toward his squad. The evening air, slightly cooler now, began to dry his shirt as he crossed Roberts Drive, and then MacArthur, retracing his steps.

Dr. Doom. It made perfect sense. Angry guy who felt that he'd been treated unfairly by the world. He knew everything about local history. Hated the way the village was being developed. But Nate felt a tinge of sadness as well. A brilliant mind. What a waste. Duminski could have done so much good.

The walk took only a few minutes. The front end on the squad was a little crumpled, but the vehicle seemed otherwise fine, though it was dirty and had grass remnants and bits of purple clover blossom stuck to it. The holes in the field appeared to be the work of kids who had been digging in the undeveloped area. A couple of shovels lay abandoned for the evening nearby, along with a few sandbox-sized toy trucks and a plastic army helmet.

Although the vehicle could not move forward to get out of the hole because of the piled earth, Nate was able to extricate it by putting it in reverse. He made a circle in the tall weeds, looking carefully for any additional holes, and then headed back toward the cemetery. Proceeding toward the east side, he found two squads, an ambulance, and several FBI vehicles parked along the access road about a hundred meters north of Eagle Lake Avenue.

Nate exited his squad and walked toward the hub of activity, where he encountered Chief Beckman.

"We got him, sir," said Nate. "It was Donovan Duminski."

"Yeah, I heard Salazar collared him," said Beckman. "Jesus, what happened to you? You smell awful! And I heard something about your squad!"

"I had a little trouble. But I chased —"

"Damn, this is a great day!" said Beckman, interrupting. "We got the collar! The Fibbies I bet are steaming! Daniels was all 'Congratulations!' and everything, but you could tell he hated to say it! Man, that was great!"

"Sir, they said a woman was attacked tonight."

"Uh-huh," said Beckman. "God, I need a cigarette! Ten years since I've had one, but it would sure taste good now!"

"Who was it, sir?"

"That gift shop woman, Grace Hall."

Thirty-three

"What?"

Nate turned toward the flashing ambulance, took a step, then paused, not sure he wanted to see whatever he might find there. Then he raced forward.

As he rounded the open door at the rear of the ambulance, he saw Schnabell overseeing the situation. On a gurney in front of the two men lay Grace.

She was alive.

"I don't need to go to the hospital!" she berated one of the paramedics. "I'm fine. I've been through a lot worse!" Her usual bandana was off, exposing her smooth head. A large bandage had been applied high on her forehead above her left eye. The area around the eye itself was turning bruise-purple. Below the eye, another bandage was in place, and Nate noticed a bright red line encircling her neck, its imprint suggesting a rope.

She saw Nate, smiled. He choked back a sob, turned to Schnabell. "What happened?"

"She was cutting through the cemetery," said Officer Schnell. "She was attacked just over there along the cemetery road." He pointed to a spot only a few feet from where they stood.

Nate looked to Grace. "Cutting through the—" The idea was so incredible and his emotions so frayed that he could not finish the sentence.

"My nausea was bad," explained Grace. "I needed to get some medicine."

Nate shook his head. "But cutting through the cemetery when we've got a serial..." He stopped short. "Why the hell did you even need to go through the cemetery? Why not just go to Walgreens?"

"Er, Nate," said Officer Bell, "I don't think she was looking for that kind of medicine."

Nate stood silently for several moments, not understanding. Officer Schnell connected the dots for him.

"Ms. Hall indicated that she occasionally uses cannabis, purchased locally, to alleviate the nausea symptoms associated with her medical treatments. She declined to identify the individual from whom she had purchased her current supply, but did indicate that he lived somewhere north of the cemetery."

Grace covered her eyes with a hand. "I'm sorry. I was just feeling so...shitty. Thought I'd be back before dark. Sometimes exercise makes me feel better. But I guess I wasn't walking very fast tonight."

Nate moved beside the gurney, placed a hand gently on her shoulder. "Grace, what happened?"

"Other than me being an idiot? I was just walking, and I looked out toward Rochester Street. I think maybe I heard a horn or something. All of a sudden, someone bashes me with a rock and then slips a rope around my neck. I got off one good scream before it got too tight."

"That's what alerted us," said Officer Bell.

Nate turned to Schnabell, incredulous. "No one saw her go into the cemetery?"

"We were focused on the Blood graves," said Officer Schnell. "We thought whatever was going to go down was going to go down there. She was way back here on the access road."

Nate turned back to Grace. "When everyone came running, Duminski took off?"

"Who?"

"Donovan Duminski," elaborated Nate. "I spotted him running away from the scene. We chased him down in Field Park."

"I never saw who it was," said Grace. "I think I've heard that name, though. Isn't he some sort of pervert?"

"Now he's some sort of psychopath," said Officer Bell. "They'll put him away for good."

One of the paramedics hopped out of the back of the ambulance. "We're going to load you now, Ms. Hall."

"No the hell you're not!" said Grace. "I'm fine! I'm not bleeding—anymore. I'm not dizzy. Thanks for patching me up, but I'm going home."

"Ms. Hall, you should really be checked out in the ER," said the EMT. "You were hit pretty hard with that rock. They can do a more thorough evaluation to make sure you don't have a concussion. They may even want to do a CT scan. They'll also determine whether your cheekbone is broken or whether there's damage to your trachea that you may not realize right now."

"That sounds just peachy," said Grace, "but I just want to go home."

The EMT looked to Nate and Schnabell for help.

"Look, Grace," said Nate, "let them take you. I'll follow the ambulance, hang around at the hospital until the tests are done." He turned to Schnabell. "You guys get her statement?"

"Not yet," they said simultaneously.

"I can take care of that, too," said Nate. "Then I'll make sure you get home safely afterwards."

Grace closed her eyes, sighed. "Fine."

*

At Waukesha Memorial Hospital, Nate noticed that the staff seemed to put everything else on hold—everything that wasn't a life-or-death situation—to evaluate and treat Grace. A few were surprised and concerned at seeing a uniformed police officer arrive with her.

"She can't be dangerous," one whispered to Nate when they wheeled Grace out for a test.

Nate shook his head. "Someone tried to hurt her."

The nurse nodded. "What makes people do awful things to each other? I swear, I ask myself that question at least once a day at this job."

While they waited, Nate took her statement. And they waited some more.

"Well, I guess the fact that we haven't seen any doctors or nurses in the past twenty minutes is a good sign," said Grace, an ice-filled collar draped around her neck. If they really think you're dying, they swarm you like bees. They've obviously moved me way down the list in importance."

Nate smiled. "How's the nausea?"

"Actually, it's okay. And without cannabis! Guess being attacked by a serial killer took my mind off it. Not that I'd recommend that treatment as a regular remedy."

"And the head...does it hurt?"

"They gave me some meds to take the edge off," she said with a grin. "Good thing you're driving."

The doctor arrived a few minutes later.

"Cheek is just bruised. You might want to put ice on the neck a couple of times a day. Let us know if you have trouble swallowing or if any significant swelling develops. I'll give you a prescription for some pain killers. Otherwise, the facial bruising is just going to take a little time to resolve."

"And no concussion, doc?" asked Nate.

"No symptoms," said the doctor. "Nothing to warrant a scan. But on the discharge papers, there will be a list of things to watch for over the next couple of days. Vomiting, headaches, that sort of thing. Anything doesn't seem right, you either give us a call or get back in here."

The doctor told Grace she could get out of the hospital gown and into her street clothes, and Nate quickly excused himself to wait in the lobby of the ER. He paced back and forth in front of the admitting desk, smiled at the woman sitting behind it.

"You guys were great," he finally said to break the silence, but he meant it, too. "You really treated Grace like royalty."

"Well, thank you, sir," said the receptionist. "When she fills out the post-visit evaluation survey, we'd enjoy hearing any positive comments. And..." She reached for a brochure on the desktop. "...If you or she would like to say thank-you or show your support in other ways, we have a program where designated financial gifts can support our upcoming building projects."

Nate thanked her, glanced at the brochure, and pocketed it as Grace was wheeled through the double doors that led back to the ER.

Grace shrugged. "I told them I could walk."

The ride back to Mukwonago was fairly quiet, and Nate had expected that Grace might fall asleep. However, when he glanced toward the passenger seat, she was always alert.

"It's almost one," said Nate. "After everything that happened today, you've got to be dragging."

"Surprisingly, I'm not sleepy at all," said Grace. "That's a good sign, right? If I had a brain injury, I'd be nodding off like an octogenarian."

"If you had a brain injury, you probably wouldn't be able to use words like octogenarian. Speaking of brain injuries, do you have someone you can call to come and stay with you tonight? Just to be safe."

Grace laughed. "No one I can call at one in the morning. Hey, why don't you crash on my sofa?"

"Me? You sure?"

"I guess I would feel a little better having someone there," Grace admitted. Then, suddenly, she gave a muffled sob.

Nate glanced over, saw a tear run down her cheek. "Hey, are you okay?"

Grace nodded."It's just...I can't believe this is all over. Donovan Duminski. You guys got him! I guess the reality of it all is just hitting me now."

They made a quick stop at Nate's condo on the way into town so that he could grab a change of clothes, and then a second stop at the police department so that he could drop off the damaged squad and pick up *Higgins*.

"This car is really...vintage," said Grace as she buckled herself into the passenger seat of the Beretta.

"It was my first car, back when I was eighteen. 239,000 miles and counting! I probably should have traded it off by now, but I'm sort of sentimentally attached."

Grace examined the passenger side door. "Is...is that a round Tinker Toy connector?" She pointed to the end of the window crank.

Nate smiled. "The regular end piece broke, and that was about the right size and already had a hole for the screw. But I guess I should get it fixed right one of these days."

A few minutes later, he pulled into the driveway of Grace's house.

"Do you mind if I use your shower before I hit the hay?" asked Nate. "After all the running earlier, I've been pretty ripe all night."

"Go ahead," said Grace, showing him the way before heading off toward her bedroom. "Extra towels in the bathroom cabinet."

Nate set his neatly-folded spare clothing on the closed toilet seat cover, stripped off his stinking uniform, and set the water running. Stepping into the steaming jets, he felt immediately better.

What a freaking night!

He washed his hair and then heard the click of the door.

"Hello?"

A moment later, the shower curtain rattled, and he was no longer alone.

"The bandages!"

"They gave me extras so that I could change the dressings."

She was not emaciated as he had imagined many cancer sufferers to be. Rather, Grace was slender and, even with the new injuries, breathtakingly beautiful.

She picked up the dispenser of body wash. "Let me help."

What a freaking night.

Thirty-four

"You're lucky the department has insurance," said Beckman, examining the damaged squad car with Nate on Friday morning. "And you're lucky I'm in a good mood. We'll get you another vehicle from the pool."

Nate found himself in a good mood as well, but he also felt a bit conflicted. He wondered about the appropriateness of his actions the previous night. It wasn't as if he'd pulled over a woman for speeding and then offered to forgive the infraction in exchange for a date...or more. That would definitely be an abuse of power. Instead, he wondered whether spending the evening with someone who had just been the victim of a crime was an ethical violation. Had he abused his position as an authority figure? Had he taken advantage of her vulnerability? He reminded himself that it was Grace who had stepped into the shower with him, all on her own. But he wondered whether she would have done so if he had been just Nate Janowsky the insurance salesman who she routinely passed on the street or smiled at in Sarah's coffee shop.

The thought of the coffee shop made him crave a large mocha latte with whipped cream. Hell, he deserved it after helping to catch the phantom the previous night. And the caffeine would surely help. He hadn't fallen asleep until half past two.

Then he thought of how doughy he had probably looked in the shower. Perhaps it was time to get serious about getting in shape. He stopped at a convenience store and picked up a Diet Coke instead.

After that he parked near the *Mukwonago Chief* office, intending to update Star on the previous night's developments.

Well...not *all* of the night's developments.

"Wait, you wrecked your squad?" asked Star incredulously as he narrated the events.

"Front bumper's messed up. Hood's a little crumpled. One headlight out. Air bag will need to be replaced. It's not like I totaled it."

She laughed anyway.

"So...Donovan Duminski." She typed data into a document as he proceeded. "You said he was a teacher?"

"Former. History. Got tossed twelve years ago for inappropriate conduct with a student. I don't know how much is on the record. No charges. They just got rid of him."

She opened a new window, tapped away. "Yup. But...looks like he's had a few little run-ins with the law since then. DWI nine years ago. A second one seven years ago. Hm, this is interesting. A couple of citations for trespassing and disorderly conduct."

"I wasn't aware of that."

"Looks like he was sort of a Peeping Tom."

Nate nodded. "I guess that makes sense, now that I hear it. A guy like that, wandering around in the dark, would know everyone's night routines. Made it easy for him to corner his victims at their most vulnerable."

Star made a face. "A real slimeball."

Nate offered a perfunctory smile. "Of course, he says he didn't do it. None of the killings or last night's attack."

"Not a surprise. They say there's honor among thieves, but I've yet to see it."

Nate stood. "I've gotta get back. Chief's going to give his triumphant press conference at ten. He's holding it at the high school auditorium. Figured it would just create a traffic jam at the station with all the news vans and crews."

"Yeah, I was about to head up there myself," said Star. "Hey, I was just thinking, it's Friday. Want to grab a fish fry tonight to celebrate the end of this nightmare?"

He wanted to say yes. He felt an attraction to Star. Her independence, her intelligence, her feistiness. And she was beautiful on top of it. He had felt a real chemistry when they had kissed. But now, he wasn't sure what was going on with Grace. Had the previous evening—or more accurately, earlier this morning—been a one-night thing? It seemed to him that there had been an expectation of...something more.

Star noticed his hesitation. "Forget it."

Nate shook his head. "No, it's just—"

"Look, it's no big deal."

"I...I may have a conflict." He realized how insufficient his reply sounded.

"No worries," said Star, looking at the floor. Then she brought her face up bearing a perfunctory smile of her own. "Maybe another time. See you up at the press conference."

*

The auditorium at the high school seated over 800 individuals, and nearly every seat was filled for Chief Beckman's conference. News cameras were set up in aisles and any spare space. The podium in front of the chief was a forest of microphones. "The Fatal Phantom," as the networks referred to the killer, was national news.

Beckman, Nate noted, was equal to the moment. He comported himself as a knowledgeable law enforcement professional who maintained a well-oiled machine and knew all the pertinent facts. He delivered the known details of the case clearly as the cameras blinked and the shutters clicked. He ticked off the details of the Sewell, Mullenberg, and Barker killings, building to the thrilling triumph the previous night when suspect Donovan Duminski had been chased down by village officers—not the FBI—after an unsuccessful fourth murder attempt. Nate was certain that Beckman was already wondering whether Bruce Willis or Liam Neeson would play his part once the epic was turned into a movie.

But Beckman's next announcement surprised most of the attendees, including Nate.

"Mr. Duminski was taken to the Waukesha County Jail yesterday evening, where he steadfastly and vocally professed his innocence to last night's assault, and to the insinuation that he was responsible for the three recent murders. He was clearly distraught, and a meeting was set for this morning to determine whether he should be placed on suicide watch. Unfortunately, just minutes before the start of this press conference, Mr. Duminski apparently took his own life in his cell at the Waukesha County Jail."

A loud murmur swept the crowd. Chief Beckman cleared his throat, and quiet quickly was restored.

"We will be providing more details as they become available. I would like to thank the many officers of the Mukwonago Village Police Department for their tireless efforts in maintaining calm during this crisis, and in helping to bring justice to the community by solving the murders. I am happy, and in fact, greatly relieved that we were able to close this case prior to the upcoming Fourth of July weekend, as well as next weekend's Maxwell Street Days, as this closure should allow village residents a well-deserved opportunity to enjoy these events without fear of a serial killer on the loose. Our small town summer has returned."

Thirty-five

Mukwonago's fireworks show was always during the Summerfest weekend, and so for the Fourth of July on Saturday, Nate drove Grace to the fairgrounds in East Troy, where they sat on a blanket in the outfield of the ball diamond and watched that community's extraordinary show. The field was full of bodies on blankets, the weather perfect, and the mosquitoes remarkably few.

Grace wore a baseball cap and lightly-tinted glasses to help hide some of her cuts and bruising, taking the glasses off during the fireworks spectacle. Around her neck, she wore a fashionable scarf to cover the rope burn. He was pleased to see her smiling easily during the evening and hoped that this meant the trauma she had suffered would be neither lasting nor overwhelming.

He saw a few people he knew, which was unavoidable. East Troy was only six miles from Mukwonago. Years earlier, the high schools from the two communities had been in the same athletic conference and had been fierce rivals. In the past few decades, Mukwonago had grown significantly faster than East Troy, however, and they now competed only occasionally, and almost never in the traditional three sports: football, basketball, and baseball. While Mukwonago's high school enrollment topped 1,600, East Troy's was around 500.

But Mukwonago folks still came to East Troy for the restaurants, the music performances and farmers markets on the village square, and to relax during the summer months on Booth Lake, Army Lake, or Lake Beulah. And East Troy folks traveled east to shop, visit the doctor, and enjoy Mukwonago traditions like Midnight Magic, the Jack-o-lantern Jaunt, and the Village Run.

"Too bad that little ice cream place isn't open at this hour," said Grace on the drive back to Mukwonago. "Wouldn't ice cream taste perfect right now?"

"It would," Nate agreed. "Maybe Dairy Queen is open."

She swept her phone into view, tapped the screen for a few moments. "They closed at 10:30. Six minutes ago."

"Bummer."

After a few silent moments, she continued.

"Hey, do you think you could help me out next Friday evening?"

"What's up?"

"I got a space at Maxwell Street Days for next Saturday and Sunday. Lots of times, it's pretty slow in the store. Thought I'd try to get some of the merchandise in front of more eyes. I could use help packing stuff up on Friday."

"I guess," said Nate, nodding. "I don't think I'm scheduled to work."

He pulled into her driveway.

"You want to come in?" she asked.

"I'd better not. I *am* scheduled to work early tomorrow."

"You seemed to do fine on just a few hours of sleep yesterday," Grace said coyly.

"That's sort of my point," said Nate. "I'm about ten hours short over the last couple of days. I'll end up falling asleep behind the wheel of my squad. And Chief Beckman won't be too happy if I wreck another one."

Grace leaned over, gave him a kiss. "Thank you so much for the other night. For being with me at the hospital. That would have been horrible if I'd been all alone. And for taking care of me afterwards."

Nate smirked. "I think you *took care* of me."

Grace laughed. They kissed again, this one more passionate than the last. "Totally worth it. You know, Mukwonago really feels different tonight, doesn't it?"

"How do you mean?"

"I don't know." She struggled to find the right words. "I guess it's just nice to go to bed and not have to think about who might be out there in the shadows."

"It's crazy, isn't it?" asked Nate. "I mean about Donovan Duminski. He was my teacher. He was sort of a dick, kind of full of himself. But I never thought he'd become a serial killer."

"No one knows what goes on in people's minds," said Grace thoughtfully. "The worst is the ones who kill for no reason. They're just twisted."

"I guess. Makes me wonder what drove Duminski to cross that line. I mean, it's one thing to be angry that the town was being overdeveloped. But to start killing people over it..."

"He obviously had deeper issues," suggested Grace. "I mean, didn't he get fired for doing some crazy stuff with a teenager?"

"Yeah," said Nate. "But like you said, it's different now. Tonight, no worries about the shadows."

They kissed a third time, this one longer and steamier yet. A kiss that very nearly convinced him to say 'To hell with it, I don't care if I fall asleep on the job tomorrow.' But then he sat back.

"I really gotta go."

"Spoil sport." She gave him a final smooch, let herself out of the car, smiled. "Sleep well."

He watched her to the door, then backed down the driveway. In truth, he wasn't as tired as he had let on. And he wasn't exactly sure why he hadn't stayed at Grace's. He had gone to work on just a couple hours of sleep many times. Grace was beautiful, despite the bruises and bandages. The other night in the shower had been other-worldly...as had the rest of the evening.

Nate wondered whether a part of him was simply reluctant to let himself commit too fully for fear that this detour through paradise was an aberration, something that had slipped by the universe's gatekeeper, and when Nate's uncanny good fortune was discovered, the universe would correct itself, returning him to the rather monkish existence of the big, doughy guy that he had grown used to. Or perhaps he feared that Grace only found herself attracted to him because of the events of the past few weeks. He represented security. Once life fully returned to normal in Mukwonago, he would no longer be the knight in shining armor, and she would lose interest.

Maybe he was afraid. It wasn't her cancer and whether that might roar back. He would be willing to face that. But where was this relationship going? Change and the unknown always brought with them a little anxiety, didn't they? And where did he *want* the relationship to go?

He had just turned north onto Main when his phone pinged.

When can we talk?

It was from Star. Suddenly, the thought of sleep was the farthest thing from his mind. He pulled over to the roadside, texted back.

How about now?

Thirty-six

When he arrived at her flat, Star was wearing running shorts and a gray t-shirt. It was after eleven, and it was the first time he had seen her not wearing the prosthetic left hand at all, revealing a smoothly-healed stump. He found it curious that he did not feel awkward or intimidated in seeing her like this, and wondered if it was because she herself behaved so naturally.

"You got here quick," she said, closing the door behind him and pointing to the refrigerator. "Beer if you want it."

He did. Opening the fridge, he grabbed a bottle of Spotted Cow and used a metal opener mounted on the end of the counter. She was already seated on the sofa, taking a sip out of a bottle of iced raspberry tea.

"You're dressed up nice," she said as he sat. "Out on a date?"

"I wouldn't call it a date. Went to the fireworks in East Troy."

"All by your lonesome?"

"No. Just dropped off Grace."

"Gift shop Grace?" asked Star, raising an eyebrow.

"Yeah. Not a big deal." He didn't know why he felt the need to qualify his evening out by saying "Not a big deal". After all, how he spent his time was his own business. For some reason, her asking had put him on the defensive. "It was just fireworks."

Star chuckled. "I'll bet."

Nate took a deep swig, vexed by her tone and what felt like an interrogation. "So what do we need to talk about?"

She set her tea on the coffee table. "Well, I went to the press conference and got the official police report just like everyone else. Everything tied up in a neat little bow, especially after Duminski decides to blow out his own candle."

Nate narrowed his gaze on her. "It sounds like you're ready to add a 'but' at the end of all that."

"I'm a journalist," said Star. "I'm not always a good journalist. Or a smart journalist. But I'm trained to be skeptical, to look for the story hiding behind the story."

"Are you suggesting that because everything sort of fell into place, that there's more to the story?" asked Nate. "Or perhaps I should ask whether you look for conspiracy theories in everything."

"I just want to know what your thoughts are," said Star. "Is there anything that didn't get spilled to everyone, anything that you can tell me without getting your ass kicked?"

Nate shook his head. "I think you know everything I know. Grace was cutting through Oak

283 / Rod Vick

Knoll Cemetery on the way to her house. Duminski attacked her, intending to make her his fourth victim. Bashed her in the head with a rock and then slipped a rope around her neck to finish the job. Almost succeeded, too. We assume he was going to drag the body over to the Blood family graves. But Grace got out just enough of a scream to alert police, and Duminski took off running."

Star smirked. "The official report doesn't mention why Gift Shop Grace was out and about, but I've heard the scuttlebutt."

"It's not like she's the only person in the world who uses marijuana for nausea or anxiety," said Nate testily.

"Easy Atticus, I'm just filling in the details! So did it surprise you that Duminski was the killer?"

Nate sighed. "A little, yeah. I guess you're always surprised when it's someone you know. I mean, he has kind of a jerk. But that's not exactly a rarity. I run into a couple dozen jerks some days before lunch, and almost none of them is ever going to commit murder. But on the other hand, I suppose Duminski should have been pretty high on the list. He was an expert in local history and not too happy with all the development. Plus, there's his history of wandering around the community at night."

"Yeah," said Star. "Makes me glad my windows are on the second floor."

"And when I talked to him at his workplace, he did seem a little distraught. I suppose some would even say unhinged."

"And now he's dead," said Star. "Like I said, all tied up in a nice, neat bow."

Nate narrowed his gaze on her. "Yeah. It is. But there's something else, isn't there? Something about it that's bothering you."

Star smiled. "Like you said, I'm the conspiracy nut. But just humor me a moment. What was different about the attack on Gift Shop Grace?"

Nate thought for a few moments. "Well, for one, it was unsuccessful."

"Anything else?"

Nate shook his head. "I don't know what you're getting at.

Star laughed. "Maybe it's just me. I guess I look at everything with a 'What if?' attitude. So I started thinking about the four attacks. What made the first three successful? I mean, whoever did it was really planning things out. Coming up with the riddles. Figuring out everyone's routines. It was the routines that were key. What did that Bryer kid say…"

"Bryer? Sandy's boyfriend?"

Star nodded. "He said she had a regular running routine. Every Monday, same route. Every Tuesday, same route. Every Wednesday. Every Thursday. It's the curse of the anal retentive. That's what really made her murder possible. The killer could observe her for weeks, learn her routine, know exactly where would be the best place to wait for Sandy on Thursday evening. No variables to create problems and increase the risk of getting caught."

Nate saw now where she was going with this. "And Carl always mowed Kiwanis Park on Friday evenings just before sunset."

"So the killer knew exactly when he would be there, where he would park his car, what he would bring with him. Just watch from the shadows, week after week. Learn the routines."

"And Corrine?"

"From what people said, she was in her garage prepping for weekend rummage sales every Thursday and Friday night," said Star. "An unvarying pattern of behavior. But..."

"But the attack on Grace was different," said Nate with sudden understanding.

Star nodded. "That's right. Cutting through the cemetery wasn't part of her regular routine. It was a one-off. A random deviation. There was no way that Duminski could have known she would have taken that route!"

Nate's mind raced. "He could have followed her."

"How would he have known that she intended to cut through the cemetery?" asked Star. "And it would have been awfully risky trailing her through town without knowing where she was going. Chances of him being seen would have been pretty high. That doesn't sound like our very meticulous killer. What if she hadn't gone anywhere near the cemetery? What was he going to do, strangle her at the Post Office and then drag her all the way to Oak Knoll to toss her onto the Blood family graves?"

"What if Duminski was just waiting in the park for…anyone?" suggested Nate. "And Grace just happened to be the first person to come along?"

"What if no one came along?" asked Star. "Come on, does that really sound like the same person who planned the first three attacks? Carefully study the pattern. Eliminate the variables. Commit murder. Leave no clues or loose ends. That's how the killer did it the first three times. What caused him to vary the routine for number four? Or did he?"

"What do you mean?"

"What if Duminski didn't kill the first three?" suggested Star. "What if he only attacked Gift Shop Grace, and the real serial killer is still out there?"

"God, I don't know why I stopped by," said Nate, finishing the beer. "Now you've got me completely creeped out!" Then he was struck by another bizarre inspiration. "Wait! What if the killer *did* try to kill Gift Sh—" He stopped himself. "Did try to kill *Grace*, but her scream scared him off. And Peeping Tom, a.k.a. Donovan Duminski, got caught in the crossfire! Grace said she didn't see her attacker. What if we chased the wrong man? The first shadow we saw?"

Star looked at Nate, her eyes wide. "And Duminski killed himself not because he was guilty and ashamed..."

"...But because he was innocent, but knew that with his history, everyone would believe he was guilty," said Nate, finishing the thought.

They sat in silence for a minute.

"Of course, this is just a theory," said Nate. "They always told us that the most obvious explanation is usually the correct one. And Duminski is still the most obvious."

"Is he?"

Nate sighed, tried to take a swig from his bottle before realizing that he had already emptied it. "Well, that neat little bow is looking a little more frayed, I have to admit. Geez, are all journalists this obsessive?"

"I'd say 'only the good ones,' but since I've already dishonored the profession at least once, perhaps I'd better refrain from comment."

"Not that we can really do anything even if we believed in your theory with absolute certainty," said Nate. "We have no real evidence."

"Although if a new letter shows up on Monday, I suppose then we can start soiling our delicates," said Star.

"Pleasant thought," said Nate, clearing his throat. He felt comfortable where he was sitting, and he was less tired than he had been when he had arrived, but his beer was empty, it was midnight, and all the bombshells seemed to have been dropped. So he stood. "What now?"

Star stood as well. "I don't know."

The subdued lamplight gave her unbrushed, cascading hair a sepia-golden hue, and suddenly, he was unsure whether they were talking about their murder theory or something else.

"Are we done here?" she asked.

What did he want to say? What should he say? A part of him wanted to stay. Right at this moment, it felt like about 98 out of 100 parts. He felt there must have been a part of her that wanted him to stay, too. She could have texted him any time. They could have met in the *Chief* office tomorrow morning. Who calls a cop into their apartment late at night to make academic conversation about murder theories? Of course, it was Nate who had replied *How about now?* Was he misreading the signals again?

We humans can't even figure out simple communication clues between each other when we're sitting in the same room. How the hell do we ever solve murders?

Or maybe the murder wasn't solved.

"I guess we're done."

Thirty-seven

Monday afternoon, Star texted:

No letter

Nate had replied with a thumbs up emoji. That likely meant that their midnight theory—that the real killer was still at large—was just the insubstantial byproduct of alcohol, imagination, and a month of murder-fueled anxiety. The real killer was, in all likelihood, at the county morgue, and when they had finished with him there, he would be released to next-of-kin who would hold a small, private funeral—not in Mukwonago. Donovan Duminski, never popular among the locals, would be even less so now that he had left the world in the wake of such macabre circumstances.

Monday evening was the memorial service for Carl Mullenberg, who unlike Duminski, had been much-loved. It had been more than two weeks since his murder, but after the autopsy, he had been cremated, so there had been no rush to have a service. In addition, his children and grandchildren were traveling significant distances, and so a date had been selected that would be convenient for all the family members involved.

Nate observed that Mullenberg, like Sandy Sewell, attracted a large throng of individuals committed to paying their respects. Most of the local Kiwanis chapter appeared to be present at the funeral home. On both sides of the urn there were large foam boards covered with photos. The first group seemed to chronicle Carl's youth, which clearly involved a lot of fishing and standing around unsmiling in uncomfortable clothes next to stern-looking relatives. A second board held photos of Carl as a young man and included pictures of his wedding to Victoria as well as photos of the proud father with his three young children engaging in activities ranging from fishing to mini golf to baseball. Two additional boards had more recent photographs of Carl, often with a grandchild on his lap, a fishing pole in his hand, or foraging through the backyard or along beaches with his metal detector.

Nate passed through the long line, chatted a bit with Carl's children, and then took his customary back row seat for the service.

"We've got to stop meeting like this!"

Grace flashed him a subtle smile and settled into the seat next to him.

"It's really powerful, isn't it?" said Grace, nodding toward Carl's children at the front of the line. "So much love. It's easy to understand why."

"Did you know Carl at all?" Nate asked.

"Why do you think I'm here?" asked Grace, pretending to be insulted.

"I thought maybe it was one of those things you did just to be nice," said Nate. "Come to every funeral. Show your solidarity with the community."

"Believe me, I'm no fan of funerals," said Grace."I'd much rather be in a quiet place sharing a cool drink with someone interesting." She gave him a meaningful glance, and Nate couldn't resist a little smile. "Carl would stop by the store once in awhile. He'd bring in old jewelry he had found to sell on consignment."

"Everything was a treasure to Carl," said Nate forlornly, staring at his hands. Then an idea came to him and he turned to Grace. "You never saw the person who attacked you, right?"

Grace gave him a puzzled look. "Yeah. You know that. Why do you ask?"

"Well, I wanted to run an idea past you." Nate tried to choose his words carefully. "I mean, you never saw your attacker. What if it wasn't Duminski?"

"What would make you think that? Didn't you chase him down?"

"What if he was just in the wrong place at the wrong time?" asked Nate. "Think about it. With Sarah, Carl and Corrine, the killer was real careful to target people based on their habits. Sarah always jogged that route on Thursdays. Carl always mowed the park on Friday. Corrine always worked on that rummage sale stuff in her garage. But the killer couldn't have predicted you'd be there in the cemetery. It doesn't fit the pattern."

Grace's face seemed to drain of color. "Why does there have to be a pattern? Aren't psychopaths unpredictable? God, Nate, someone tried to choke me! Duminski was there! He ran! How can it be any clearer than that?"

He patted the air with a hand to encourage her to keep her voice at a whisper. "I know, it sounds even crazier now that I'm talking about it with you."

"And it scares me, Nate!" said Grace, hugging herself and shivering. "I was just starting to feel like I could relax again, and now you say something like this?"

"I'm sorry."

She hugged herself again. "I'm shaking."

"Here." He took off his sports coat and draped it around her shoulders.

They sat without talking for a few moments. More people began moving toward the chairs as it drew to within five minutes of the memorial service.

"So is the department hunting for someone new now?" asked Grace, seeming to have calmed a bit.

Nate shook his head. "I haven't told it to anyone else yet. I wanted to run it past you to see what you'd think before I did. I mean, you're a part of this, and I wanted someone I could trust."

Now she offered a small smile. "Thank you. So this is *your* little theory?"

"Well, it was actually Star who came up with it."

Nate noticed Grace's nostrils flare slightly. "The newspaper woman?"

"The newspaper woman," Nate replied with a sigh.

Grace was silent for a bit and seemed to be mulling this over. "Well...she's probably seen a lot of crazy stuff before. Probably has pretty good instincts." This notion appeared to calm her again. But then another thought seemed to strike her. "Unless..."

Nate blinked. "Unless?"

Grace shook her head. "No. It's nothing."

"Come on. What were you going to say?"

Grace hesitated, then lowered her voice and forged ahead. "Well, I mean, it might be just like you say. But...there was that big ethics scandal in Madison that she was part of."

"I don't see what that has to do with what's happening here," said Nate.

"Think about it," said Grace.

He took a moment, trying to make the connection.

"Are you saying that Star is floating an alternate theory to try and generate controversy?"

"You've got to admit, she's been the belle of the ball ever since those murders started," said Grace.

"Right away, she gets a bombshell story to launch the newspaper she's just bought. The serial killer story keeps people reading, keeps advertisers pouring money into the paper. Then the national news starts picking up her stories and running them. It's sort of a journalist's dream. But then they catch the guy. Pretty soon, her dynamo of a newspaper is just a sleepy little rag that's printing the news about street construction and teeball leagues. Unless she can keep the excitement going."

Nate's heart skipped a beat. "You really think she'd do that?"

"I don't know," admitted Grace. "All I know is that, based on what I've heard, she buggered the news once. How do we know she wouldn't do it again?"

He had to admit that it was at least as easy to believe that someone might publish a phony theory to generate readership as if was to believe that Donovan Duminski was an innocent bystander who'd been mistaken for a serial killer. But he knew Star better than that, he told himself. She had admitted her past mistakes. He found it hard to believe that she would bend the facts a second time. On the other hand, he had been on scenes of domestic abuse and in courtrooms where people guilty of despicable crimes so effortlessly spun believable lies to portray themselves as blameless.

The funeral director summoned people to the seats.

Grace leaned against his shoulder, whispered. "Don't pay any attention to me. I'm still not recovered from everything that has happened."

"Who can blame you?" said Nate, his eyes noticing the red marks on her neck, though most were hidden by a green scarf she wore.

"It's just a nightmare. No, forget it. Star's right to consider alternate theories." She shivered again. "Damn it! I'm just angry and speaking out of turn because it scares me to think that this isn't over. And because...well, because of Star."

"What do you mean?"

Grace focused a gentle gaze on him. "Well, she's a good-looking woman. And you spend a lot of time with her. I suppose there a little envy at the bottom of it, makes me want to say things that will hurt her."

Nate opened his mouth to respond, but no words came.

"I'm sorry. I was being petty. And I made you uncomfortable."

"No, this is my fault," he said, finding his voice. "I shouldn't have brought it up. To you of all people. Pretty damned insensitive of me, after the trauma you suffered."

"No, I'm glad you did," said Grace, calmer now. "In fact, you reminded me of something."

"What is it?"

Her eyes darted suddenly away. "No. Now I shouldn't be bringing it up. It's nothing."

"It's obviously not nothing."

She hesitated. "Well, I only mention this because…like you say, what if Star *is* right, and the killer is really someone else? It made me think…Sandy and I were friends. Not in school. I was…a *few* years older."

Nate smiled.

"But if you worked in Mukwonago, you couldn't help but get to know Sandy," Grace continued. "Plus, she liked my little shop. Stopped in frequently. Sometimes just to talk."

"So you were sort of like an older sister to her."

"*Slightly* older," amended Grace with a wry smile. "Anyway, you know Sandy loved everyone. But this one time we were talking, and she mentions this guy from high school. I don't remember all the details, but it was some guy she broke it off with, I guess. He didn't take it well. Twelve years later, she said she'd still get a call or a message from him. She said it was sort of creepy."

"What do you think she meant by that?"

Grace shook her head. "No idea. I just know she felt uneasy. Maybe even a little threatened. I mean, it's probably nothing. But if Duminski could hold a grudge for twelve years, I suppose so could a guy who got his heart stomped on. Just throwing it out there."

"You don't recall this guy's name?" asked Nate.

"No. But I'll bet Allie Crossman might know. Unlike me, the 'older sister,' Allie was right there in the trenches with Sandy during the high school years."

A man in a blue suit stepped to the podium at the front of the room. "We're here this evening to celebrate the life of Carlton Benjamin Mullenberg, better known as Carl."

"Oh, I hope Star is wrong," whispered Grace. "Last Thursday...I never want to have to worry about going through something like that again."

"Like I said, I shouldn't have brought it up."

Grace rubbed her arms as if she were freezing. "Will you drive me home afterwards?"

"Sure," said Nate.

She slid her arm through his. "And...and maybe stay?"

Nate patted her hand.

"Absolutely."

Thirty-eight

Nate had a headache as he cruised the north side of Mukwonago on Tuesday morning. Part of it, he suspected, was sleep deprivation. He had gotten only a few hours of sleep the previous Thursday night after the trip to the hospital with Grace. On Saturday, he had been up late going over conspiracy theories in Star's apartment. Then he had taken Grace home on Monday night after the funeral.

You are a piece of work! he told himself. *You're not twenty-five anymore, you know!*

In fact, if he recalled the time period honestly, he had never had the opportunities at the age of twenty-five that he'd had in the past couple of weeks. At twenty-five, he would have been more likely to fall asleep with his video game controller in his lap and snooze for ten hours.

He stopped at Sarah's for coffee. Large. No sugar.

As he sat in his squad, taking several large gulps of the hot, black liquid, Nate considered the other part of the reason for his headache: the competing theories.

On one hand, there was Star's theory that the killer was still at large, based on the deviation in routine that had accompanied the attack on Grace.

On the other hand, there was Grace's theory that Star was looking for a way to keep the serial killer story alive and pumping blood into her fledgling newspaper.

Just thinking about the two issues—and their advocates—made his head throb.

It was also possible that both were wrong. That Star was sincere in her concern about the deviation in routine, but that she was, in fact, wrong. Duminski had been the killer. And Duminski was dead.

He took another big gulp and now wished that he had bought something to eat. He went back into Sarah's and emerged with a plain doughnut and a second large coffee.

As he devoured the doughnut, Nate glanced again at the Al Capone papers in his passenger seat. A fortune in lost gold and diamonds might tempt a lot of people to do nasty things to their neighbors. What if Star was right, he wondered? What if the killer wasn't Duminski, but it was more than a case of Duminski simply being in the wrong place at the wrong time. What if the real killer had *known* that Duminski would be in the cemetery, that it was *Duminski's* nocturnal habits that the killer had studied and relied upon?

But who would want to throw Duminski under the bus? And why?

It seemed to Nate that there must be a lot of people in Mukwonago who didn't care for Duminski. Nate thought of the new information that Grace had supplied at Carl's memorial service: the jilted boyfriend. It seemed like a longshot. A guy gets dumped by a girl in high school. He's emotionally devastated, carries the anger for more than a decade. Then he kills her and tries to pin it on the local perv.

Nate had seen stranger motives lead to violence. Social media posts that led to fistfights or shootings. People cut off in traffic who pulled out guns and committed murder. He recalled the case of a woman in a nearby community who was stabbed by her husband because she put too much paprika on a roast chicken.

The doughnut was gone. Feeling guilty as hell, he trudged back into Sarah's and got another.

Back in the car, he attacked the doughnut, hating himself for giving in to temptation, hating himself for obsessing over what should be a no-brainer.

You should really stop. The evidence points to Duminski. The simplest answer. You're wasting your time.

But Star had planted a seed of doubt.

He drove the short distance to Curls Galore, an older home not far from the village center that had been remodeled into a hair styling shop. Allie Crossman, Sandy Sewell's best friend in high school, owned the shop, and when Nate walked in, she had just put an older customer under the dryer.

"Hi Nate," said Allie, who always had a big smile for everyone. "I don't have you down for an appointment and I've got Mrs. Keber coming in in ten minutes."

"No worries, Allie, I was just wondering if I could ask you a question or two real quick."

Allie's smile faltered. "I'm not in trouble, am I? This isn't about my car registration or something, is it, because I've really been meaning to take care of it, but it's been so crazy lately."

"You're not in trouble," said Nate, smiling gently. "Hell, Allie, I know you wouldn't steal a crouton if you were starving. It's just all these crazy killings, you know? I'm trying to wrap up a few details about Sandy."

"I thought it was all wrapped up," said Allie. "I thought Duminski did it, and now he's gone."

"That's right," said Nate. "We just wanted to make sure there was no one working with him." It seemed a reasonable lie. "So I just wanted to ask around, see if you knew of anyone who really hated Duminski."

"I suspect everyone in Mukwonago."

"No, I mean back in the day. You know, when you were in high school."

The look on Allie's face suggested she had no desire to pursue this line of questioning, but she answered nonetheless. "I think a lot of students thought he was a good teacher, even though he was sometimes a real jerk. But he said some awful things.

He had students he picked on, not in a fun way if you know what I mean."

"Do you remember any of them?"

Lines formed on Allie's forehead as she concentrated. "Oh, it's been quite a few years. Maybe Oliver Fletcher. He never seemed to have his work done, and Doctor Doom really gave it to him."

"Anyone else?"

Allie shook her head, first slowly, then with more surety. "I've tried to suppress a lot of my memories from high school."

Nate laughed. "Fair. What about Sandy? She have any enemies?"

Allie looked comically stricken. "Sandy? Are you kidding? Everybody loved her! Well, there might have been a couple of people who were jealous of her grades. I remember that valedictorian race being pretty competitive. But Sandy was just too organized for them. Had a color-coded calendar that she made, with study times for each class for every night of the week. Dictated her class notes into an old tape recorder and then would play them back whenever she had free time. In the car. At breakfast. She was sort of obsessive."

"Sounds like she carried those habits into adulthood," said Nate. "They made her a successful realtor."

"Unfortunately, I guess they got her killed, too." Allie looked at the floor for a moment and wiped something away from the corner of an eye.

303 / Rod Vick

"Had a special running route for every day of the week. She'd run to Field Park, stretch, then off on whatever the route of the day was. Maybe if she'd been a bit more spontaneous…"

Nate nodded, and they let the thought dissipate under its own weight.

"Now that I think about it, there might have been a couple of girls who got their noses put out of joint when Sandy got voted Homecoming queen," added Allie. "But not enough to kill anybody over. And besides, Sandy never actually got crowned."

"I heard. The Duminski thing. Any boys who Sandy rubbed the wrong way?"

Allie perked up. "There's another thing! Roger Bach was really upset about that!"

"Roger Bach. Where have I heard that name?"

"He and Sandy were dating at the time," explained Allie. "When Duminski assaulted Sandy, Roger was furious. Told everybody he was going to kill Doctor Doom!"

"Did Roger ever try anything?" asked Nate.

"Not that I know of. But then Sandy withdrew from Homecoming court, and I know Roger was mad about that, too. Sandy spent a couple weeks at home, and when she came back, she was still pretty fragile. For awhile, she sort of kept to herself. Didn't do much socially. Especially with guys. She really wasn't interested in dating anyone for a long time. Roger was pretty crushed. He'd really fallen for Sandy.

When she broke it off, he was hurt and angry. Said some really awful things."

"Threatening things?"

Allie shrugged. "I can't remember, exactly. I just know they were awful."

"Thanks," said Nate. "I'll let you get back to work. You don't happen to know whatever happened to Roger, do you?"

"He went downhill pretty fast after that," said Allie. "I think he'd been some kind of track superstar his junior year. But after the Duminski thing, I think he started smoking and drinking. Didn't even go out his senior year. Think he lives in Big Bend now."

"You've been very helpful," said Nate, moving toward the door. "Please keep this conversation between you and me."

"I'm a hairdresser. We don't engage in gossip!" She gave him another big smile.

Thirty-nine

He was treading on thin ice.

Nate understood that Beckman would not be pleased if he knew Nate was nosing around, asking questions about the Duminski case. As far as Beckman was concerned, the case was closed, and he would want it to stay that way. It represented a victory for the Mukwonago Police Force, and if Nate uncovered some legitimate new leads, he might put that victory in jeopardy.

But he needed to know. Not only whether Duminski had acted alone or was even guilty, but he wanted to know that his trust in Star was deserved. If she was just suspicious by nature, but barking up the wrong tree, that was okay. If it turned out she was right, and someone else was involved in the murders, Star would earn redemption for many of her past mistakes.

If, on the other hand, he found out she was simply milking the story to sell papers, well, that would hurt. In fact, it would be devastating.

He waited until the end of his shift and headed down Edgewood Avenue to Big Bend, turning right onto Wynn Drive shortly after entering the village. A minute later, he pulled into RB Welding. Big Bend was one of several satellite communities that surrounded Mukwonago and sent its teens to Mukwonago High School. Its significantly smaller size—about one-quarter the population of Mukwonago—and more modest development made it an appealing residential area. It contained the requisite churches, taverns, gas stations, restaurants, and small businesses common to many small towns, but lacked the big box development and traffic issues of larger communities. There was, however, an elementary school that fed into the Mukwonago system.

The name of the community stemmed from a horseshoe bend in the Fox River. After flowing south out of Waukesha, the Fox was joined by the Mukwonago River on the east side of Mukwonago. From there, the Fox River meandered in a generally eastern direction until right before Big Bend, where it suddenly surged north, made a sweeping horseshoe bend, and continued south for a mile before making another spectacular horseshoe bend. A few twists and turns later, and the river continued on its way toward Waterford and other points south.

The center of the village contained the original business park, although several of the buildings sat empty and most of the manufacturing and development seemed to have moved to the newer industrial park off Edgewood on the village's east side. The business park at the center of the village had

307 / Rod Vick

a forgotten and lonely feel to it, although Nate was pleased to see that RB Welding was still open for business.

Roger Bach was a business owner. Nate reasoned that this suggested he had the brains and organizational skills to pull off a complex exercise in revenge against Sandy and Duminski, two people he apparently loathed.

The metal building had a large, open garage door on its front and what appeared to be a smaller door to its right. A modest window next to the smaller door showed a disheveled office area. A chain link fence cordoned off the rear of the building, and a yellow cat wandered along the structure's rust-flecked east side.

Out front stood a man Nate estimated to be in his forties or fifties wearing a welder's smock, smoking a cigarette. He stood just five-nine-ish but easily weighed two-fifty. A yellow bandana served as a sweatband, pushing curly locks of greasy black above a chapped, red face.

"Can you tell me where I might find Roger Bach?" asked Nate after a slow walk from his squad.

The man met his gaze impassively. "I'm him."

If he'd been an actor in a sitcom, Nate figured this would have been an excellent place for a spit-take. Roger Bach had graduated from high school just twelve years ago, which made him about thirty. This guy looked like he could have kids that old.

"You graduate from Mukwonago with Sandy Sewell?"

"Yeah. So what?."

The years had not been kind to Roger Bach. "So you're probably aware that she was killed a few weeks ago."

Bach exhaled a cloud of smoke. "I heard. I ain't stupid."

"We're trying to wrap up the investigation and I was hoping you could answer a few questions."

Bach spit out a mirthless pebble of laughter. "What the hell are you talking about? The guy who killed her got caught! By you guys! Right in the act of trying to snuff someone else! The investigation is over!"

"But he never confessed," said Nate. "Now he's dead. And we're beginning to wonder whether we got the right man."

Nate was also beginning to wonder whether he was cruising for a suspension—or worse.

"That's bullshit," said Bach, taking a final drag on the cigarette and tossing it onto the ground, where he crushed it with a boot.

"Maybe. Maybe not. I heard you weren't too happy when Sandy dumped you."

"Yeah, I'm an angry S.O.B. Jesus, that was half a lifetime ago!"

"But you tried to make contact with her more recently. You called her. You texted."

"You're nuts!"

"But she wasn't too interested. Even after all those years, was she? Maybe those anger issues that were bottle up for half a lifetime finally boiled over!"

"This is just stupid!" Bach's face had grown redder. "Yeah, I get angry! But I get it out like everyone else!"

"How do you do that?"

"In my case, I play softball."

"Softball?"

"And I drink a lot of beer. But I led the league in homeruns three times! I can rip the cover off that mother! In fact, I was playing a game the night Sandy got killed. I got all sorts of witnesses."

This was not going the way Nate had hoped.

"Besides," said Bach, "I could have never murdered her."

"Why's that?"

"I coulda never got close enough to her. When we was in school, she noticed everything. She was like freakin' Sherwood Holmes."

"Sherlock."

"Whatever. I'm just saying that she woulda spotted me before I got close enough and woulda probably woke the neighborhood with a rape whistle or something. I said some things, back when we broke up. I was stupid. Sort of cancelled my ticket forever with her. Yeah, I tried to get in touch a couple of times to maybe patch things up. She wanted no part! So it couldn't have been me. The only way ANYONE woulda been able to get close to her was if he was a friend! And I ain't no friend!"

Nate sighed. "All right. Fair point. Thanks for your time." He turned to go but Bach's voice brought him back around.

"You want the God's own truth? When I heard the next day that she got killed, I shed a few tears. Felt bad for what I'd said about her...and knowing she died thinking what a creep I was. Yeah, I'm a creep. A real bastard. But for what it's worth, I don't believe all that stuff about history that I read in the paper."

"What do you mean?"

"It just seems like bullshit to me, killing people because they don't know history shit. It said in the papers that Sandy went out running every night. Like I said before, she noticed everything! I'll bet she seen something she shouldn'ta."

Nate turned that thought over in his mind. "Thanks again for your time."

It was almost 7:00 by the time he returned to Mukwonago, and Nate was hungry. But instead of turning north off Veterans Way onto highway 83, which would have taken him to his condo, he proceeded through the intersection and turned left into Field Park. He parked along the paved roadway that ran parallel to the park's north border and exited the squad.

An idea had begun to form, but its shape was still too elusive to pin down. He walked toward the stone walls that formed a pedestrian gate at the intersection's southwest corner. Sandy had come to Field Park every night to stretch. And just across the street, Carl Mullenberg had been murdered in Kiwanis Park. Sandy, of course, had been killed before Carl, so she could not have seen his murder. But had she seen something else?

Nate squinted toward the north where the shed stood. He remembered the tale of the jockey who had stolen Capone's gold. How some believed it might be buried beneath the shed. Had Carl and Sandy both seen something? Perhaps without even realizing, at the time, that what they were seeing was important?

But as Nate squinted toward the far-away shed, this seemed unlikely. Even in daylight, it would be hard for Sandy to make sense of any activity so far away. And at dusk or afterwards, when Sandy would have been in the park, it would be impossible.

And even if Sandy and Carl had been killed because they had seen something going on at the shed, that didn't explain Corrine Baker's murder.

The more he thought about it, the less sense it all seemed to make. "It just seems like bullshit to me," Bach had said. Nate was inclined to agree.

The simplest explanation.

Donovan Duminski was the killer. Case closed.

Forty

He had stopped by at Grace's after his epiphany in Field Park.

"Yeah, I talked with Roger Bach. It just made me feel dumb. You can relax. It was Duminski."

Of course, Grace had been extremely grateful for this information, as well as the fact that he had stopped by personally to deliver it rather than simply phoning.

"You've been so good to me," she told him. "You've been there for me when I really needed it. This past year has been such a roller coaster, but you…"

Sometimes, words were insufficient.

*

3:13 Wednesday morning, Nate woke suddenly. For just a moment, he had trouble finding his breath.

"Nate, what is it?" said Grace, sitting up beside him, rubbing his bare back.

He had relaxed in sleep and his mind had let the distractions fall away. And a truth had surfaced, so stark and startling that it had awakened him.

Roger Bach's words rushed back to him. "She noticed everything...The only way ANYONE woulda been able to get close to her was if he was a friend! And I ain't no friend!"

And that was the thing. Donovan Duminski was the easy answer. The history expert. The guy with the troubled past and a grudge to settle. The night wanderer who might know the routines of others. And he had been there in the park the night that Grace had been attacked.

But he had not been the one thing that he needed to be in order to get close enough to kill Sandy Sewell.

He had not been a friend.

If Roger Bach stood no chance of getting the drop on her, then neither did Duminski.

He couldn't be the killer.

But now Nate couldn't steal Grace's serenity. Not after just making a present of it to her a few hours earlier. Later, certainly, when he had more information, when she was stronger, but not now. Not tonight.

"Nothing. Just a bad dream."

Forty-one

He had been unable to sleep after his three a.m. realization. Nate had closed his eyes, tried. But his mind had been too unsettled, at war with itself. Roger Bach, insisting that Sandy was too sharp, that she would have noticed a threat, no matter how subtle.

He tried to play devil's advocate. Maybe Bach was wrong. Maybe she had let her guard down, become distracted. Perhaps she had passed too close to a clump of bushes and Duminski had leaped out unexpectedly. Yet, no one had heard a scream. And there were no bushes.

The only way ANYONE woulda been able to get close to her was if he was a friend!

If that were indeed true, the pool of suspects was enormous. In fact, Bach, Craig LaForte and Donovan Duminski were probably the only three people who *couldn't* have murdered Sandy Sewell.

Let it go, he pleaded with himself. *There are no guarantees, no sure things.* Things that couldn't have possibly happened *do* happen all the time. Sure-footed roofers who could allegedly give the tightrope-walking Flying Walenda's a run for their money fall off roofs. Champion gymnasts trip over cracks in the sidewalk and require knee surgery. Surgeons leave Rolexes in patients.

When it got light, he showered and dressed but still said nothing to Grace. Until he had something concrete, he wasn't going to add to her worries. However, it was clear that she sensed something was upsetting him.

"The bad dream?" she asked.

He nodded. "I'll get over it."

"Want to tell me about it? Would that help?"

"I will eventually."

He drove to Phantom Glen Park, the site of Sandy's murder. Neighbors had reported no vehicles in the park that evening. The killer had arrived on foot or by boat, perhaps in the stolen canoe. What had happened in the park was subject to conjecture. Sandy might have jogged to the end of the street, entered the parking lot on the south side, and jogged through it to the east, intending to make a loop that would swing back out onto Andrews Street and send her on her way. The parking lot was lighted along that route, and there were few hiding places. Leaping out into the light to assault a moving target would have been extremely chancy. As careful and well-planned as the murders had been, that didn't sound like the killer.

A section of the parking lot extended south toward the lake. This area would have been darker had Sandy deigned to make a wider loop to add a little distance to her route. Or perhaps she had ventured out onto the pier to gaze at the stars. Despite the darkness, there was still little cover for an attacker. And while she would have been cornered once she was on the pier, she would have surely cried out at the approach of Duminski, and that would have been heard by neighbors.

She noticed everything. She was like freakin' Sherwood Holmes.

He drove to the station, found Dick Andrews at his desk. "Can I ask you something? And if you don't mind, can this be just between you and me?"

Dick initially looked a little worried by the request, but then quickly relaxed. "Yeah, sure. No sweat. Watcha got?"

Nate looked around, found a chair, pulled it close and kept his voice low. "I know this is going to sound like a silly question. But you were a little closer to all the details of the Duminski investigation. Just how sure are we that we got the right guy?"

Dick's expression was one of amused incredulity. "This is a joke, right?"

Nate said nothing.

"Dude, he was right there in the cemetery. He ran. He had bad history with Sandy. He was a peeping Tom." He ticked the items off on his fingers.

"All of that's circumstantial."

"Not the letter."

Nate's mouth dropped open slightly. This was new information to him. "What letter is that?"

"That first letter Duminski sent to the newspaper," said Andrews. "It was right there in the documents file on his computer. We found it when his home was searched after his arrest."

Nate nodded slowly. That was a game-changer. "Yeah, I guess that pretty well settles the matter if the letters were on his computer."

"It was just the first letter," clarified Andrews. "Probably deleted the others but missed it by accident."

Nate stiffened. Again, this did not seem to fit with the killer's pattern of careful planning. Would someone who had probably spent weeks studying the habits of potential victims and designing murders bereft of clues really forget to delete one of only four letters?

He exited the station. Although he was supposed to be patrolling, he drove to the apartment complex where Duminski had lived. His unit on the first floor was easy to spot, since yellow police tape was still fastened across the door. Nate went to the unit on the right, knocked.

No answer.

He crossed the hall, knocked on a second unit. He heard movement inside, and after a few moments, a heavy-set man of about forty in a blue-green work shirt opened the door.

"Yeah?"

"Sir, I was wondering if you could answer a question or two about your neighbor, Donovan Duminski?"

In an almost practiced monotone, the man responded, "Never heard of him. Didn't know him."

"Anything you could tell me might be helpful."

"Never heard of him. Didn't know him," repeated the man.

Realizing that this was all he was going to get, Nate thanked the man, who promptly shut the door. He then moved to the apartment just across the hall from Duminski's. A woman of about seventy-five came to the door, identifying herself as Vivian Gartener.

"Mr. Duminski is dead, isn't he?" asked Vivian. When Nate responded that he was, the woman said, "Then I suppose it wouldn't hurt to talk about things."

"Did Donovan Duminski strike you as a very organized person?" asked Nate. "A careful planner?"

Vivian thought about this for a moment. "It's not like we spoke often. But he seemed a very bright man. Used to be a professor or something, I think. Did he really do the awful things they say?"

"That's what we're trying to determine. You said you thought he was bright. That doesn't necessarily mean he was organized."

Vivian shook her head. "I couldn't say. I know he was very busy."

"With his job as a grounskeeper?"

She nodded. "And with his mother."

"His mother?"

"This was really her apartment," explained Vivian, pointing across the hall. "He moved in with her years ago. After he'd divorced, I think. At least that's what I heard. He needed somewhere to go, and she needed help."

"In what way?"

"Her health wasn't good. Dementia and diabetes. Poor thing. Needed a lot of care. Was pretty much bedridden the past two years."

Nate glanced at the police tape. "Where is she now?"

"One of the long-term care facilities," said Vivian. "They moved her after he was arrested."

Nate thought about this for a moment. "You say she has dementia? Do you think she would be able to answer some questions?"

Vivian's face drooped doubtfully. "I wouldn't think so. From what I understand, she doesn't speak much. Her mind is pretty well gone."

Nate clenched his jaw in frustration. "And he took care of her all by himself?"

Vivian nodded. Then she stopped. "Well, not completely. On weekdays, someone would stop by during the day when he was at work, make sure she had her meds, clean her up, move her limbs around, that sort of thing. He had one of those four-digit electronic boxes that hung on his doorknob where she could get the key to let herself in."

"Did you know the code?"

She smiled. "Yes, for emergencies. Actually, a lot of us did. Because of his interest in local history, it was really a little joke. 1-8-3-6."

Nate blinked absently. "I don't get the joke."

"1836," said Vivian. "The year the village was founded. Or so the Professor said."

He thanked Vivian and returned to his squad, moving out into village streets to begin the patrol he should have begun half an hour ago. Nate had hoped that his trip to visit Duminski's neighbors might have given him answers that put his mind at ease. Instead, Vivian's testimony had left the door open on the possibility that Duminski had been set up. If his door code were really that loosely guarded a secret, the killer could have entered his apartment during the day while Duminski was at work. The mother, bedridden, would either not have known or not have been able to communicate it to others. And if Duminski's computer were as easy to access as his key safe, it would have taken only minutes to leave a copy of the first letter tucked away in a documents file.

Stop it, Nate. You're being paranoid! What's next? You'll start investigating whether NASA faked the moon landing?

But Roger Bach's words reverberated. *The only way ANYONE woulda been able to get close to her was if he was a friend!*

And almost everyone was a friend. It was like walking the beach, looking for a cinder speck amongst the grains of sand.

Worst of all was not knowing what to do with this information. He knew that Beckman would be angry that he'd been devoting his time to what seemed a far-fetched conspiracy theory—unless Nate could produce something more solid in the way of evidence. Yet, he really needed to share it with someone, partly because the weight of this information was such a heavy burden to bear alone, and partly because he wanted another—perhaps more objective—opinion to tell him whether he was right to be concerned, or whether he was full of beans.

The first person to come to mind was Star.

He wondered if perhaps Star wasn't the best choice if he were looking for an objective opinion. She had already suggested that Duminski might not be the killer. Plus, she had a history of both overzealousness and ethical lapses, although she seemed to have come to terms with the latter. Still, she was smart, she knew the case, and he had to admit, he enjoyed her company.

He found a spot a block from the *Chief* office and exited the squad. Halfway there, he bumped into Grace, on her way back to the gift shop with a coffee from Sarah's.

"Where you heading, big guy?" asked Grace coyly.

Nate saw no reason to be evasive. "*Chief* office."

Grace hesitated, and he couldn't tell whether her troubled expression was because he was going to see Star, or because she suspected he might have discovered something that meant she was still in danger. "This isn't anything to do with those murders, is it?"

"Look, I just want to be sure. If there's any chance it wasn't Duminski and that you're still in danger, I want to be on top of it."

She attempted a brave smile, but Nate could see she was upset. "And I was just thinking to myself, 'What a nice day. Think I'll go get a latte at Sarah's. Then it'll be even better!' Guess I should have stayed in the store."

"I'm sorry. I could have made up some excuse. But I wanted to be honest."

She shook her head. "No, I'm glad you were. Did you learn something that made you more suspicious?"

"Just a lot of little things," said Nate. "Like the fact that Duminski's apartment was pretty easy for anyone to access to plant evidence."

Grace nodded, and then a thin smile appeared. "You know, I'm glad you're so thorough—even though what you're learning scares me all over again. But no matter what the truth is, I'll feel more secure in the long run. Thank you. I'd give you a hug if you weren't in uniform and we weren't standing right in the middle of the village. And if I wasn't afraid of spilling this delicious coffee!"

Nate smiled. "I appreciate your restraint."

Then Grace's smiled disappeared. "Wait. There wasn't another letter, was there?"

"No, nothing like that."

She relaxed again. "Thank goodness! Almost gave me a heart attack! Did they ever figure out how Duminski did it?"

"Did what?"

"The letters," said Grace. "How Duminski magically got them to the *Chief* office without anybody seeing?"

"I'm sure they figured it out."

She snuck a kiss onto his left cheek and then hurried off toward her store.

And suddenly, he felt funny in the stomach again. To his knowledge, no one had really spent much time addressing that point after Duminski's death. Because Duminski wasn't a regular fixture in the downtown area, his appearance there would have been noticed. On the other hand, someone who regularly did business there or owned a shop in the downtown area would draw little attention.

Of course, someone who worked at the *Chief* would draw the least attention of all, and would in fact sometimes have hours alone in the building during which   time letters could be made to "magically" appear.

Abracadabra.

He stood for a minute, rooted to the spot. Then he turned and walked back to his squad.

Forty-two

Friday afternoon, he helped Grace load boxes of gift items into the back of her minivan, its back seats removed, for the trip to tomorrow's Maxwell Street Days in Field Park. They ate delivery pizza after they finished.

"I hope you don't mind if we don't hang out this evening," she said during their supper. "I've still got lots of things to price and organize. And then I've got to get to bed early—to *sleep*! Have to be up by five so I can get ready and get in line over at the park by six. In fact, it's going to be a long weekend, so we probably won't see much of each other until Monday."

In truth, he was rather relieved that Grace had something to keep her busy over the weekend—other than himself. For most of his adult life, there had been few relationships that had progressed beyond a third date. He had always imagined what a devoted boyfriend he would be if a woman ever continued to see him for a longer period. But now he found himself wanting some down time. He wasn't sure why. Grace was beautiful, affectionate. She seemed to need protecting. He wondered if, perhaps, this feeling of needing separation was something natural, something all relationships experienced.

His thoughts turned to Star. Nate had decided against stopping by at the *Chief* office after meeting Grace on the sidewalk. It seemed absurd, but what about the "magical" envelopes? Star could have easily planted them for Judith to discover. But murdering people just to jack up circulation in a small-town newspaper? That would require an especially twisted mind, an individual for whom the term 'psychopath' would truly be apt.

But, as Grace had observed, many individuals visited the *Chief* office every day, and so there were dozens of other possible suspects who might have left the envelopes discreetly. And if not Star, whoever it was had probably more in mind than selling newspapers. Even if the killer were not Duminski, maybe someone else had been pushed over the edge by anger at rampant development and the loss of the village's historical homes and businesses. Or perhaps there was some personal revenge motive that would make itself clear once all of the evidence was collected.

Still, Nate kept circling back to Capone's supposed lost gold and diamonds. Killing to protect local heritage? Maybe. But Nate also knew that the majority of murders, whether drug deals gone bad, insurance scams, convenience store robberies or others, were over money.

Heading home from Grace's, he realized that the Mukwonago Community Library was still open for another half hour. He already had the information on Capone from the Red Brick Museum, but he wondered whether the library would have Capone material he didn't already possess.

The Mukwonago Community Library was one of Nate's favorite places. A beautiful newer, brick building, it stood at the intersection of Washington Avenue and Division Street. Prior to the building's construction, the site had been home to a tan, brick, two-story school building that had served as the village's first dedicated high school. It had been used as an administration and storage facility in its last years, and Nate had never attended classes there. However, he had seen the inside with its high-ceilinged classrooms with tall windows and wooden floors. And the small gymnasium had had a stage on one end, three rows of fold-out bleachers, and a parquet wooden floor. The high school teams had played their football and baseball games on the adjacent lot that still featured a couple of ball diamonds.

Prior to the razing of the old school for the construction of the new library, Mukwonago's village library had been in a house on Grand Avenue, right next door to the old fire and police department—which had also been torn down to make way for more modern businesses. While the old "Floyd and Jessie McKenzie Library" had been charming, it could not have held a candle to the new facility, which had a vast catalog of books, meeting rooms and the latest in tech that would help researchers, students, writers, and others.

Nate stepped inside, smiling at the shelves of new titles just in front of him. However, his business was at the circulation desk, and so he stepped to the left.

"May I help you?" asked a young woman behind the counter.

"Hi, I'm doing a little research. You wouldn't happen to have any information on Al Capone, would you?"

"Let me check," said the woman, who consulted the screen in front of her and tapped at a keyboard. After a moment, she replied, "It looks like we have several books on Al Capone. Would you like me to print their call numbers?"

Nate smiled. "Sorry. I'm actually looking more for something local. Al Capone was supposed to have spent some time in Mukwonago back in the 1940s. I was just wondering whether you had any materials on that."

The young woman nodded. "For that, you'll have to try the reference desk." She pointed. Nate thanked her and ambled over to a desk near the back of the main room. A slightly older woman with glasses sat behind a monitor there, and Nate posed his question to her.

"Yes, we do have some information on Mr. Capone in Mukwonago," she said. "But…"

She tapped away for a moment.

"Hm. It's out."

"Out?" said Nate. "I didn't think reference materials could be checked out of the library."

"If I recall correctly, the library director granted a waiver for this request."

Nate groaned, then recovered himself. "Who checked them out?"

"I'm sorry," said the woman, offering a smile that really seemed to suggest that she was sorry. "It's our policy not to give out that information. Confidentiality, you understand."

Nate, who was in civilian clothes, reached into a pocket, pulled out his badge and flashed it.

"I think you're going to have to grant me a waiver, too."

The woman frowned, but she printed out the name. Nate's heart pounded. Whoever had checked out the material might have been looking for information on Capone's treasure. And that could be a motive for murder.

She handed him the sheet and he read it.

Star Calloway

Forty-three

Nate slept fitfully on Friday night, despite the fact that he was alone and could have slept as late into the morning as he wanted. Star had checked out the Capone materials. Did that and the ease with which the letters had mysteriously appeared in the *Chief* office suggest that Star was behind all of this? Was it just a coincidence that the murders had started shortly after she had arrived in Mukwonago?

He finally dozed off fully just as a yellow rim was coloring the horizon in the east, and when he woke again, it was after ten. The last time he had slept in that late was when he was a student at Waukesha County Technical College, the morning after a buddy's bachelor party.

He decided he needed a vacation, that he could no longer process information about the Duminski case objectively. One minute he felt he was onto something important. The next, that he was tilting after windmills.

Grace would be busy all day at Maxwell Street. While the open air market had been a once-a-month Mukwonago summer tradition for decades, this was the first time Grace had taken her wares to the event.

Her items would see much more traffic than a typical day in the gift shop, as Maxwell Street was attended by thousands—weather permitting. And the forecast for the next two days was clear skies and a daytime high of eighty. Summer in Mukwonago didn't get any better than that.

Nate was grateful to be off for the entire weekend. After having a "brunch" of Frosted Mini Wheats with skim milk and a Coca Cola, he caught up on two week's worth of accumulated laundry, vacuuming, dishes, and a trip to Pick & Save to replenish his bare cupboards. He watched an afternoon ballgame on TV, and this seemed to take his mind off the issues that had been troubling him. Late in the afternoon, as he hosed the grime off *Higgins*, the familiar aroma of neighbor Pete's grill distracted him in a different way—and made his mouth water. And as usual, Pete extended an invitation.

"Damn it, Pete, you know I can't say no to your grilled brats!"

By six, Pete, his wife Emily, and Nate sat in lawn chairs, enjoying double bratwursts and slowly downing Coronas.

"Thanks again, Pete," said Nate, tilting his bottle toward his neighbor in a kind of salute. "I really needed this. It's been a crazy couple of weeks."

"Well," said Pete, "thanks for all you do to make this a safer community."

Nate shook his head. "Don't give me too much credit."

"Oh, don't be so modest, Nate," said Emily.

"You chased him down," said Pete. "You told me that."

"I didn't actually catch him, though," noted Nate. "And I sort of ruined my squad."

"But the good guys got the bad guy, and that's all that matters," said Pete.

"I guess."

"You guess?" Pete took a sip of Corona, eyed his friend skeptically."What do you mean 'I guess'? The bad guy is dead."

"Assuming we got the right guy."

This statement appeared to slightly alarm Emily. "Is there any question about that, Nate?"

Nate sighed. "I don't know. That's been bothering me all week. I think we got the right guy. But then I start wondering whether there wasn't some other motive for all the murders. Something a bit more tangible than giving the community a mortal spanking for not knowing its history lessons."

"Like money?" asked Pete.

"Something like that. You know a lot about local history, Pete, so I'm sure you've heard of the Capone stories. And his supposed stolen treasure."

"I've heard a little," said Pete, nodding.

"It's just a crazy theory I had, that somebody might have found where the jockey hid the treasure and killed those three people to cover it up and keep it for himself."

Pete and Emily laughed politely.

"For the chance at a million bucks, some people would do some pretty ruthless things," said Pete. "Heck, for a million bucks, who knows what I'd do?" he gave a wink.

"I doubt you'd do anything too nasty," said Nate with a knowing smirk. "Anyone who really knows you knows that beneath all the tough talk, you're a softy. And I'd heard the lost fortune was more like two mil."

"Yeah, I'd need at least five to start whackin' people," said Pete sarcastically.

"When Carl was killed in that shed, I thought maybe that had something to do with Capone's loot and the theory that maybe it had been buried underneath by a jockey," said Nate. "But that didn't really add up. The killer knew a lot about village history and would have known that the shed had been moved a decade or so ago from its earlier location at the southeast corner of Kiwanis Park, right next to the intersection."

"And before that, from Field Park, across the street," added Emily.

Nate stiffened. "What?"

Emily laughed. "You weren't aware? Well, that's understandable. After all, it was before any of us were born. But yes, it originally stood in Field Park."

"Where in Field Park?"

"You okay, Nate?" asked Pete, noticing his friend's sudden intensity.

"Yeah Pete, but, holy cow, this could be important!"

Emily made little circular movements in the air with her fingers as she replied. "Just across the street, not far from that big stone gate."

"Where did you hear this?"

She thought for a moment. "I was at an art show in…Wales, I think."

"Figures!" said Pete.

"Right there along the Glacial Drumlin Trail. Lots of nice work. So much talent! One older gentlemen, he painted pictures of unique barns from all over southern Wisconsin, but he'd try to make them look like they did when they were first built. If they were sort of run-down, he'd make them look like new, and he'd put horse-drawn carriages or vintage tractors next to them. Or people dressed like they did a hundred, a hundred and fifty years ago. Well I saw this one and I knew right away it was our barn from Kiwanis Park, almost right across the road! But it wasn't all colorful, like it is now. He painted it gray, with horses grazing next to it, but he had it standing over in Field Park. You could see the big stone gate in the background.

"He was very nice. We got to talking, and I told him that he had the location wrong. He shook his head no, said that it had originally stood in Field

335 / Rod Vick

Park, and he recited all his sources. I don't recall them, however. But he was very convincing. Said he did meticulous research on every barn he painted. Said they stored saddles and bridles and the like in it for the races."

"You didn't buy the painting?" asked Nate.

Emily sighed. "No. I had my eye on another one. And Pete said I had to stay within the budget. But the artist—I think his name was Frank—he said he spent some time in Field Park at the shed's original location, making sketches, getting measurements. I think he said its original spot was where the flagpole is today."

"The American Legion flagpole?" asked Nate. "The one on top of the stone steps?"

Emily nodded. "That's right. Sort of looks like a Mayan pyramid."

He considered this information for a beat, and then stood. "I'm sorry, but I've got to go. I've got to check something out."

"Hey, buddy, are you okay?" asked Pete.

"Yeah," said Nate, backing toward his side of the driveway. "Thanks for the food. And the Corona."

He hurried into his condo, changed into slacks, strapped on his service revolver and threw a sports coat on over the Hawaiian shirt he had been wearing. Then he hopped into *Higgins*.

He didn't know exactly where Grace's sales booth was in Field Park, for she had insisted on unloading her merchandise herself. But she had mentioned the north side of the park along the main road. If she had meant the road that entered off of Rochester Street and made a sweeping arc past the pavilion and the ball diamond, that would put her near the stone gate on the intersection of Rochester and Veterans Way.

Right in the vicinity of where Emily had indicated the shed had once stood.

What if that had something to do with the lost Capone treasure? What if it really had been buried there, and the killer had learned that Grace was going to have her Maxwell Street Days stand right at the location? Might that explain why they had tried to kill her?

And if the killer wasn't Duminski, then Grace might still be in grave danger.

It was about 6:30—half an hour after the official closing time for the day—when he pulled into the Park View Middle School parking lot, got out, and crossed to Field Park. He began his walk down the main aisle and hadn't gone far before he saw the vinyl "GRACE'S GIFTS" banner attached at the roofline of a white commerce tent whose white sidewalls were tied closed for the night. He quickened his pace, pulled back the edge of a sidewall, peered inside. There were hundreds of trinkets and craft items on tables and portable shelving, but no Grace. He closed the flap, looked toward the back of the narrow space. There was another ten-by-ten, white commerce tent with sidewalls, presumably filled with additional merchandise and packing boxes.

And directly behind that tent, the base of the Legion flagpole.

"Grace?" Nate called out.

She did not reply, but a woman tidying things up in the space next door to Grace's booth did. "I think she went home for the day about half an hour ago!"

He was relieved to hear this.

"Thank you. Good to know."

The woman, a cigarette bobbing between her lips, who seemed about fifty, rotund, very tan with sun-damaged skin, placed hand-lettered wooden signs into large, clear plastic storage boxes. "I been doing this for fifteen years. Never missed a Maxwell Street. Love it. Very nice girl. Too bad about the cancer."

Nate nodded. "She's a fighter. Hopefully she's got it beat."

The woman inhaled deeply, let out an enormous cloud of smoke. "At least she was lucky to get a good spot."

"Yes," said Nate, beginning the little shuffle toward the gate that was intended to subtly end the conversation, but the woman persisted.

"First-timers usually get stuck on one of the side aisles. People hold onto the good ones year after year. But your Grace was lucky a good spot opened up. But not so lucky, I guess, for Corrine. She was a regular, too. Good person."

"Yes, well, I…" He stopped cold. Stared back at the woman. "Corrine? Not Corrine Baker?"

"I think that was her name, yeah."

Nate's face drained of color. He turned, ran through the stone gate, picked his way across the street, threw himself into his car.

The details swirled. Corrine Baker, a Maxwell Street regular, is killed for no apparent reason. Grace ends up getting her spot—which may be in the vicinity of where the shed once stood.

Were these simply coincidences? And if not, what did they mean? Was somebody trying to put Grace in harm's way? Or was something else happening?

He took out his mobile to call Grace, but something stopped him. Something about Carl Mullenberg. He had died in the shed, but not in Field Park. Not at the shed's original location. Carl had died at the far north side of Kiwanis Park, more than a quarter mile away. How was Carl connected?

Ellie, from the museum, had mentioned something.

He had one of those metal detector things. After every Maxwell Street Days or big event up at Field Park, he'd be out there the next day, looking for coins that people had dropped. Sometimes he'd find car keys, too, and help get them back to their rightful owners. Other times he'd find an old thing, an antique ring or belt buckle, and he'd donate it to the museum. Once he found a railroad spike that looked to be from the 1880s. Imagine that! I have no idea how it ended up in Field Park!

Had Carl found something else in Field Park, something more valuable than an old railroad spike? Something that put his life in danger? Something that connected him to Corrine and Grace?

Nate's mind raced. *This can't be right. I must be having some sort of episode. It doesn't make any sense. Things like this don't happen.*

Sandy Sewell flashed to mind. She had visited Field Park every evening, had done her stretching exercises at the memorial flagpole. The same flagpole that stood just behind Grace's Maxwell Street stall.

Field Park connected them all.

I've got to warn Grace!

Again he raised his phone. Again he hesitated.

The smoking lady had said people kept their sales stalls a long time. There must have been dozens of other stalls that Grace, a first-timer, could have been assigned. It was an amazing coincidence.

Unless Grace had asked for that stall specifically after Corrine's death.

His thoughts ran a dizzying race.

Carl had occasionally stopped by at the gift shop to talk about items he had found in the park. That's what Grace had said.

Grace was a good friend of Sandy's.

The only way ANYONE woulda been able to get close to her was if he was a friend!

He felt his heart beat in his temples, the beat so loud he was certain that passersby on the sidewalk could hear it. Suddenly, he opened his door and lurched out into the Parkview Middle School lot, jerked open the driver-side rear door, began pawing through items strewn about the backseat. Sandwich wrappers, receipts, paper bags, pens, Coke cans. He had shoveled it all into his personal vehicle from the squad before he had turned it over to be repaired. After a few moments, he found what he was looking for.

The brochure from the hospital the night he had met Grace at the ER. He had glanced at it briefly that night and then tossed it into the back of the squad. It featured opportunities to donate to worthy hospital causes and programs, including several building or renovation plans dedicated to individuals who had passed on. The first time he had glanced at the brochure, a name had clicked as vaguely familiar, but his mind had been elsewhere. He'd given it no more thought. Wasn't even sure where he might have heard the name. But now he was afraid he understood why the name sounded familiar. He opened the brochure.

Opportunities to support our mission include memorial donations to:
- *The Dr. Alex Castleman Radiology Wing*
- *The Dr. George R. Zenzimmer Solarium*
- *The Dr. Susan Ayers Oncology Lab*

Memorial donations!

He took out his phone, typed Dr. Susan Ayers into the browser.

Top Cancer Doctor Ayers Felled by Disease She Battled in Others

Dr. Susan Ayers, 51, passed away earlier this week at Green Meadows Hospice from complications relating to cancer.

Ayers, a cancer specialist, guided hundreds of individuals, most of them women, through their own battles with cancer, accumulating an impressive success rate that complemented what colleagues frequently described as a remarkably caring and empathetic relationship with her patients. She was recently named one of the Top 100 Doctors in Wisconsin.

Unfortunately, Ayers herself was diagnosed with breast cancer two years ago, and while she initially responded well to treatment, the cancer

resurfaced with a vengeance
several months ago.

    Ayers attended college at

    Nate found he could scarcely breathe. Dr. Susan Ayers had died more than six months ago—a month before Grace had said she was diagnosed with her own cancer. Nate felt sick to his stomach, turned from the car, retched in the parking lot on his hands and knees. After eating that double brat, he was surprised that nothing came out.

    But when he got to his feet, he found that his confusion had been, in part, replaced by anger and hurt. Grace must have seen Ayers' name in the Top 100 Doctors article and chosen her at random, not realizing that she had recently died. Yet, Nate had seen the bottles of medicine on Grace's dresser, cancer medications with Ayers' name on them as the prescribing physician.

    She even faked the bottles. They were just props.

    And that day in her gift shop, when Grace had been sick in the bathroom.

    She was faking then, too.

    But why? Why would someone pretend to have cancer?

    The answer came to him almost immediately. No one would suspect someone who was battling cancer, weakened by chemotherapy and the ravages of the illness. No one in the community. Certainly no one she might approach out of the dark on a summer night. And with a shaved head and eyebrows, less chance of leaving behind DNA evidence.

Jesus!

He got back in the car, raced off, not knowing exactly what he was going to say, but knowing he had to confront Grace. He had to hear it from her. And he had to remember that she was dangerous.

Unless...

Could there be some other interpretation, some alternative explanation? How often had he thought he had figured out this case, only to find that he was wrong?

He screamed into her driveway, banged on her front door, one hand inside his coat, resting on his gun. No answer. He went around to the back, checked at the windows. It appeared that no one was home.

Nate noticed that her minivan was gone as well. *The store!* He returned to his car, raced toward the center of the village. There he spotted the minivan in the small parking area to the rear of the shop. He pulled in beside it, removed his weapon from its holster, mounted the back steps. The door was unlocked and he opened it cautiously.

"Grace?"

No answer. He called a second time with the same result. Nate stepped inside and was greeted by an aroma that was equal parts paint thinner and cinnamon holiday candles. He cleared the short hallway, then saw something that made him shiver.

"Oh no!"

At the end of the hallway where it opened into the main front room of the store, a woman lying on the floor, the upper part of her body hidden by the wall. Nate rushed to the corner. The woman lay face down on the floor behind the check-out counter, her smooth head partially covered by a red bandana.

"My God!" Nate knelt, leaned forward, felt with the fingers of his free hand for a pulse.

Off balance, he was completely surprised and unprepared to respond when a damp cloth was clamped over his mouth and nose from behind. He hesitated just an instant, then tried to stand—whoever was behind held on just long enough.

And then there was only darkness.

Forty-four

When he came to, there were no lights on in the store, and only a dusky gloom showed through the windows. His mind cleared quickly, and Nate guessed that he had not been out long. The shelves were mostly empty along the perimeter of the shop's large main room, since much of the inventory was at Field Park.

"Grace." He spoke the word without emotion.

"Don't cry out. I'll have duct tape over your mouth in half a second."

Her voice was near. He detected movement in the shadows to his left, but she did not come clearly into view. He lay on the oak floor on his back, in the middle of the room, his wrists secured behind him, his ankles tied together.

"Why, Nate?" she asked. "Why did you have to be so frickin' anal? Everyone in the goddamn village was all-in on Duminski. But not you. And I guess not that newspaper bitch, but her credibility is worth piss anyway. Why couldn't you have just accepted the easy solution? All the evidence pointed to Duminski."

"Obviously not all the evidence," said Nate. "Jesus, Grace, why?"

"Don't you have it all figured out?"

"Look at me, Grace. I'm lying on the floor of your shop, my hands tied behind me. Do I look like I have it all figured out?"

"I really liked you, Nate." Her voice drifted softly out of the growing darkness. "But you had to be a damn Boy Scout."

"Obviously not a very good one. Their motto is 'Be prepared'."

"Don't you hate it, Nate, when you love, but aren't loved in return?"

Nate said nothing, and after a few uncomfortable moments, Grace continued.

"I always loved this town. Really loved it. I mean it's beautiful. Not a big city. Farmland just outside the village limits. Nice parks. Historic homes. Picturesque lake. The Mukwonago River. Growing up here was like growing up in a Currier & Ives painting. I had such a happy childhood."

"Then why, Grace?" asked Nate. "Why all of this? And who was that behind the counter?"

"Bob was the one, Nate," she continued, ignoring his questions. "My Prince Charming. We lived in the Emerson House—the most spectacular historic home in town! And he treated me like a princess. Until she came and ruined everything."

"Who, Grace? The woman behind the counter?"

"She wasn't from here. Racine. Her husband was a developer who was starting to buy up land and bulldoze old homes in the area. That's how they met. Bob was on the village planning commission and had to work with her husband—and sometimes Felicity came with him."

"Is that the woman behind the counter, Grace?"

"How did I not know? How did I not suspect? Then one night after a meeting, Bob told me everything. Most of the meetings on the current project had been concluded more than two months ago. But *they* had been meeting. She was younger, pretty, blonde. Bob said there just wasn't anything there between us anymore—for him. He wanted a divorce. The week after that, Bob died."

Nate knew the longer one kept a dangerous individual talking, the better one's chances. But there was no cavalry coming to save him. He wasn't on duty, so no one expected him to be anywhere. But he had to buy time, try to figure something out.

"How did he die, Grace?"

"He was working under the car, in the garage. But the jack slipped. Crushed his skull. They said it was terrible, but in those old houses where the little barn in back is turned into a garage, sometimes the concrete floors they pour over the dirt isn't very structurally sound, and it cracks and shifts over the years. That was what must have happened. A badly-placed jack on uneven flooring."

"But that's not what really happened, was it, Grace?"

"He was just out in the garage, checking the air pressure on the tires with a little gauge, bent over near the front passenger side. Never heard me coming, I was so careful. I'd never swung a baseball bat so hard. Only once. He seemed dead, though maybe he wasn't. And I felt such a release. All the hurt of the betrayal, gone in that one swing! Of course, then I had to jack up the car, remove a tire, arrange his tools around him, bring the car down on his head and make it look like the jack had tipped. Then I cleaned up and walked out to the garage and screamed. A couple of neighbors came, jacked up the car again, tried to resuscitate Bob, but it was of course too late for that. And by moving him around, they created enough chaos at the crime scene that there was no way the police could conclude anything other than an accident. I marveled at how easy it had been to stage the whole thing and get away with it."

"Jesus, Grace! Look, undo my hands. You know I'm your friend. We can get you help."

"Help?" Her voice had a sharp edge. "Do you know when I needed help? After Bob died. But that's when I started to learn what a bastard he had really been. He'd always said he had life insurance. Well, doesn't a good husband have enough insurance to make sure his widow is taken care of if something happens? But Bob's was barely enough to cover funeral expenses. Then I got sick. Not cancer, which

I'm sure you figured out was bogus. Ulcers and stomach issues that required hospitalization and surgery. Couldn't work, lost my job, had tons of medical bills. And then I lost the house. That hurt. Nothing has ever hurt so bad."

"Grace, I'm sorry." No matter how he struggled, he could not get the zip ties to budge.

"I'm sure you are," she said soothingly. "I really believe you are. Because you're a good man, Nate. You would have had enough insurance so that I wouldn't have to worry about losing the house. You wouldn't have cheated." Then the edge returned. "Or would you? You seem to have an interest in the news bitch."

"I had to talk to her about the letters," explained Nate. "She's just a friend."

"That's what Bob said. At first."

"But Grace, despite the betrayal, the loss of your house, the health issues, you got through it! You opened your own business, became a respected member of the community."

"A crummy little gift shop that operates in the red most of the year," she said ruefully. "After all I've been through, you'd think the community would be more supportive. But no, it's always. 'Oh, I could order this cheaper online,' or 'I could make something like this for a third of the price.' They're happy to come in once a year around Christmas and pat themselves on the back for shopping locally and expect smiles the rest of the year while I'm scraping together pennies to pay the store's electric bill…and living in a shack one-fifth the size of the Emerson House. I loved this town, and what did it give me in return?"

"I don't know," said Nate. "When I looked at you, I thought you had it all."

She laughed bitterly. "And now I'm going to. Our friend Carl, who visited me frequently, was kind enough to let me know that he had found something underneath the flag monument in Field Park. He wasn't sure what it was, but he had discovered it after some big event in the park when he was sweeping the place the next morning with his detector. He brought in a 1929 Indianhead $2.5 gold coin, though I don't think he realized it was gold. Today they're worth more than $200 each. Said he thought there was more, maybe a metal box. I told him not to tell anyone and hold off until I got it appraised, and then if he wanted, we could check it out together. I got pretty flirty, and so he was happy to agree.

"Long story short, I did a little research on my own, batted my eyelashes at the right old-timers at the Red Brick Museum and the library, and I put two and two together. The thing that cinched it was learning the original location of the shed. Had to be the Capone legend treasure. And right then, I figured out exactly how the village was going to pay me back."

"Poor Carl." Nate said it softly, but he felt his anger returning.

"Yes, 'Poor Carl,' but Poor Carl had to go. He knew the location of the treasure and could implicate me. And Sandy had to go. It would only be a matter of time before the woman who noticed everything would start poking around where Carl had disturbed the earth at the base of the flag monument. And Corrine, so that I could get her vendor space and have an excuse to put up a tent where I could excavate without drawing attention. If someone had seen me digging in the park all by myself and called the police, do you think I'd have been allowed to keep any of that treasure?"

"But why the letters?" asked Nate, straining, trying to buy more time. "Why the whole charade about protecting local history?"

"I needed someone to take the fall. Someone whose guilt would be readily accepted by the community."

"And you pinned it all on Duminski."

"Like everyone else, Mr. Duminski was a creature of habit," said Grace. "Every night, just after dark, out for a walk. He'd always start by cutting through the cemetery, either heading along the access road toward the south, or around the corner to the west. He wouldn't always do the Peeping Tom thing, but once in awhile, it was as if he couldn't help himself. I knew he'd be cutting through the cemetery on Thursday night, and so I waited until I saw him—he didn't see me at all. I twisted the rope back and forth to create the marks on my neck, then hit myself with the rock. Yes, it hurt. It hurt like hell. But I knew I wasn't doing any lasting damage, and considering the payoff, it was a small price. Then I screamed, and as I expected, Duminski took off running. You guys did the rest. I hadn't expected that he would kill himself, but that was really a stroke of luck. It seemed like an admission of guilt, and he could no longer provide any details that might create suspicion about my story. But then you got nosy. What pointed you toward me?"

"One of the other vendors mentioned that the stall had belonged to Corrine. It sounded like just a bit too much of a coincidence."

"You're one hell of a detective, Nate. When you started asking questions, thinking that maybe something wasn't right, I got scared. I thought you were going to figure it all out before I could finish. I tried to distract you, to get you to waste your time chasing down nonsense leads by making you suspicious of Star and mentioning the old boyfriend as a suspect."

"The old boyfriend helped me realize that whoever killed Sandy had to be a friend."

A sad laugh out of the darkness. "I guess it's true. There are no perfect crimes."

"Grace, it's over." He adopted a serious, authoritative tone, hoping it would make her see the sense of things. "There are too many loose ends. Star is suspicious. And now you've got another body, this time in your shop. This isn't going away neatly. Let me help you make the best of it. I'm still your friend."

"You *are* going to help me make the best of it," said Grace. "You're going to help me provide a distraction. You and Sarah."

This startled Nate. "Sarah?" Then he understood. Sarah was the woman behind the counter. "What the hell, Grace! Not Sarah! Oh God, no! You fu—" But as his voice rose, Grace stepped out into his field of vision and, despite his squirming, stretched a length of duct tape across his mouth, securing it with a second strip.

"Sarah was so good," said Grace, standing above him, although now she was not bald. Now she wore a dark wig with hair that fell across her shoulders, a wig that gave her an entirely new look. "When I was sick, she brought me soup. And all I had to do was call this afternoon and ask her to stop by after she closed the coffee shop. Whatever it was, she was ready to help in an instant. After she was dead, I shaved her head. You see, I want to get all the police on this end of town, away from Field Park where I'll be digging and then making my getaway. So I'm going to set the store on fire."

Nate erupted into muffled sounds of alarm, his eyes bulging above the tape as the implications of this statement became clear.

"I know. It sucks. But you're not going to just let me go. And I can't have you spoiling things for me. In a calm sea, you went looking for storms. And you found one."

Nate tried to calm himself, think it through. However, his panic rose again when he reminded himself of the careful and calculated murders that Grace had already committed. Her earlier victims had had no chance. His prospects were likely no better.

"It's really very simple," said Grace. "In an hour, the automatic thermostat is set to turn on the furnace in the basement of this building. I've arranged it so that when the burner comes on, it will ignite flammable materials. This will almost instantly engulf the basement in flames. To assure this, I've filled it with shredded newspaper, wrapping paper, cardboard boxes filled with pine needles, anything that I could collect over the past few months that will burn like tinder. A little while ago, I doused it all with mineral spirits, which are almost as flammable as gasoline."

He recalled the smell of paint thinner when he arrived, had thought nothing of it at the time.

"And the rest of this place is all old, dry wood, which will catch like a box of kitchen matches. It'll be very quick. You won't suffer long."

The panic was so overwhelming that it was difficult for Nate to even think complete or coherent thoughts now. Not being able to respond with anything beyond muffled grunts heightened the sense of helplessness, magnified the terror of what was to come.

"Because all of these old wooden buildings in the downtown area could go in minutes, and because they're all so close together, every cop and emergency vehicle in the county will be in the center of town. The Chief office, Won-a-go Biking, Espresso Love, the Red Brick Museum...they'll be absolutely frantic, hoping they don't lose every one of their precious downtown buildings. Ironic, isn't it? The idea that our ignorant neighbors will claw like wildcats to try and save the historic buildings whose heritage they're almost completely ignorant of!"

He felt dizzy. No, he didn't want to pass out. Not yet anyway. Perhaps in an hour, he would beg for sleep, for darkness, even if it was for eternity. Yet, even in his current panicked state, a part of him still hoped, still wanted to fight. But he was a boxer down for the count, unable to even rise off the canvas.

"And while the whole community is focused on its burning center, I'll be finishing my business. In just a few minutes, I'll head back to Field Park. It'll be dark. All the vendor stalls will be closed up and deserted until eight tomorrow morning. I'll slip into my back tent, do a bit of digging, and then disappear. This wig should make me virtually unrecognizable. And no one will be able to say which way I went, even if they do see me. They won't be able to describe a car or testify that they saw a stranger walking down the road. Because I'm not taking the minivan. And the car I'm taking is parked at the end of a path that no eyes will be watching at this time of night. While the diamonds won't be so bad, I imagine the gold coins will make my backpack rather heavy. That's all right. Just a couple of miles. And I'm a strong girl. Good thing I don't have cancer!"

Nate saw the glint of the outside streetlight on her teeth as she smiled.

"And the really beautiful part is that thanks to Sarah, they won't even start looking for me right away," Grace added. "They'll find her charred, hairless corpse and think it's me! And they'll find you, all tied up! 'Oh no! Nate and Star were right! The killer is still at large! It wasn't Duminski! And poor Grace! What a terrible way to go, after all she's been through!'"

Then Grace laughed, and Nate felt like he was going to be sick.

"Before anyone suspects I'm not dead, I'll be out of the country. With enough money to start living my best life. Somewhere with beaches, don't you think? Oh, not for you, of course. You'll spend eternity right here in Mukwonago. But they'll probably put up some sort of memorial to you. Make you a hero for future generations. You should thank me! It wasn't like your police career had a very successful arc before this."

She stepped into the hallway, out of his field of vision. He tried to roll more forcefully now that she was gone, to see whether he could get onto his stomach. Perhaps then he could push himself caterpillar-like into a standing position. However, the roll almost wrenched his left right arm out of its socket, an indication that she had fastened the zip ties on his wrists to some fixed object on the floor.

A moment later, she returned. "Everything looks good. So I'm going to leave you now. Looks like about fifty-one minutes." She leaned over him, rested a hand on his forehead so he couldn't head butt her or thrash about, inspected the duct tape on his mouth. "That ain't going anywhere." She looked him in the eyes. "I really am sorry about this." Then she bent even closer, kissed his cheek, rose, scuttled down the back hall and out the back door. He heard the click of the lock sliding into place.

Then there was only the darkness, the streaks of yellow across the floor from streetlights, and a horror that grew with the passing of each second.

Forty-five

He spent a couple of minutes trying to make noise, but he knew his muffled attempts weren't carrying. It seemed to Nate that the thumping of his heart surpassed any sounds that issued from beneath the tape.

He prayed, he schemed, he bargained, he cursed himself. Why hadn't he stayed with Pete and Emily? Right now he'd be sitting under the stars, probably on his fourth or fifth Corona, probably on his third or fourth brat. He just had to keep poking the hornet's nest. And the outcome would be the same. Grace would get away with millions in gold coins and jewels and end up on a beach somewhere. The only difference: Because he had persisted, he wouldn't wake up tomorrow morning, have brunch at Blue Bay, listen to the Brewers game on the radio, order a pizza for supper, maybe see if Star wanted to stop by to share a slice or two, just to laugh at their absurd theories about the Duminski case. Tomorrow he would be a bag of charred meat in a chilled drawer at the county morgue.

Then he cried, and his vision blurred.

Gotta try something!

He rocked back and forth. Maybe he could break whatever was tethering him to the floor. Then at least he would have a chance of crawling or rolling toward a door or window. He rocked until his joints screamed and he was almost certain the zip ties were biting into his wrists badly enough to bleed. What did it matter?

How much time was left? Grace had said that fifty-one minutes remained right before she left. Had ten minutes elapsed? Twenty? More? What would it feel like when the building erupted into a fireball? He prayed that Grace was right and that the end would be quick. An end that could come at any moment.

He began to shiver uncontrollably.

Then he heard something, or thought he did. It had almost sounded like someone had tried the front door knob. But perhaps it was just the sound of a trucker shifting gears as a big rig passed on Rochester. Or his imagination, grasping at straws. However, then he heard it again. Someone was definitely there. Hope flared like a sun. He tried to push louder sounds through the duct tape.

The rattling at the door stopped.

Panic set in again. Had someone only stopped by to see if Grace's Gifts was open? Not this late on a Saturday. Not at a completely dark shop. Had they gone away?

Half a minute later, sounds from down the hall. The back door. Then they stopped, too.

Don't go away! Please, don't go away! He squeezed his eyes shut.

Suddenly, glass exploded into the room from the direction of the front windows, and something heavy thumped onto the floor. When Nate opened his eyes, he saw a figure crawling through the window opening.

"Shit, Nate!" cried Star, almost tripping over him. She pulled off the duct tape and he sucked in a couple of rasping breaths.

"Star! My hands! You gotta get my hands! This place is a time bomb!"

She partially turned him, eyed the ties.

"Let me see if I can find a scissors."

Star headed to the checkout counter, emitting a gasp when she arrived. "My God! That can't be Grace!"

"It's Sarah! Grace killed her! She's going to burn down this place! She shaved Sarah's head to make everyone think it was her!"

Star found a box cutter, returned, freed Nate's hands, then cut the ties around his ankles.

"Get out! I'll meet you on the sidewalk!"

"But—"

"Go!"

She went to the front door, unlocked it, exited. Nate went to the counter where he found that Grace had left his cell. He pocketed it, but saw no trace of his gun. Then he stepped behind the counter, picked up Sarah Cutler, carried her out to the sidewalk.

He called 9-1-1.

When he finished, he carried Sarah's body farther from the gift shop, laid her carefully near the curb, then faced Star.

"I…"

The emotion was too much for him. Minutes ago, he had been certain he was going to die a horrible death. Now he was breathing the cooling night air of his hometown in July, perhaps destined for breakfast at Blue Bay after all. Unable to speak, he gathered Star into a hug and held on for almost a minute.

Sirens began to wail in the distance.

"How?" asked Nate as he finally broke from the hug.

"Too many coincidences," said Star. "The more research I did, the more everything led me to Field Park."

"Sounds like you followed some of the same trails I did. I noticed you checked out a few Capone items from the library, too." He decided to omit the part about how this had made him suspect her.

She nodded. "When I found out Corrine Baker was a Maxwell Street regular, I called Marcie Shoal who coordinates the vendor spaces for the Kiwanis. Found out that Gift Shop Grace had asked for Corrine's old spot. That seemed just a little too creepy. I went over to the park today to check things out, and then I followed Grace to the store here. Saw you pull in a little later. But you never came out when Grace left…so I got worried."

"That's sweet. Seriously, thank you!"

A squad arrived. A fire truck wasn't far behind. Nate spoke to Rob Salazar, the patrolman. "Basement's full of flammable shit soaked in accelerants. When the furnace timer comes on, it's going to light everything up."

"I'll see if the gas company can do an emergency shutdown," said Salazar. "And I'll have the trucks hose down the building and the ones next door."

Nate returned to Star, grabbed her right hand. "Come on!"

They jogged a wide path around to the back of the building, dove into *Higgins*.

"We've got to try and stop Grace."

Star glanced around the interior. "This is your car?"

"Made the last payment seventeen years ago."

She buckled up. "Let's hope Grace is on foot."

While he drove, Nate called it in. "Everyone's at the center of town right now. It'll probably take a few minutes for the county to get someone over to the park. Hopefully we can get there while she's still digging up the treasure. If not, she's going to be harder to catch."

He brought Star up to date on what Grace had told him.

"What a sick bitch!" said Star, shaking her head.

"No argument here."

He pulled up to the park, sprinted to Grace's vendor stall. She was already gone, but using the flashlight app on his phone, they saw where she had dug a hole inside her rear tent, no more than two feet deep and right up against the base of the flagpole monument.

"Shit!" Nate paced back and forth in front of the vendor stall. "Shit!"

"She didn't say where she was going?" asked Star.

Nate shook his head. "She was kind of vague about it."

"What exactly did she say?"

Nate tried to remember. He had had a lot on his mind at the time, being tethered to the floor and confronting his mortality.

"She mentioned something about a car that was parked at the end of a path. That's where she was going from here."

"You're right. That's pretty vague. Do you think she was talking about the bike path here along Veterans Way?"

"There was more," continued Nate. "She said no eyes would be watching it at this time of night. That doesn't sound like the bike path. There are streetlights the whole length. And on a Saturday night, plenty of traffic, plenty of eyes."

"What about the gravel road through Kiwanis Park?" asked Star. "Maybe she hoofed it through there and was parked at the vet's or the greenhouse."

Nate shook his head. "No, no. She said something else. She mentioned the gold coins and how they were going to make her backpack kind of heavy, but she didn't really have cancer, so it would be no big deal to carry it a couple of miles."

"A couple of miles?" repeated Star. "That's a nice long path. And no streetlights. Where do you find something like that in the village?"

"You don't," said Nate, his eyes lighting up in a sudden epiphany. "You find it in Vernon Marsh!"

Dick Andrews pulled up in the squad with which he'd been cruising the park after hours, making sure no one disturbed the vendor sites. He leaned out the open window, jabbed a thumb toward the south.

"What the hell is going on in the middle of town?"

"Possible arson," said Nate. He pointed to the Grace's Gifts tent. "Long story. Did you see a woman enter or leave this stall?"

Andrews shook his head. "I did see someone walk through this area awhile ago. It was from a distance. Couldn't tell if it was a man or woman."

"How long ago?"

"Maybe ten, twelve minutes."

"Thanks."

Sirens continued to wail and a county squad screamed past them as they cut across Rochester to Nate's car. Nate made another call on the way.

"I used to run around on the trails in Vernon Marsh all the time when I was a kid," he said as they fastened their seatbelts. "There are trails that snowmobiles and hikers sometimes use that Grace could catch in the woods right behind Pick & Save. No one would be on them at this time of night. If she headed east, they'd eventually turn into a gravel road that would take her toward the river. Then it cuts across the marsh on a kind of isthmus that ends at a parking lot on the end of Frog Alley Road. I'll bet anything that's where she's headed. They're sending a squad out to check and see if there's a car there."

"And we're going after her, right?" asked Star.

"You bet your ass," Nate replied. "With squads on Frog Alley and us coming from behind, she'll have nowhere to go."

Forty-six

They sped east on Veterans Way, turning left onto a gravel road just before reaching the railroad crossing. A wooden sign near the entrance read VERNON MARSH WILDLIFE AREA.

Nate knew that Vernon Marsh, tucked along the village's north side, stretched north and east toward Waukesha and into the Town of Vernon, covering more than 4,500 acres. While much of it was wetland, there were some wooded areas and meadows. Gravel access roads and footpaths snaked through portions of it, as did the Fox River, and several miles of Canadian National Railroad line.

As a kid, Nate and his pals had built forts in the woods, picked asparagus, drunk straight from the spring, played hide-n-seek, and dared each other to walk out on the massive railroad trestle that towered above the Fox River. But their play had always been during the daylight hours. At night, one could easily get lost traversing the unlighted trails, or find oneself off the trail in a boggy area, unsure which direction led back to civilization.

A hundred yards north, the gravel road widened into a roughly circular parking area, although there were no cars at this hour.

"That had to be Grace that Dick saw in the park," said Nate, slamming the car into park and reaching across to the glove compartment, where he grabbed a flashlight. "He said she had a ten or twelve minute head start. She'd go through the woods on foot. Hopefully by taking the road, we cut some time."

They exited the car and walked to the beginning of the trail. A length of rusted, inch-thick wire cable was locked between two posts to prevent vehicles from going any further. They stepped through the pedestrian gate and started down the slope into the dark, green woods.

"Hey, I'd been meaning to ask," said Nate as they descended. "You attacked a co-worker with a shovel? What was *that* all about?"

"It was about stupidity," said Star. "My former boss came to my house to pick up my keys. I was shoveling snow, angry and embarrassed, said I'd drop them off Monday. She said she'd take them now. I kept shoveling. She decided to stand right there in the driveway. Long story short, she ended up getting seven stitches in her foot. Of course, I had to pay for that, too."

"Remind me to stay on your good side." He picked up the pace as they neared the base of the hill.

"If I'd known we were jogging, I'd have switched to my blade," said Star, who wore knee-length shorts and a tank top.

"You going to be okay?" asked Nate.

"Yeah. Except for probably a fucking blister tomorrow. If I'm not keeping up, just go!"

At the bottom of the hill, a grassy trail joined from the west, the trail Grace had presumably used. The gravel road bent to the east, and Nate tried to choose a sustainable pace, straining ahead for any sign of his quarry. He shut off his flashlight so as not to alert her and send her into hiding. The nearly full moon provided sufficient illumination to keep him on the path. It was still relatively low in the southeast, and an infinite treasury of stars spilled out behind Nate as he ran, although on this occasion, he failed to register their majesty.

He scuffed heavily along on the gravel, knowing that Grace would be hurrying too, and that the sounds of her own ragged breathing and heavy footsteps would camouflage his own. The sirens wailing from the center of the village well before an hour had elapsed would have alerted her to the failure of her plan to torch the shop. She had to assume that Nate might have survived, might have revealed enough of her plan that someone would pursue her. Instead of a leisurely walk, she would be running like a hunted fox. And in this case, the fox was weighed down by an extra twenty pounds or so of loot—like carrying a bowling ball. Maybe a ball and a half.

The woods overhead grew more dense, and he had to be careful about where he stepped. A minute later, the brush thinned on either side revealing a straight path—two parallel dirt tracks worn in by service vehicle tires and foot traffic and an old meadow on both sides, rapidly being consumed by new tree growth. Another couple of minutes and the woods thickened again, a darker overhead canopy than even the previous stretch. Beyond this, Nate knew that the trail would slope down toward wetland and the isthmus that led across the marsh toward Frog Alley Road.

His lungs burned and the humid marsh air made him sweat like a marathoner. He had not run this far since the early days of his police training. He wondered if it was adrenaline that kept him going.

Emerging from the last wooded thicket, he finally switched on his light. "Grace!" She stood there, barely fifty yards away, wearing the long wig, struggling to adjust a modest backpack on her shoulder, a stunned look of surprise on her face.

"How the fuck!"

Nate slowed to a walk, put up his free palm in a halting motion. "It's all over, Grace! Come on! Let's walk out together!"

Grace reached into a pocket and pulled out a revolver. "Stay where you are, Nate! I've got your gun!"

"You don't want to do that, Grace! It'll just make things worse!"

She shook her head. "No it won't, Nate. You can either walk away now. Or I'll shoot you. Either way, I walk across to Frog Alley and drive away. Same result for me. But one of those is way worse for you."

"Not going to happen, Grace. Look across the marsh!"

Although a mile away, there were no trees or buildings to obstruct the view, and it was easy to see the flashing lights of squads that had just now reached the parking area on the east end of Frog Alley.

Grace turned back to him, her eyes radiating hatred, but an instant later, she turned and darted out of sight to the right.

Where the hell does she think she's going?

Nate jogged to where he had seen her disappear, approaching with caution, in case she were hiding and hoping to draw him in for a closer shot. He discovered a pathway that led off toward the railroad tracks. He plunged down it, racing over soft ground with six-foot tall reeds sprouting on either side. He needed the flashlight to keep from breaking an ankle, even though he knew the illumination made him an easier target. Half a minute later, the ground shot up at a steep angle toward the ballast-covered bed of the railroad tracks. Sweeping the flashlight around, he discovered Grace running toward the long trestle that spanned the Fox.

If Grace made it across the trestle, she might increase her chances of escape. No police presence awaited her there, and there were residences in the Hidden Lakes subdivision as well as farmhouses she could quickly pillage to steal a car—probably permanently silencing the owners to keep them from reporting the crime. Or perhaps Grace had anticipated potential problems and already had a "Plan B" car of her own waiting.

Nate scrabbled out his cell with his free hand as he ran, intending to report Grace's change in direction. But in trying to run and dial one-handed, the phone twisted out of his fingers, bounced on the rocky roadbed, and slid into the tall grass.

"Goddamn!"

He spent exactly three seconds unsuccessfully searching for that needle in a haystack, then lurched to his feet and continued the chase. It was difficult to run, since the rocks that supported the tracks were often an inch or two lower than the tarry ties, creating the real danger of twisting or breaking an ankle. The rocks themselves, often the size of golf balls or larger, and frequently scattered on top of the ties, added to the footing difficulties.

On the plus side, he saw that Grace was having as much trouble as he was, if not more. She was clearly exhausted not only from the running, but from carrying the heavy backpack, and even after pausing to look for his phone for several seconds, Nate had still gained ground on her.

"Grace, stop!"

She made an animal sound and stumbled forward with renewed effort.

From the east, somewhere still miles away, came the faint howl of a train horn.

No, no, no!

The thought of having to pursue Grace across the trestle with a train closing in terrified him. As a kid, they had made some daring runs across the bridge, whose tracks were probably thirty feet above the river. And the span across seemed as long as a football field. In those long-ago days, one had been forced to step gingerly from tie to tie, gazing through the foot-wide spaces in between at the southward-flowing river waters far below. Since then, the railroad had laid boards between the rails to form a walkway, which made the trek easier, but rendered the height no less intimidating or the thought of meeting a train any less terrifying. Nearly thirty years ago, a whole group of his friends had been in the very middle of the trestle when a train appeared around the bend from the east. They had all begun to run as best they could, trying to avoid slipping between the ties and fracturing an ankle or shinbone, leaving them helpless on the bridge. The train had come closer and closer, its horn blaring, and Nate and the others had only just made it across and tumbled down the steep embankments on either side when the train rumbled over. Nate's younger sister had been with them, had been the last coming across, and Nate had to wait anxiously for the entire train to pass before he was able to confirm that his sister had slid down the embankment on the opposite side of the tracks, getting off the trestle with seconds to spare.

The train horn sounded again, this time much closer.

"Grace, stop!"

She ignored him, reaching the trestle and the wooden walkway. This made for easier going, but she still clearly struggled with exhaustion and the weight of the pack.

"Don't Grace!"

She continued onto the bridge. Nate reached it seconds later, now only ten yards behind.

"Stop!"

In response, Grace unleashed an angry scream, limped ahead.

Shit.

Hesitantly, he followed her onto the span. She, on the other hand, seemed to move with increased urgency, and reached the center of the trestle as Nate detected a low rumbling.

"Grace, you don't have enough time!"

With another animal cry, Grace suddenly whirled around, Nate's own revolver in one hand, pointed and fired. From the way she handled the firearm, Nate could tell she was inexperienced, had perhaps never held a gun before. But that did not make her any less dangerous. A kill shot could come from a skilled marksman or some bozo waving a pistol in drunken reverie. Either way, you were just as dead. He side-stepped at the flash, part reflex, part instinct. The step took him off the planking and his foot slipped between the ties, his weight carrying him off balance. Although he fell onto the planks, he felt something in his ankle snap. Pain shot through his shin.

He tried to push himself to his knees. This was his nightmare, come to life. Trapped near the halfway point, unable to run, a train screaming closer. But Grace was on the move again toward the far side. A bright light suddenly pierced the night ahead of her and the mechanical thunder grew in intensity.

The train horn wailed again, loudly, urgently.

Desperate, Nate pushed himself to a standing position, balancing on one foot, the other throbbing and useless.

"Grace, come back! You're not going to make it!"

He took a couple of hops back in the direction he had come, tried to put weight on the foot, fell to his knees. Although terrified, he was unable to keep from looking back. The headlamp of the diesel engine lit up the trestle like a football stadium. The horn sounded so loudly that Nate's skin vibrated. At the same instant, Grace realized the futility of reaching the other side before the train arrived, turned and began running savagely back toward him.

"Drop the pack, Grace! It's slowing you down! Drop the pack!"

She shook her head, cried out again, gritted her teeth, tried to run faster.

"Drop the pack, Grace!"

His shout was drowned out by the latest warning blast from the train, whose brakes squealed wretchedly, but Nate knew it would be another half mile at least before the one hundred or so cars could be brought to a halt. He watched in horror as Grace disappeared beneath the wheels of the giant. In seconds, one hundred tons of screaming metal would slam into him. Once more, he tried to rise, a futile gesture, for the massive engine was still speeding forward, just feet away, a wall of metal and sound, the light blinding. He closed his eyes.

The impact came from behind, someone slamming into him at a full sprint, two arms encircling him in a running bearhug, toppling him sideways and off the trestle.

He felt the wind of the train as it roared past, and then, a long fall.

Forty-seven

"Another double brat, hon?" asked Emily.

Nate sighed. "You know you really don't have to baby me like this, Em."

"Nonsense," she said with a smile. "You're our neighbor. And you're a hero!"

"Geez, Em, don't say that!" said Nate.

"Yeah, Em!" chimed in Pete. "You're gonna give him such a big ego that it'll throw him off balance and he'll bust the other leg!"

They sat in deck chairs at the front of the double condo unit, Pete's grill smoking off to one side. The weather was a bit cooler—mid 70s—but the sun shone brightly. It was a little after noon, and Nate had a Corona in his one, fully-functioning hand.

"The leg's not busted," said Nate, pointing to the gray, plastic shell encasing his right foot to halfway up the calf. "Dislocated and badly sprained. Be in the boot for four weeks."

"That's right," said Pete. "Only sprained. It's your arm that's broken. Pardon me, Mister Hero."

Somehow, a week ago, when Star had tackled him off the trestle an instant before the train engine would have reached him, and they had tumbled together into the Fox River far below, Nate had broken his arm. He still didn't know exactly how. Ironically, Star had broken nothing.

But she had saved his life. Twice. First by rescuing him from Grace's shop, and then on the trestle.

The horrors of that night still shook him up occasionally. They had found Grace, or rather what remained of her. He shuddered both at the image of her being sucked beneath the engine's pilot, the look of raw terror on her face, and how close he had come to the same fate.

They had found her shredded backpack as well, but so far, no trace of the Capone treasure. Nate suspected the dozens of diamonds and gold coins had been swept away by the current or lost in the mucky bottom of the river.

A blue car pulled into his driveway, parked, and Star emerged, wearing running shorts and tank top along with a Milwaukee Brewers cap. She reached back inside to grab a shopping bag.

"Thought I'd stop by to see how the recovery is going," she said, sauntering toward the group. Nate introduced her to Pete and Emily. "I brought some chips and guac. I made the guacamole. Only recipe I'm really adept at. Hope I'm not intruding."

"Grab a seat!" said Pete, sliding another chair in Star's direction. "And break out that guac! Would you like a double brat?"

"We have hamburgers too, dear," said Emily, rolling her eyes at her husband.

"I'll have a burger, thanks," said Star.

"Corona?" asked Pete.

"We have wine spritzers too," added Emily. "And I think some soft drinks."

"A Coke if you've got one," said Star. Emily excused herself to get one out of the refrigerator.

"Another Corona for you, Nate?" asked Pete. Nate nodded, and Pete checked the cooler. "Guess I'd better make a refrigerator run too. And I'll be back in a sec."

After Pete disappeared into the house, Star gave Nate an awkward smile. "Scuttlebutt around town is that when Vic Wrangell retires in December, someone I know is the odds-on favorite to get the lieutenant's job at the cop shop."

"You solve one major serial killer case, and people all of a sudden get these horrendously misguided ideas about your competence," said Nate wryly. "Truth be told, I wouldn't have solved it without your help."

"Yeah," said Star, smiling. "We made a pretty good team."

Nate took a deep breath. "And...thanks for, you know, saving my life. I mean, I can't imagine how it must have felt for you to run out there onto that trestle and—"

"When I saw you go out there on that bridge, I thought you were crazy," said Star. "Then when I ran out there, I thought I was crazy."

Nate nodded, looked at the ground for a moment before continuing. "I just...it just...I mean, I can't believe..."

Star leaned off her chair, threw her arms around Nate's neck, kissed him deeply, passionately. He was surprised for a moment, but then kissed her back.

They came apart slightly, looked at each other.

He smiled. "What I mean is, I'm so glad I didn't die."

Star returned the smile. They kissed again. Then they heard the sounds of Pete and Emily returning, and Star slid back into her chair.

Emily handed the Coca-cola to Star. Pete gave the Corona to Nate.

"Jesus, Nate, you're all red! You need some sunscreen?"

Nate shook his head, smiled at Star. "Hey, are you busy tomorrow?"

"What did you have in mind?" she asked.

"I was thinking brunch at Blue Bay. Then catch the Brewers game on the radio while we relax on the deck. Later, order a big pizza from Mario's for supper."

Star smiled. "That sounds like my perfect day."

Notes about the book: What's real?

Most of the places in this book are real. There are, however, a number of fictional locations that should not be confused with real places, nor are they intended to represent real places.

All of the characters in the book are fictitious, with the exceptions noted below.

While most names in this book identify fictional characters, Arthur Grutzmacher was a real Mukwonago resident and did indeed donate his extensive collection of Native American artifacts to the Red Brick House Museum.

The Mukwonago Red Brick Museum is not only a real place, but a really cool place. And the real volunteers are even cooler than the fictional Vern and Ellie.

The Emerson House, the Caul House, and Grace's Gifts are all fictitious places.

Grant really did visit Mukwonago and a cannon really did blow up in an attempt to salute him.

There really was an Ira Blood, and the Blood Family graves are as described in the book.

Sarah's coffee shop does not exist, and in fact, I never actually gave it an official name for the book.

Pete Moore is a fictional character, but Pete Mohr was real, the owner of Mohr's Standard Service Station in downtown Mukwonago years ago. In fact, my dad, Gordon Vick, used to work there pumping gas—back in the days when gas stations did that. Thanks to Andy Hemkin, Pete's grandson, Andy's wife, Cheryl, and their son, Scott, for agreeing to let me use Pete Mohr's name and story in the book.

The Heaven City history is accurate, and Chicago-area gangsters apparently did frequent the complex. However, the Al Capone-related events and his betting on horse races in Field Park are fictionalized. The shed that currently stands at the north end of Kiwanis Park really was moved toi its current location from the south side of the park. However, to my knowledge, it never stood in Field Park nor was it used in conjunction with horse races.

A good deal of historical information in this book comes from *A Chronicle of Mukwonago History* by D.E. Wright, *Place of the Bear* by D.E. Wright, and *From Mequanego to Mukwonago* by Kathryn Bergmann. I am thankful to both individuals for their extensive research into local history and their love of Mukwonago.

I am also indebted to Jon Stock, an MHS cross country teammate of mine, whose mother, Hazel, owned the three books mentioned above. Jon was kind enough to pass them along to me when Hazel passed on, and I will do my best to be a good caretaker of them. They were invaluable in my research for this book. Thank you, Jon.

Thanks to Mukwonago Police Chief Kevin Schmidt for help in understanding how the Mukwonago Village Police Department works. He should not be confused with the fictitious Chief Beckman in the novel.

Photos of Some of the Real Places Mentioned in the Novel

Legion Flagpole in Field Park

**The Blood Family Memorial Tree Stump and
Book with "Blood" on Cover**

The Kiwanis Park Shed

Repainted many times over the years. But can you see the "typo" in this rendition? (It says "EST. 1839. The village was founded in 1836, not 1839.)

About the Author

Rod Vick lives in Mukwonago, Wisconsin with his Lovely Wife, Marsha. An occasional speaker at conferences and orientation events, he also runs half-marathons, enjoys watching his daughter Haley perform as a professional singer, and attending Packers games, ax-throwing competitions, and escape rooms with his son, Josh.

Like Kaylee O'Shay Books on Facebook

Like We Are Mukwonago on Facebook

All of Rod Vick's books are available on Amazon

Visit us at:

www.kayleeoshay.com

and at:

www.coolgreenink.com